STAGECOACH GRAVEYARD

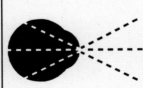

This Large Print Book carries the
Seal of Approval of N.A.V.H.

STAGECOACH GRAVEYARD

THOM NICHOLSON

WHEELER PUBLISHING
A part of Gale, Cengage Learning

Detroit • New York • San Francisco • New Haven, Conn • Waterville, Maine • London

GALE
CENGAGE Learning

LIBRARY OF CONGRESS CATALOGING-IN-PUBLICATION DATA

Nicholson, Thom.
    Stagecoach graveyard / by Thom Nicholson.
        p. cm. — (Wheeler Publishing large print western)
    ISBN-13: 978-1-4104-2528-7 (alk. paper)
    ISBN-10: 1-4104-2528-2 (alk. paper)
    1. Bounty hunters—Fiction. 2. Outlaws—Fiction. 3. Large type books. I. Title.
PS3614.I3535.S73 2010
813'.6—dc22   2010003204

Published in 2010 by arrangement with NAL Signet, a member of Penguin Group (USA) Inc.

Printed in the United States of America
1 2 3 4 5 6 7 14 13 12 11 10

*To my darlin' Sandy and
the grandkids, Cason, Lilly, and Xander*

Chapter 1
It's Just Business

"Git a-goin, ya no-good glue-factory rejects. Haw, Lucy. Put a strain on yur lines or I'm a-gonna flail the hide right offa yur butt with this here bullwhip — see if I don't. Come on, now. Drag this here coach over the top and earn yur hay fer a change. Haw! Put yur shoulders into it. Come on, mules, let's git a-goin' now. Hee-haw, hee-haw, giddyup now."

The mule skinner spit a stream of brown juice to the side and wiped his mouth with the back of his gloved hand without missing a beat as he cursed and shouted at the six mules straining to pull the heavy Concord stagecoach up the six-degree slope and over the crest of the latest hill of the many that tormented any traveler making the perilous journey from the diggings at Virginia City, Nevada, to the southern terminus of the Reno and Carson City stage line.

The mules pulled against the leather

traces and slowly the team and stage crested the grade and reached the flat summit of the pass. As he always did on the run to Carson City from the mining camps at Virginia City, Squint Richards halted the mules and let them catch their breath before starting the long downward trail to the flat-land below.

"Good mules," he grunted to the sweating and winded animals. "Take a blow and git yur breath back. You're gonna need it when we hit Deadman's downgrade."

Squint, who derived his name from his droopy left eyelid, the result of an encounter with a mule's hoof many years earlier, stood and looped the reins around the hand brake of the stage. He stretched a kink out of his weary back, spit a glob of brown tobacco juice over the side of the coach, and spoke to the shotgun guard riding beside him. "Dave, we might as well stretch our legs as well. Once I get them no-account mules started down the grade to the bottom, we ain't stoppin' till we hit Carson City."

Without awaiting an answer, Squint climbed out of the driver's box, stepped down to the axle hub of the four-foot-high front wheel, and then jumped to the ground. He stomped his feet on the rock-strewn roadway and stretched up on his tiptoes, raising his hands high above his head.

Squint slowly walked toward the lead mules while Dave suppressed the amused smile that threatened to cross his lips. The mule skinner would have been over six feet tall if his legs had grown in proportion to his stocky torso. They had not, so the feisty driver was barely four inches over five feet and was extremely sensitive to any adverse reference to his size. Dave had seen Squint plow into some thoughtless character who ridiculed his height at a bar, even though the man towered over Squint by many inches and outweighed him by many pounds. Most of the time the rugged mule skinner would thoroughly clean the clock of anyone who uttered a disparaging slight against his stature. Even when he lost, as he did the last time he got roused, by Lebo Ledbetter, the local bully, the offender knew he had been in a scrap.

Dave set his shotgun against the driver's seat and stood to climb off the other side of the stage. He swung his leg over the side of the stage and paused, his mouth agape. Three men, their faces covered by kerchiefs, stood at the side of the road, two pistols and a rifle pointed directly at him. For an instant, nobody said a word or moved. Then one of the outlaws motioned with his pistol for Dave to get down from the stage.

Dave Gunther was not a particularly brave or stupid man. Yet he had hired on to the Reno and Carson City stage line as a shotgun guard, knowing it was dangerous work. The last lucid thought he made in his life was that he had better start earning his salary. He grabbed the shotgun and jumped to the ground, hoping to catch the holdup men by surprise, but to no avail. The robber holding the rifle shot a round into Dave's spine, shattering it, while a second outlaw fired a round from his .44 Colt directly into Dave's heart. The bullet passed on through Dave's body and buried itself in the wood of the coach frame, next to the bottom step of the driver's box.

Squint ran around the front of the mule team, clawing at his holstered .44 and shouting, "Dave, what's goin' on?"

The outlaw who shot Dave with the rifle spun on his heel and fired a hasty shot at the charging Squint before the surprised driver even got his pistol clear of its holster. The bullet caught Squint high on his right shoulder and spun him to his left, right off the roadway and down a steep, rocky slope toward a sheer drop-off of some two hundred feet. Squint dropped and rolled down the slope until he got all tangled up in a lone piñon bush growing out of the rocky soil. The shock of the bullet or the fall or both combined left Squint unconscious by the time his limp body wrapped itself around the bush. Squint was lucky; if he had missed the piñon, he would have rolled off the slope and fallen the two hundred feet to the bottom of the cliff, landing among the rubble of two stagecoaches and a freight wagon that had been pushed to their doom in earlier robberies.

As the last echo of the gunfire faded across the hilltops, the man who had shot Squint pulled down his neckerchief, exposing his face. "Well," he said aloud, "that takes care of that, don't it?"

The center outlaw holstered his pistol and dropped his mask as well, wiping his hand across the bushy mustache covering his upper lip. "Damn, Luke, that was some shootin'. Ya didn't seem to aim yur rifle afore ya shot." He stepped to the edge of the road and looked down at the still form of Squint, twenty feet below. "Ya reckon he's dead?"

Luke Graham jacked another bullet into the chamber of his Winchester Yellow Boy rifle. "He has to be — I hit him square in the brisket. Ya wanna climb down thar and check him out?"

The leader of the trio shook his head. "Not me. You wanna scramble down there, Bob? I noticed ya didn't fire a shot durin' the whole show. What's the matter? Git cold feet?"

"Nope," Bob answered, his youthful face creased in concern and worry. "Not me. 'Sides, Charlie, I don't like the ideer of killin' them two. I was just about to whop the guard on the noggin with my six-gun when you and Lucas filled him full of holes. Up to now we ain't killed no one. Now we're murderers, as well as highway robbers."

"Well, tough beans to the both of 'em," Luke answered. "They was the ones who started it. If they'd had a lick a' sense, they'da give up peaceful-like. We gotta take care of ourselves. It weren't personal or nothin'. It was just business."

Charlie nodded his head in agreement. "Luke's right, Bob. Now shake a leg. Git up thar and throw down the express box while Luke and me gets these mules unhitched. I wanna get offa this here road as quick as we can."

Working with practiced dispatch, the three outlaws completed their assignments and gathered around the steel express box. A heavy lock stood between them and the

12

contents inside. Luke aimed his Winchester and blasted open the lock. Charlie quickly flipped up the hasp and lifted the heavy lid. Inside lay two leather pouches filled with gold dust and a stack of twenty-dollar greenbacks.

"Damn," Charlie muttered in satisfaction, "there's gotta be two thousand here, iffen there's a penny." He quickly placed the loot in his saddlebags and turned to young Bob. "Grab a holt of them mules' lines, boy. Me and Luke'll push the stage over the side and then we're gettin' outa here. Luke, put the guard's body in the stage." Charlie positioned the tongue of the stage toward the edge of the drop-off as Luke wrestled the limp body of Dave Gunther onto the floor of the passenger compartment.

Pushing on the rear wheels, the two outlaws rolled the stage to the edge and over the side of the roadway. As the stage tipped forward, it gathered speed and quickly rolled down the rocky scree to the sheer drop-off. It rolled over the limp body of Squint, breaking his right leg below the knee, and then sailed into space, falling in a trailing shower of dust and small rocks until it smashed into the ground two hundred feet below. The stage broke apart, scattering its shattered pieces among the worthless remains of the earlier victims.

The three outlaws watched in morbid fascination as the dust settled and the sound of the crashing stage and falling rocks echoed from the far wall of the canyon. Satisfied, Charlie swung up onto his saddle and spoke to the others. "Let's skedaddle. I wanna git offa this road afore someone comes along. Bob, you bring them mules along." He rode off, not bothering to see whether his instructions were carried out. Of course they were, and the entire party headed back down the steep grade the stage had just ascended.

About a quarter mile back down the hill, a shallow stream twenty feet wide carried runoff from the last vestiges of snowmelt across the rocky roadbed. Charlie turned his horse into the stream and was quickly lost to view from the road by the trees and brush growing along the banks of the cold, rushing water. Without comment, the others followed, nobody speaking, nobody concerned by the foulness of their evil deed. Instead, their thoughts were on the hot meal awaiting them back at their ranch hideout.

The three horses and six mules muddied up the clear water as they splashed through the stream, following its path toward the base of the mountain, but the debris quickly washed away as if it had never been disturbed. Any evidence of their passing was soon gone. As the sound of their horses' hooves faded in the rippling water, the area grew quiet, and forest birds began to fill the air with their twittering songs.

All was calm for the next ten minutes. Then two men rode over the top of the hill from the opposite direction, the second in line leading a heavily laden packhorse. They stopped their mounts at the top, looking around in puzzlement. The older man, his face covered by a gray-streaked beard and sun-weathered skin, took off his sweaty hat and scratched his balding head.

"I swear them shots had to come from here'bouts, Lem. We wouldn't have heerd 'em if they'd been farther down the slope, yonder."

"Yu're probably right, Hank. But what were it all about?" The second man, not yet in his forties, swung down from his horse and walked to the edge of the road, examining the chopped-up dirt caused by the wheels of the stage as it had rolled over the edge of the roadway. "Looks like somethin' went over the edge here. Hey, lookie thar! Thar's a body down thar! And down to the bottom of the cliff. Look at them wrecked stagecoaches. Gawd bless. I shore hope thar

15

weren't no folks on 'em."

Hank hurried to join Lem by the edge of the road. "Shore enough. Damned, I woulda hated to be on any a' them stages. How ya suppose it happened?"

"Reckon some skunk of a highwayman tried to hold up the stage from Virginia City and they ran offa the road?"

"Three of 'em all at once?"

"Well, one at a time, then?"

"Naw, I don't reckon so. These here wrecks musta happened over time. That don't make it no better, though. It looks like a stagecoach graveyard down thar."

"Git yur rope, Hank. I'm gonna try and shimmy down thar and git that body afore it falls on over the cliff."

Lem looped Hank's rope around his chest and waited until the older man was settled on his saddle with the rope wrapped around his saddle horn. Carefully he edged his way over the side of the road and crabbed his way to the still form, wedged against the lone piñon growing out over the drop to the bottom of the ravine.

Lem grabbed the limp body of the driver and called up to Hank, "Take a strain, Hank. I've got 'im. Pull us up."

Dragging the two men up the rocky slope was hard work for Hank's horse, but eventually its efforts brought Lem and Squint to the rocky roadway, Lem gasping to catch his breath. Hank passed him a canteen of water, from which the hot, dusty Lem gulped several swallows. "Thanks, pal. I thought fer a minute I was gonna hafta let the body go over the side like the stage. I'd never a' made it if yur hoss hadn't done most of the work."

Hank rolled Squint onto his back. "What are we gonna do with this here dead fella?" He suddenly did a double take. "Whoa, now, this jasper ain't dead."

CHAPTER 2
MORE BAD NEWS

Colleen O'Brian walked angrily down the wooden boardwalk of Main Street in Carson City, her lips pursed with suppressed rage. She had just finished talking with Samuel Malone, the president of the Silver City Bank, and what she heard had made her spitting mad. So mad that she had stomped out of the florid-faced banker's office and slammed the door with force greater than that which would become a refined lady. She shook her head vigorously, whipping her auburn hair around her face. "To hell with that pompous old bastard. All the business we've given him and he can't extend our loan a measly thirty days." She glanced around guiltily to ensure that nobody had heard her cuss like a drunken mule skinner.

Fuming, she wiped a hand across the bridge of her freckled nose, then stepped over a lazy dog that lay sprawled across the boardwalk in front of Trammel's Dry Goods Store. She paused to look at her reflection in the fly-speckled glass of the front window. Colleen O'Brian was taller than most women, with what she considered an excess of bosom and hips on an otherwise lean frame. Her mouth was wide and generous, just like her father's, but her eyes were the emerald green of her late mother. Her hair was also the same fiery auburn of her departed mother. It spilled over her shoulders in the afternoon breeze. She did not pluck her brows as some of the girls had done back at Ms. Emily Trotter's Girls' Academy in St. Louis. Thus when she frowned, as she was doing now, it seemed as if she were glaring out from under a single long brow. She sniffed in derision at her reflection and headed toward her father's office, down one more block.

Malcolm O'Brian was working on his accounting ledger when his daughter stomped into the office, swishing her long hair back from her face without breaking stride, straight to his scarred, wooden desk.

Malcolm puffed on his pipe, as much a ploy to give her time to relax as to steel himself for the obviously bad news. "No luck, I take it, huh?"

Colleen tapped her foot against the

wooden floor, her arms folded across her waist. "That moneygrubbin' weasel Malone — all I got was some huffing and puffing about responsibility to his stockholders and other customers. All the business we've given him too. It makes me so mad I could spit nails right through a barn door."

"Settle down, honey. I didn't expect anything else. We're on the ragged edge and everybody in town knows it. These holdups and destruction of our rolling stock would have driven most lines under already. However" — he held up a letter with a work-hardened right hand — "I got some good news in the mail. Uncle Joe will loan me ten thousand dollars against twenty percent of the business. It'll be here within a week."

Meg collapsed into a broken-down chair next to the old desk, relief washing over her face like a flood of sunshine. "Oh, Pa. That's wonderful. God bless Uncle Joe." She stood up, a fresh look of optimism on her face.

"One other thing. Uncle Joe wants to send his wife's nephew, a young man named Carson Block, out here to work. I suppose that he thinks this Carson can sort of watch out for his interests. I said I had no problem with it. Do you?"

"Whatever you say, Pa. Just what we need, though, some dude from back East to mess things up. Well, I guess I'd better tell Roy to get the relief team hitched up. Squint should be pulling in with the four o'clock stage any minute now."

Malcolm pulled a silver pocket watch from his vest. "As a matter of fact, he's already ten minutes late. I sure hope he didn't run into any trouble coming over Graveyard Pass."

"Pa, don't you start calling Roberts Pass that awful name. It's bad enough that half the folks in town are callin' it that."

"Ya can't blame 'em, honey. That's exactly what it looks like to every man, woman, or child that passes by them wrecks down at the bottom of Roberts Mountain. I sure hope we've seen the last of whoever was doin' that. It's been two weeks since the last holdup."

"Pray to God you're right. But why would they stop? The law hasn't seen fit to catch even one of them. I declare, I sometimes wonder if Sheriff Schrader isn't hoping we'll fail to meet the contract with the silver combine."

"I can't believe that, Collie, honey. He's tried, even though his responsibility ends at the edge of town. If we only had a county marshal, he'd be the one to really get involved in our problem."

"I wonder when the county board is going to appoint another man to replace Marshal Digby."

"Probably just as soon as the governor finds someone crazy enough to take it. Why risk getting plugged in the back some dark night, like Digby, for fifty dollars a month when you can make twice that in the silver mines?"

"Be that as it may," Colleen asserted, "we need some help, especially if these holdups and stage destructions start up again."

"Well, honey," Malcolm replied, "keep your fingers crossed they don't. We're too close to losing everything we've worked so hard for as it is. A few months of peace will do wonders for our profit margin." He glanced out the window. "I wonder where Squint is. He's never been this late before."

Colleen walked to the front door and swung it open for a better view down the street, toward the steep hills to the east and north of Carson City. "Oh, Pop. You don't suppose it's starting again?"

"Now, now, daughter. No need to get all riled up afore we know that anything's amiss. Squint may have had some equipment problems, we don't know. All we can do is be patient until he shows up." Despite Malcolm's soothing words, his eyes were filled with concern as he sneaked a quick peek at his open pocket watch propped up next to the pile of unpaid bills.

Scarcely had Colleen resumed her seat when they both leaped up as a skinny boy burst into the office. Gasping for air between words, the young boy finally got his message out. "Mr. O'Brian, come quick. Two men has ole Squint on a litter down to the doctor's office. They said to tell ya that he's shot up bad and the stage is wrecked."

Malcolm and Colleen hurried side by side to Dr. Waldren's office at the far end of Main Street, the youngster trailing close behind. Both were clearly shaken by the news and neither chose to speak as they hurried past other pedestrians on the wooden boardwalk.

When they arrived at the doctor's combined home and office, the two men had already carried the unconscious Squint into the doctor's treatment room. They stood awkwardly on the front stoop, discussing what course of action they should next consider.

"You fellas found Squint Richards, did ya?" Malcolm queried.

"Yep," Hank replied. "Me and Lem come upon him at the summit of Roberts Pass, right where all them stagecoaches are dashed to pieces at the bottom of the cliff."

"You bet," Lem chipped in. "We almost didn't see him. He was just a-hangin' over the edge of the drop by a little ole piñon, just about ready to slide over the edge. I went over the cliff and fetched him back up. All he had twixt him and eternity was my lasso around his waist." Lem rubbed his grimy hands on his denim pants, somewhat self-consciously. "Yep, Hank lowered me over till I got ole Squint by the arms. Then he dragged us up the slope with his hoss. I was plenty scared, lemme tell ya."

Malcolm shook both men's hands and spoke gratefully. "That was mighty fine of the both of you fellas. Did you happen to see what happened?"

"Naw, I guess the stage was held up and pushed over the edge. Squint musta been throwed over afterwards, or else he fell off the stage as it were goin' over. Nobody was around when me and Hank got there."

"You boys spot Dave Gunther? He was supposed to be riding shotgun fer Squint."

Both men shook their heads simultaneously. "Nope," Hank answered. "We jus' found ole Squint and figgered we'd better git him back here to the doc's as quick as we could. He had a hole in him the size of a silver dollar and was bleeding like a stuck

24

hawg. We didn't go down to where the stage was wrecked, but we didn't see nobody from up at the top, did we, Lem?"

Malcolm nodded. "You probably did the right thing. If Dave went over the cliff in the stage, he'd never have survived the drop anyway. Would you two wait here until I check on ole Squint and then go to Sheriff Schrader with me and tell him what you know?"

"Sure," Hank answered. "We was headed to Silver City, but now there's no way we can git there today."

"When we're done with the sheriff, I'd like for you to go with me out by the river trail. I want to check the wreckage and see if we can find Dave. I'll give each of you ten dollars for your troubles."

"Fair 'nough," Hank answered. "We'll give ya a hand, won't we, Lem?"

"You betcha."

Malcolm turned to his daughter. "Colleen, why don't you go on back to the office? If there were any passengers on Squint's run, some of their kin may show up lookin' for 'em and you'll have to tell them what has happened."

"Pray to God there weren't any," Colleen answered. "There's not been many passengers since all these robberies started."

"I doubt if there were any, since I told Squint not to say when he was leavin' Virginia City, and most customers wouldn't want to stand around waiting until he decided to go. I sure hope there weren't any. That's all we need now. Anyway, go on. As soon as I get these two fine fellas over to the sheriff, I'll come to the office and tell you how Squint is."

Malcolm watched his daughter hurry off and then entered the doctor's office. The sweet, biting odor of chloroform permeated the air. The doctor came out of the treatment room, wiping his hands on a small towel, stained red with blood. His glasses were pushed up on his bald head and a frown framed his dark brown eyes.

"Howdy, Doc. How's Squint?"

"Shot up good and proper, Mal. Also got a busted leg. Looks like the stage wheel ran over him."

"He gonna make it?"

"I think so. The bullet seems to have bounced off a rib, and sliced open his side, but it apparently didn't puncture his lung. If he doesn't get an infection, I'd say his chances are pretty good."

"Can I talk to him?"

"Nope, I've got him under the chloroform. I've got to sew him up and get him bandaged. He'll sleep for the rest of the night, I reckon. You can talk to him in the morning, not before. You might as well tell Sheriff Schrader the same, so he won't be coming around late tonight."

"I'll do that, Ralph. But if Squint wakes up or takes a turn for the worse, you fetch me right away, will you?"

"I'll do that, Malcolm. Go on now. I got me some work to do."

Malcolm returned to the two prospectors outside. "Doc says Squint'll be out until tomorrow. You two come on with me. We'll let Sheriff Schrader know what happened. Then we'll head out to the pass by way of the river road. We might get lucky and find poor ole Dave still among the living."

"Not iffen he went over the cliff in that stage. It was plumb smashed to pieces, weren't it, Lem?"

"You said it, Hank."

The two men reported what they knew to the Carson City sheriff, who duly noted the main points in a small notebook. "Ya say ya didn't see nobody or the teams when ya got to the top of the pass?"

"Nope, Sheriff. It was just like we said. No sign of nobody." Hank bit off a chew of twist tobacco, offering a bite to the others, all of whom refused. "Me and Lem didn't

27

go down the Virginnie City side, we was too intent on gittin' Squint back here to the doctor, but we shore didn't see hide nor hair of nobody."

Sheriff Schrader looked resignedly at O'Brian. "They had to go back toward Virginia City, Mal. I suspect they cut off the main road long afore they got there. No tellin' where your mule team ended up." He paused. "I'll bet a week's wages they'll be at the bottom of one of the silver mines afore the week is out, though."

"Anything you can do for me, Otto?"

Schrader shook his head. "Mal, you know my authority ends at the city limits. I'll send in a report to the territorial attorney general, and ask him to send us a county marshal. It'll probably get as much attention as my last request."

Fuming, O'Brian smacked his fist into the palm of his other hand. "Come on, fellas. Let's get on out to the bottom of that cliff below Roberts Pass and see if we can find Dave. We're not accomplishin' anything here."

"Sorry, Mal," the sheriff called to the angry stage owner's back as he led the others out of the office.

The three men rode along the trail that followed Runoff Creek at the bottom of

Jefferson Mountain. It was getting close to sundown before they arrived at the base of the steep cliff, where the destroyed stage lay among the wreckage of earlier crashes.

Malcolm tied his horse and the extra mount that he had borrowed from the livery to a tree limb and surveyed the wreckage, strewn about a good-sized outcropping on a level portion of the cliff about thirty feet above the trial. The slope was steep, but not impossible to ascend on foot, so the three men scrambled their way to the flat and walked over to the latest wreckage. The wheels were gone and the coach body was split open, almost completely torn in two from the impact of the fall from the road high above them.

Lem poked his head inside the stage body. "Ain't no one here. A bunch of blood all over the floor and seat, though."

"Damn," Malcolm groused. "Spread out. Dave may be around here somewhere. Dave, Dave," he shouted, "you hear me?"

"He ain't hearing you, Mr. O'Brian," Hank answered from behind a pile of debris that was once a fine Concord stagecoach. "He's a-lyin' over here, stone-cold dead."

Malcolm hurried to Hank's side. It was Dave, ejected by the crash to fall in a pitiful heap beside the debris. O'Brian rolled the body over on its back. "Shot through the heart, damn them. At least he didn't have to ride the stage off the cliff whilst alive."

Malcolm looked up at Hank and Lem standing over him, looking in awe at the dead man. "Give me a hand, boys. Let's get Dave up on the horse and take him on back to Carson City. I gotta go tell his poor wife what happened to him."

It was well past sundown before the three men and their grisly cargo arrived at Carson City. Mal delivered Dave's body to the undertaker's on Second Street and paid off Lem and Hank. "You fellas did me a good service and I'm mighty grateful. You ever need a favor, come find me." He passed over the ten silver dollars he had promised the two and watched as they headed for the bright lights of the nearest saloon.

Sighing in resignation and knowing full well just how unpleasant the next few hours were going to be, he turned his horse toward the freight office. Colleen would be needed with Dave's wife; the poor woman had delivered a little girl only months earlier, and she was sickly. He wondered how much he could safely spare from the cash his brother was wiring him, to give to the poor widow. She would need some, which was certain. Dave never would have taken the guard's job if he hadn't been in desperate need of some hard cash. Malcolm mentally crossed his fingers that Squint had not signed for any money to be delivered to the Carson City Bank. If so, that would have to be replaced from the ten thousand he had coming as well.

After Dave's wife finally fell into an exhausted sleep, Malcolm and Colleen walked back toward their living quarters above the freight office. Colleen spoke first. "Poor Mrs. Gunther. She was crying like her poor heart was broken forever. I certainly am grateful that her preacher and some of the ladies from her church were so prompt in coming to her side. I was about to break down myself and I only met Dave one time, the day we hired him."

"Well, come on, hon, let's get some supper and then go tell Sheriff Schrader that we found Dave and he's now got murder to add to robbery and wanton destruction of our rolling stock."

"It's a waste of our time, Pa. He won't help us and you know it."

"Probably not. But it can't hurt. Then we'll just have to wait and see if ole Squint can tell us anything."

The next morning, Malcolm was at Doc Waldren's office as soon as he saw the busy doctor hang out his OPEN FOR BUSINESS sign.

"Howdy, Ralph. How's Squint doin'?"

"Morning, Malcolm. He had a pretty good night. I've already dressed his wound this morning and it doesn't look like there's any infection setting in. I think he'll make it. You tell Sheriff Schrader about the holdup?"

"Yeah. It won't do me much good, though. As long as there's no county marshal and the governor's so busy tryin' to get his reelection campaign up and running, I'm out of luck. Schrader did say he'd put a warrant out on the holdup for me if I would guarantee some reward money."

"Good idea. It might help you catch the outlaws who did this terrible thing."

Malcolm nodded thoughtfully. "I'll do it, Doc. Well, I'd better see Squint. Okay?"

"Sure. He's awake but he might be a little groggy. Just don't get him too agitated."

Squint was lying on his back, a large bandage around his right shoulder and side. He looked up as Malcolm stopped at the side of the bed.

"Hello, ole-timer. How you feelin'?"

"Like I was rode hard and put away wet, boss. How's Dave?"

"The skunks killed him, Squint. The only

reason they didn't kill you was some prospectors came upon you right after the robbery occurred and pulled you back up the cliff to safety and got you here to Doc Waldren's before you bled out."

"Poor Dave. Them bassards didn't give him a chance. Me either, fer that matter. By the way, Boss, the invoice of what I was a-carryin' is in my shirt pocket."

"Any money?"

"Jus' over two thousand, from the Lucky Strike Saloon in Virginnie City. Some letters and such, but nothin' as valuable as the money. They got it, I reckon?"

"Damn, damn. Yep, they did. Destroyed the stage and stole the mules as well."

"Them rotten skunks. I knowed one of the robbers, boss."

"You did?"

Squint painfully nodded his head. "Yep, played cards with him a time or two. Name was Luke Grimes, or was it Graham? Graham, I think. I knowed it was him 'cause he carried a fancy pistol holster with some silver Mexican conches on it. I don't reckon thar's another holster like it within a thousand miles a' here."

"Well, that's a bit of luck for our side. Sheriff Schrader say's he'll put out some wanted posters. Maybe someone'll get Luke and we can find out who's behind all this. It's time we had a little good fortune."

"There was at least two others, but I couldn't see their faces as they was a-wearin' masks. They shot Dave right off and got me as I was comin' around the lead mule to see what was a-goin' on."

"One name is better than none. You take it easy, Squint. I've got me a plan, if we can jus' get someone to catch this Luke Graham. I'm gonna send the sheriff over to talk to you, Squint. Give him a description of Graham as best you can. I'm gonna go and see about getting us a replacement stagecoach from the Butterfield folks in San Francisco. You hurry up and get well, oletimer. I'm gonna need you afore this is all over."

CHAPTER 3
DRAWN INTO TROUBLE

Marty Keller stretched his arms high over his head as he came out of the hotel. Rocking back and forth on his heels, he looked up and down the street, as was his custom since he went on the bounty hunter trail, but saw nothing that gave him concern. He took a leisurely walk to the sheriff's office, letting his breakfast settle. He felt refreshed after a long night's sleep following his hard ride from Elko, clear across the northern border of the new state of Nevada to the even newer town of Reno, the gateway to California through the infamous Donner Pass.

He had stopped in to introduce himself to the town's sheriff, and found to his happy surprise that he was Jesse Longabaugh, from Texas. Jesse had worked as a Texas Ranger in Dallas near where Marty had lived with his family. They renewed old acquaintances quickly.

"I remember when your family was wiped out, Marty," Longabaugh commiserated. "I actually was on the first posse with Captain Self, when we chased the filthy bastards all the way into Injun territory. We were all sick to our stomachs that we had to turn back at the state line. I heard you was on the trail, huntin' fer 'em ever since. Had any luck runnin' the fiends down?"

"Some, Jesse. I caught up with the gambler in Arkansas. Killed him at a card game. I got the Swain brothers in Bixley, Kansas, about a year after that. Had the pleasure of sendin' 'em both straight to hell." Marty shifted as the brutal memories of his dead family flooded his thoughts. "I've never found a trace of the leader, Al Hulett, and his Mex sidekick. It's like the earth swallowed 'em up and brushed the sign away."

Jesse Longabaugh smoothed the bristly hairs of his mustache with a forefinger and mused a moment. "Maybe they hid out in Mexico. That would explain why you ain't seen nor heard of 'em."

"I thought of that, Jesse, I assure you. But it doesn't make sense. They don't even know I'm on their trail and outlaw scum like Hulett couldn't abide lyin' around some adobe cantina swilling tequila for five years. He's bound to have come back to the States to rob and steal for some more spendin' cash. I just can't seem to cut his trail. That's why I hunt criminals for a livin'. It gives me more opportunity to cross their paths and meanwhile make a little spending money to keep up the hunt."

"Well, I don't reckon I can fault ya for that, Marty. I came in early this morning and went through all my latest wanted papers. I don't see anything that's likely to do ya any good. That's not to say somethin' won't come in on the next stage. Since the big gold strikes around Virginia City we've had more'n our share of owlhoots causin' trouble in these parts. You're welcome to stick around as long as you want and see what turns up."

"Thanks, Jesse. That's a fair offer and I think I'll take you up on it. My horse damaged a hoof crossing the hardpan north of here. The blacksmith says he'd be better off if I didn't ride him for a week to ten days. I wouldn't have pushed him so hard if I had known that McNeal was gonna turn himself in to your custody as soon as he arrived in town."

"Well, once he heard you was on his trail, I guess he decided to do something smart for a change."

"Yeah, and cost me a thousand dollars and

a month of hard ridin'."

Jesse grinned right back. "Well, I sure do appreciate you herdin' him my way. I guess I do owe you a meal or two in thanks. That reward money'll come in handy, as I'm trying to save up enough to buy some land down around Carson City and start myself a little ranch."

"I guess a reputation isn't always a bad thing. I want you to know, Jesse, that talk about me always bringing in my man dead just isn't true. I try and get them to surrender first. I just don't let them get me before I get them. I still have men to kill."

"I believe you, Marty. Remember, I knew you from before. All I ask is that you try and stay out of gun trouble while here in Reno."

Marty grinned at his latest friend. "And I do promise you, I'll really try and stay clear of problems when I'm not on the job. It's bad enough when I'm after some killer. I don't need the aggravation when I'm trying to rest up. I doubt if many folks around here know me, so I'll stay quiet and cut a low profile."

"Appreciate it, Marty. I'll watch the posters that come in and let you know if I run across any that might be of interest to you." The sheriff held out his hand, a friendly smile on his face. "Welcome to Reno, Marty. Once you're settled in, maybe we can ride up into the hills and shoot that famous rifle of yours."

"Anytime, Jesse. You'll get one for yourself, once you see how far out it can touch a target."

"Well, I'm looking forward to it. Now, however, I'd best get some work done. Why don't we plan on sharin' supper together, say about seven, at the Chinaman's Café?"

"Works for me, Jesse. See you there about seven."

Marty left the sheriff to his duties and walked toward the livery at the north end of town. He was worried about Pacer. The big gray was about done in when they had arrived yesterday evening. Marty had grown to appreciate and rely upon the faithful animal's strength and endurance on the trail. He also had a soft spot in his heart for the Tennessee gelding, and the affection was reciprocated.

The smithy, a muscular black man with gray-streaked ringlets of dark hair tightly coiled about his head, greeted Marty with a polite nod and a welcome. "Morning, Mr. Keller. Ya come to check on yur hoss?"

"Morning. Sam, isn't it? Yes, I have. How's he doing this morning?" Marty continued on back to the stall where Pacer was stabled. The animal softly snickered as his master came into view. "Mornin', Pacer. How you doing, fella?" Marty stroked the velvety nose and scratched behind Pacer's right ear, a very satisfying and soothing spot for the horse.

"I's brushed him down right good, Mr. Keller. I'm afeered he's got what's called the 'curbs,' on his right rear leg. Thass why he was limpin' so when you brung 'im in lass night."

"Damn, that's a strain on the main ligament, isn't it? Is it permanently disabling?"

"Nope, I'd reckon I can have him up and about in ten days or so. I's got a poultice I larned from an Injun that use'ta live hereabouts. I'm already makin' some up to put on this here fine animal's leg. I reckon it'll cost you five dollars to give him the full treatment."

The brawny black man looked intently at Marty. A man who did not care would pass on the cure and let nature take its course, usually to the horse's detriment. Marty did not hesitate. "Certainly. Spare no expense. Whatever it takes to get ole Pacer back on his feet."

"Mighty fine, Mr. Keller. I knowed you was a man who likes his hoss. I'll git started

40

right away. Ya check in every day. I'll feed yur hoss the best grain I got and take right good care of him, ya can count on it."

"I know you will, Sam, and thank you. Here's ten dollars. Give ole Pacer anything he wants or needs. I'll make it right by you."

"Ya can count on me, Mr. Keller."

Marty walked out of the livery barn and paused before crossing the street. He took a mental reckoning of his available funds. He needed some new clothes and several boxes of ammunition. He also wanted enough to play cards at the local saloons. He had learned the hard way to steer clear of those games where card slicks and high rollers dominated, but to instead play with the locals. Their stakes were lower and he gained much more useful information.

He would also need to stock up for the trail once he decided on taking up man-hunting again. "I sure hate to draw any more from the bank," he muttered to himself. Shaking his head at how much he spent, when once he and Meg had lived comfortably on fifty dollars a month, he headed for the dry goods store across the street.

By noon he had bathed, shaved, and put on new store-bought clothes. He rented a horse from Samuel and rode out of town to

41

look over the surrounding countryside. He headed west, toward the forest-covered mountains, away from the rocky desert from Salt Lake. During his hunt for McNeal, he had learned more about the barren wasteland than he ever wanted to.

The mountains to the west of Reno were cool and green, and for Marty the time elapsed quickly as he rode through the lush terrain. He barely made the Chinaman's Café on time for his meal with Jesse Longabaugh. They reminisced about their days in the famed Texas Rangers and their shared memories.

Finally, Jesse put down his coffee cup and quickly glanced at his pocket watch. "Well, I'd best make my rounds. Wanna walk with me, Marty? I'll try and keep the drunks offa ya."

"Might not be a bad idea, Jesse. It'll show the locals that I'm your friend and maybe they'll think twice before they try to brace me if they find out who I am."

They made the town tour, stopping in most of the saloons along Front Street, where Marty was introduced to the bartenders and owners. "You fellas take care of my friend Marty here," was Longabaugh's standard line. Only one man's eyes widened as Marty was introduced.

42

"Say," he gushed, "are you the famous man —"

Longabaugh held up his hand to stop the question. "I'd rather you didn't say anything about that, Wil. This is just ole Marty, here to take it easy and visit an old friend. We clear on that?"

"Whatever you want, Sheriff." The chunky bartender winked at Marty. "If I can help ya in any way, Marty, jus' let me know."

"Thanks, Wil. I'll sorta be operatin' on the quiet side for a spell, so don't spill the beans on me." Marty cast his gaze over the back of the saloon. Several tables were filled with cowboys, miners, and townspeople engaged in games of cards. "Well, Jesse, I guess I'll try and get into one of the games here. See you tomorrow?"

Jesse nodded and Marty turned back to the hovering Wil, who was shamelessly eavesdropping on every word. "Wil, have you ever met up with a man who had the last two fingers of his left hand blowed off? Goes by the name of Alva Hulett?"

"Sorry, Mr. Keller. I can't help ya."

"Well, it was just a shot in the dark. I'd appreciate hearing from you if you ever do run up against him. Jesse'll tell you how to get in touch with me."

As Marty stepped away from the bar, the

bartender whispered to the man in front of him, "Say, do you know who that is?"

When the customer shook his head, Wil leaned even closer and, glancing around conspiratorially, continued. "It's the famous bounty hunter, Marty Keller, called by some the Man Killer. Let me tell you . . ." His eyes never left Marty's back.

At the front door, Longaburger slapped Marty on the back. "Come by my office around ten. We'll ride out to where I practice my shootin'. I'll try out your big Sharps then, if it's all right with you."

"Fine by me. You probably need the practice." He watched Jesse depart, then turned toward a table of cardplayers, all wearing the rough clothing of cowboys or miners.

Marty relaxed as much as a man in his particular profession could over the next few days. He and Sheriff Longabaugh made it a habit to ride out and shoot their weapons at various targets put up by the sheriff in a box canyon in the nearby foothills. Marty showed the sheriff how to shoot his special Sharps, with the telescopic sight and oversized barrel, that he had obtained during his period as a buffalo hunter with Bill Cody.

Marty's luck at the low-stakes poker that

he indulged himself in every opportunity at one saloon or another was somewhat better than average and it provided him with a satisfying wad of money, which he stuffed in a sock in his carpetbag under the bed in his hotel room. He repeatedly posed questions to the many men he played cards with about the outlaw Hulett, without discovering a single lead worth pursuing.

The accident happened on Friday morning as they returned to Reno from their morning target practice. Jesse was laughing and kidding with Marty, not paying much attention to the trail, even though they were following a game path around the side of a steep hillside. His horse suddenly shied at the unexpected encounter with a fat rattlesnake that had slithered up onto a flat rock right beside the trail to sun itself. As the horse stepped close, the rattler coiled up and sounded his many rattles in warning.

The startled animal threw the shocked lawman off his saddle, slicker than a wild stallion fighting his first ride. Jesse hit the edge of the path and slipped over the side, the wind knocked out of him and a burning pain in his right knee. He fell and slid for thirty feet before he jammed up against a scrub bush.

Marty was off his horse and scrambling

down the rocky slope before the dust had settled. He reached the still gasping Jesse and pulled him up to a sitting position. "Damn, Jesse, that was some fall. You all right?"

"Ooh, my leg. I think I musta broke it, Marty. Danged hoss. Spooked by a little ole snake. Um, I don't think I can walk on it. You're gonna have to help me back up the hill."

Marty eventually brought the injured sheriff to Reno and delivered him to the local doctor. Marty got the horses stabled and then returned to the doc's office. He waited impatiently until the old sawbones came out of the treatment room, rolling the sleeves of his white shirt back down to his wrists.

"How's he doin', Doc?"

"Well, he ain't got a broken leg. But he shore has twisted it. He won't be walkin' around fer a week or so."

"Can I see him?"

"Sure. Go on in. He ain't goin' nowhere."

Marty entered the room, wrinkling his nose at the medicinal odor that permeated the room. "How you doin', Jesse?"

"Hurts like the bejesus, Marty. I reckon I gone and done it now."

"Doc says you'll be fine in a week or so."

"Yeah, but my deputy is outa town, deliverin' a fugitive to Sacramento. Marty, yu're gonna have to help me fer a spell. I want ya to swear in as a deputy."

"Now, Jesse, I can't take on a job like that. As soon as my horse gets well, I'm off on the trail again."

"You can do this fer me, Marty. For old times' sake. It'll only be a week or so. Come on, raise yur hand. I'll get the city council to pay ya a hundred a month, in advance. Do it, pard. I'm really needin' ya."

Reluctantly, Marty took the oath and found himself the newest deputy of Reno. He prowled the streets at night and haunted Jesse's bed during the day, trying to will him to get well faster.

Word somehow spread as to his identity and the problems were few and far between. Everyone was watching to see if the deadly bounty hunter was as fast and lethal with his guns as his reputation.

CHAPTER 4
OUTLAW LOYALTY

The summons to Virginia City was not completely unexpected, but still Vern Barton tried not to show just how nervous and uneasy he was as he stepped into Ransom Stoddard's office at the headquarters of the Virginia City Mining Consortium on the top floor over Root's Dry Goods Emporium. Just before knocking on the door, he wiped his palms on the sides of his pants.

As usual the slender, graying Stoddard, with his icy eyes and grim countenance, was sitting behind a massive desk in the dimly lit room. While it was lavishly appointed with the very latest in furniture, with original oil paintings adorning the walls and a glassed front gun case displaying several expensive weapons, to Barton the effect was still more about money than good taste.

To add to the unnaturalness of the surroundings, an odor of malevolent evil seemed to permeate the very atmosphere.

Barton swallowed and flashed a sickly smile at his master. "You wanted to see me, Mr. Stoddard?"

Stoddard made Barton wait a full minute while he shuffled papers on his desk before responding. Ransom Stoddard raised his cold, expressionless blue eyes toward Barton, looking at him as a wolf might look at a crippled jackrabbit. His voice was high pitched and as cool as his stare. "How is your campaign going to gain control of the O'Brian stage line?"

"Everything's goin' just fine, Mr. Stoddard. We hit their last three runs out of Virginia City, gittin' the money they was carryin' and wreckin' their coaches. It's just a matter of time afore they're completely outa business."

Stoddard nodded his head, reminding Barton of how a rattlesnake bobs its head just before a strike. "Excellent. I want complete control of the freight business before Hearst can rebuild his production. With the coming railroad, whoever owns the freighting business will make a tidy profit from the freight concession. And that damned George Hearst will finally be out of my hair." He toyed with a chunk of quartz laced with golden threads. It was probably worth a thousand dollars, Barton estimated, and the wealthy mine owner used it for a paperweight.

Stoddard was embroiled in a fight with George Hearst, the equally wealthy owner of the Comstock Mine, the richest in the area, as well as several others. Barton had no idea how many men had been financially ruined or killed in the two egocentric multimillionaires' war, and did not want to ask, ever. He was content to take his money and ruin a small stage and freight operation. "Any chance you can get the contract shifted to you without all the trouble of runnin' the O'Brians outa business?"

Stoddard's malevolent glare sent shivers down the spine of the hardened outlaw. "I would if I could," he snarled. "George Hearst has convinced the rest of the Mine Owners' Association to let O'Brian have the freight concession and I have not been able to convince them otherwise, no matter what I promised. I'll kill the SOB someday, I swear."

"How's he doin' tryin' to put out his fire in the Comstock?"

Stoddard nodded his head, a contented smirk on his face "It's still burning and smoking like hell on earth. My engineers say he won't be able to get back into the mine for several months. Meanwhile, I'm hiring as many of his men as I need and he's trying to make ends meet with the production from his smaller mines. Since he hit water in the Little Bill, his production is down by over sixty percent. He's bleeding money like a drunken sailor in port and falling fast."

"I heerd that he's ordered some big water pumps from back East to pump out the Little Bill shafts."

"That's what I wanted to talk to you about. When those pumps come in from Pittsburgh, they'll be shipped by his wagons from Reno to here. I figure about eight wagons to carry 'em all. You'll take the whole string out and both O'Brian and Hearst will fall like a house of cards. Better yet, if we can get O'Brian to fail before then, Hearst will have to use my freight service and I'll simply have them diverted to your ranch, so I can use them if or when I hit a water pocket in my mines."

"When do ya think they'll get here, Mr. Stoddard?"

"It won't be long. Hearst has to get the Little Bill or the Comstock back online and soon or he'll run out of money. I'm selling his stock short every day, to keep the price so low he can't raise any funds by issuing more stock. When he goes bust, I'll make

51

millions."

Barton shifted his feet. He was anxious to get away from Stoddard. "I'll be standin' by with twenty or thirty men, awaitin' yur instructions, Mr. Stoddard."

"Good. And by the way, have you seen this poster?" He passed a wanted poster to Barton, who quickly scanned the writing and lithograph picture. It was for Luke Graham, wanted for murder and robbery of the O'Brian stage line.

"How the hell did this happen?" Stoddard questioned. "You know I wanted you to ensure that none of your men could ever be charged with something. If they're caught, they might spill their guts out to the law."

"I surely don't know, Mr. Stoddard. But I assure ya I'll git to the bottom of this as soon as I git back to the ranch."

"Get rid of this Graham. If you doubt that he can make himself scarce around these parts, put him in a shallow grave up in the woods somewhere. I'm tempted to insist that you do that anyway, just to drive home the point about being careful."

"I'll do it immediately. That'll shore make the others take notice that I mean what I say when I tell them to leave no witnesses behind."

Stoddard nodded. "That's the end of our

discussion, then. Keep yourself ready to move on O'Brian's wagons the moment I send you the word. Meanwhile, keep pecking away at any stages he tries to run from Virginia City to Carson City or Reno."

Barton took a deep breath when he exited the office. Suppressing a shudder, he headed for the bar across the street. He needed a stiff drink to loosen the tight feeling in his throat. He liked working for a man of such wealth and power, but he was still deeply afraid of the man. Barton sighed. Being poor was no party when a person had to work for a man like Stoddard.

Barton visited the dry goods store below Stoddard's office and purchased some staples for the ranch before heading south on the high mountain road toward the cutoff to his place. As he approached the cut created by centuries of snowmelt that led to the meadow where he claimed enough land to support a few hundred cows, he breathed deeply of the pine-scented air. Cedars and ponderosa pine trees grew in abundance at this altitude of the front slopes of the Sierra Nevadas. His single-story, log-constructed main house with a sod roof showed smoke from the kitchen stack, so supper would not be far away. One thing about the old Chinaman who cooked for him and his crew of cutthroat outlaws was that the small Oriental cook put a hot meal on the table every day at precisely the same time.

"Afternoon, boss," Charlie Call called out as Barton stepped off his dark bay at the front hitching post and climbed the two wooden steps to the porch. Call was the ramrod of the crew and a hardened gunnie, with several notches on his gun. He pushed himself up from the staghorn rocker and opened the front door for his superior. "I suspect ole Chink has just about got supper on the table."

Barton held up his hand, stopping Call. "First things first, Charlie. Call the men to gather round."

The fifteen men at the ranch quickly clustered at the base of the steps leading to the porch. Barton held up the wanted poster given to him by Stoddard. "You men take a look at this. It's a wanted poster for one Luke Graham, wanted in Carson City for murder and robbery. There's a thousand dollars reward, dead or alive. Care to tell me how your name happens to be on this here poster, Luke?"

Suddenly, like oil floating on water, an imperceptible space separated the unfortunate outlaw, Luke Graham, from his fellow outlaws. Luke's voice cracked with anxiety as he tried to come up with an explanation that would satisfy the anger in Barton's voice. "I don't know, boss. I swear to ya, I ain't been spoutin' off my mouth or nothin' in Carson City. I don't know how they got a hold of my name. Nosiree, I shore don't."

"You boys all have heard me say to leave no witness that could identify any of us, ain't ya?"

A murmured rumble of agreement rose from the assembled men. Everyone was watching the cowed Luke, wondering how the drama was going to play out.

Barton paused to let the tension grow for a moment, then gave an order. "You, Red Mike" — who happened to be standing the closest to Luke — "take Luke's pistol." The command was promptly obeyed. Barton gave the sweating Graham a cold leer. "I guess we had to have one jackass that couldn't obey orders. A couple of you boys take ole Luke here up to the tree line and give him a proper send-off. Luke, don't come back this way, ever. Clear?"

Red Mike spoke up. "I'll do it, Mr. Barton. Iffen you'll have Chink fix me up a sack of sandwiches to make up fer missin' dinner."

"That I will, Mike. Sailor, you go with

Mike and Luke, so there's no trouble. Luke, ya got ten minutes to pack up your kit and be offa my place. Sailor, watch ole Luke so's he don't pick up nothin' that ain't his whilst he packs his possibles. Mike, step up here. I wanna talk with ya a minute."

Luke wiped sweat from his forehead. "Mr. Barton, I got two hunnerd dollars comin' fer the last job. Ya gonna let me have it?"

"Shore am, Luke. I always make things right with my men. I'll have it in gold fer ya when yu're ready to leave."

Luke hurried away, the rest of the men trailing behind, save Red Mike, who moved to where Barton could whisper softly to him. "You and Sailor plant ole Luke up there in the trees and you two can split the money I'm givin' him. Understand?"

Mike slowly nodded his head, his over-sized mustache twitching as he spoke. "Gotcha, boss. Consider it done."

Twenty minutes later the three men rode slowly toward the green slash that marked the line between high timber and the meadow grasses. Luke was cussing a blue streak, trying to understand the calamity that he found himself in. Mike eased his horse up to where he could talk softly with Luke without Sailor overhearing. The ex-seaman lagged behind, never quite the

56

horseman that a man raised in the West came to naturally.

"Luke, shut up," Mike whispered. "Yu're in big trouble."

"What's the matter?"

"Barton told me to plant ya back in the woods somewhere."

"Jesus, Mike. Whaddya gonna do?"

"When we reach the trail that leads over the back pass to Reno, you pull a branch of a tree back as you ride past, and let it go. I'll get my hoss to buckin' and carryin' on until yu're hidden in the trees. Then I'll throw a couple a' shots in yur general direction and block Sailor from chasin' after ya. You head on up to my folks' place in Winnemucca and hide out until things cool down. Then you can head over to Californnie and do somethin' in the gold fields there."

"Will you be all right, Mike? Ya don't reckon Barton knows we're cousins, do ya?"

"Nope, I don't think so. If you play this right, we'll be okay. Once ya start, don't stop till ya reach Reno, and only stay there long enough to load up with provisions. Ya got any money?"

"I got about three hunnerd, countin' what that bastard Barton give to me. It'll have to do, I reckon."

"I'm sorry, cuz. It's a tough break. The money's been pretty easy here, so far."

"I'll make do, I reckon. I'm grateful to ya, Mike. Thanks fer gittin' me off the hook."

"Here's the trail. Keep yur eyes peeled fer the right branch. Take this bag of food. Good luck to ya." He turned to call out impatiently to Sailor, lagging behind, "Come on, Sailor. Let's git this over with."

Just as Mike turned back, a long branch pulled forward by Luke slapped back, hitting his horse and him with a stinging sweep of pine needles. Mike spurred his horse into a frenzy of bucking, hollering, and carrying on as if he were about to be violently thrown off the saddle. By the time he got his pony under control, Luke was long gone. Cursing savagely, Mike swung down from his agitated horse and tightened the cinch, all the while blocking Sailor from riding past to chase after his cousin.

"Damn, Mike, he's got plumb away. Barton ain't gonna like this."

"Weren't no help fer it, Sailor. That branch spooked my horse plenty. By the time I got him under control, Luke was gone. We'll just have to take whatever cussin' Barton wants to give us. Iffen he wanted Luke dead bad enough, he'd 'a done it hisself, don'tcha agree?"

The two men took their cussing and returned to the bunkhouse, relieved that Barton was not as riled up as they thought he might have been. Mike drifted off into a satisfied sleep, grateful that he had saved his cousin from a certain and ignominious death.

Luke rode hard and made Reno the next afternoon, before his water and food gave out. His first stop was the Silver Bird Saloon, where he downed three glasses of rye whiskey, just to wet his throat properly, then had a bath and shave before gorging himself with a big supper. After taking a leisurely stroll around the downtown area to settle his food, he returned to the Silver Bird and played cards all night, winning nearly a hundred dollars from four locals.

Encouraged by his luck, he took a room at a nearby flophouse and played again the next night. This visit to the card table was not as fortunate for Luke, and he rode out of Reno early the next morning more than seventy dollars poorer then when he had arrived.

While he was playing, the new deputy sheriff came into the saloon and stood at the bar, sipping a beer and watching the action at the tables. "Who's that jasper?" Luke asked one of his table companions.

"The deputy? He's standing in fer Sheriff Longabaugh, who broke his leg when he fell offa his hoss. A bounty hunter, name of Keller, Marty Keller. One of the sheriff's buddies from his Texas Ranger days. Ever heerd of him?"

Luke shook his head. "No, I don't think so."

"Well, he's bad medicine. Always gits his man, and always brings 'em in dead, shot through the back."

"Lousy SOB," Luke muttered under his breath.

"What's that?"

"Nothin'. Just sayin' it's a shame that someone can make money shootin' another man in the back. Don't seem right, if ya ask me."

"Well, I suppose when ya ride the crooked trail, ya gotta take yur chances with the likes of Keller. I will say he's kept the town nice and quiet since he's been on the job. Shootin's are way down." The man cackled as he laid down his hand, a full house, triple eights over fives. "Got ya agin, Luke. Yur luck ain't so good tonight, is it?"

"Dang it, Hal. Yu're makin' my luck run sour, talkin' like that. Jus' shut up and play cards." Luke watched uneasily until Keller walked out of the saloon, losing three straight hands in a row. He pushed back from the table, disgusted with his bad luck. Somehow, he blamed Keller for it. "I'm done. I ain't gonna put no more a' my money in yur pockets, by gum." He grumpily stomped over to his room, and restlessly slept until daylight. Then he hit the road for his uncle's house on the small ranch outside Winnemucca, three days' ride up the Salt Lake Trail.

CHAPTER 5
BACK IN THE
MANHUNTING BUSINESS

Marty flipped the butt of his cigar into a sand-filled box sitting outside the café. Hitching his pants up slightly, he turned toward the sheriff's office. He tipped his hat to a passing woman. "Morning, ma'am. Looks like a hot one today, doesn't it?"

"Yes, indeed." She walked on and Marty opened the door to the office. He was surprised to see Jesse sitting behind his desk, shuffling through a pile of new wanted posters that had just been delivered by the freight agent.

"Morning, Jesse. You must be feeling better?"

"I'm about to go stir-crazy, lyin' around my room. The doc says I can start walkin' on my leg now, so I decided to drop by and see if any paperwork needs lookin' after."

Jesse stacked the posters, making certain one was on top. "By the way, Marty, I got a wire from my deputy. He'll be on the mornin' train from Sacramento. I guess you can say that today's the last day you'll have to wear a badge fer me. And don't think I don't appreciate it. You saved my bacon, pard. The town owes you a lot."

"Not really, Jesse. I got good pay for two weeks of badge totin' and I've got no complaints. But now that Pacer's hoof and leg have healed, it's time I got back to my business."

Longabaugh held up a poster. "I'm gonna do you a favor in return, Marty. This jasper, Luke Graham, comes from up around Winnemucca, a town northeast of here. I've seen him in town more'n once. He used to hang out at the Silver Bird when he did his drinkin' and card-playin'. Why don't you mosey over that way and see if he's been around lately! The poster's sent up from the sheriff in Carson City, so Graham may be makin' a run thissaway."

Marty took the poster and read through the description of the wanted man. "Says he killed a stage guard during a robbery. Looks like he needs catching, for a fact."

"Yeah, the stage line that runs from here to Carson City and Virginia City has had a spate of holdups lately. I can't think of another time when anyone was kilt, though. Sounds like the robbers are gettin' even more ruthless."

"It happens when they've had a string of successes. They get more confident that they can get away with anything. It'll only gets worse unless they get stopped, hard and permanent." He nodded to Jesse. "Appreciate the tip, Jesse. I'll mosey on down to the Silver Bird and see what I can find out."

Marty stepped out into the warm sunshine and headed toward the saloon, his eyes scanning the street for any sign that something might be amiss. He had learned to tread cautiously and to be alert for the unexpected no matter what time of day or circumstances. It went with his chosen profession.

The Silver Bird was one of the less desirable drinking establishments in Reno, located next to a feed and grain store. It was dim and dirty inside with a sour smell of spilled beer emanating from the sawdust on the floor. A long bar extended along one wall fronted by half a dozen card tables. A faro table took up most of the remaining space to the rear of the saloon. At the far end of the bar, a rummy-faced old man with thinning silver hair and a rose-colored nose, from many years of swilling the hard sauce, pounded on a tinny piano.

The place was empty except for the barkeep, a swamper busy sweeping last night's refuse into a pile next to the door, the piano pounder, and a solitary boozer sitting listlessly at a table, nursing a glass of rye whiskey. Marty walked past the drinker to the bartender and waited until he had the barkeep's attention. The bartender shifted a stub of a cigar from one side of his mouth to the other and threw Marty a disinterested glance. Marty patiently waited, his face impassive. The barkeeper rested his forearms on the bar and spoke softly, his voice hoarse from a blow to his larynx many years earlier.

"What can I de fer ya, Deputy?"

Marty passed over the wanted poster. "I just talked to Sheriff Longabaugh. This fella Graham. When was he in here last?"

The bartender knew Luke slightly and had no regard for the young outlaw, since the drunken Luke had once slapped him for not serving him a drink after closing hours. "Well, let's see. I think Thursday was his last night here. Yep, I'm certain of it. He played cards until about midnight and then left. Ain't seen him since."

"He say where he was staying?"

"Luke always slept over to the Ryan Hotel when he was in town. I reckon he did the last time too. It's just up the street."

Marty nodded. "I know where it is. Thanks." He headed for the hotel, his pace picking up. He was close to Graham, on the very first day of the hunt. The eight-room fleabag hotel had an aging, slightly built clerk sitting behind the front desk, idly playing solitaire and slapping flies with a rolled-up newspaper.

In response to Marty's inquiry, he looked at the register. "Yep, Graham stayed here Wednesday and Thursday night. I think he pulled out early on Friday morning. Ain't seen him since."

A quick trip to a nearby livery verified the information. Marty returned to the sheriff's office. Jesse was still at the desk, working on his account books for several misdemeanor fines Marty had collected in his absence.

" 'Pears that Luke headed out to the east, according to the livery owner," Marty reported. "The road toward Winnemucca. You know the sheriff there?"

"Yep." Jesse nodded. "I've met 'im. He's about as worthless as tits on a boar hog, but I reckon he's almost honest."

"You give me a letter to him, so I can find out what he knows about Graham?"

"Be happy to. You leaving tomorrow?"

"Just as soon as your deputy arrives on the train."

66

"I'll hate to see ya go, Marty. Any way I can convince ya to stay here and help me keep a lid on Reno?"

"No, thanks, Jesse. I've got a blood debt that needs collecting and I'm determined to get my satisfaction."

"Ya ever need a place to light, don't forget me, pard."

"Thanks, I won't. I reckon I'll head to the store and put together some supplies for the trail. See you later, Jesse."

Marty rode into the small town of Winnemucca early Friday morning, knowing he was only three or fewer days behind his quarry. The letter from Jesse Longabaugh made enough of an impression with the local lawman, a fat-bellied, one-eyed, ex-army sergeant named Russell, that he gave Marty directions to the Lazy W Ranch, owned by Graham's uncle Harvey Whitcomb.

"You headed out there today?" the sheriff asked.

"Just as soon as I get a good meal and rest up my horse a spell."

Sitting just outside the office was one of Winnemucca's local ne'er-do-wells, Salem Rice. It was a warm day and Sheriff Russell had the small window at the front of his office open in the hope of catching any breeze that wafted by. Rice considered himself a friend of Harvey Whitcomb and thought about what he had overheard. Whitcomb might give him five dollars for the information that a bounty hunter was on the trail of his nephew Luke. Salem had no connection to Luke Graham, but he certainly could use the five dollars. He hurried to the stable and saddled his worn-out cow pony, and then lit out for Whitcomb's Lazy W Ranch.

He rode into the front yard just as the sun reached its zenith in the hot, brassy sky. He spotted Harvey Whitcomb standing by the corral while a young cowboy tried to ride a bucking bronco. Just as Salem reached Whitcomb's side, the cowboy went sailing, unseated by a mighty fishtail buck from the sweating bronco.

"Yahoo, Tyler. Ride that slab-sided flea-bag, dang his no-good hide."

"Howdy, Harvey. That cayuse acts like he don't ever plan on bein' rode, don't he?"

"Hello, Salem. You're a long way from home. What brings you all the way out to the Lazy W?"

"I come upon some information I thought you'd be interested in, Harvey. I was sorta hopin' it'd be worth five dollars to ya." Salem scuffed his feet in false embarrassment. "I'm a tad short right now."

"You rode a long, hot ways fer five bucks,

Salem. Well, give it to me and I'll decide if-fen ya made a good or bad decision."

"There's a bounty hunter in town, lookin' fer Luke."

Whitcomb turned a stern eye on the subservient Salem. "What's that? A bounty hunter? What's he want with Luke?"

"I reckon you'll have to ask Luke 'bout that, Harvey. I jus' heerd him tellin' Sheriff Russell that he was a-comin' out this way jus' as soon as he got some chow and rested his hoss. I'd figger on him bein' here by late afternoon."

Whitcomb was no fool. He knew that his boy, Mike, and nephew Luke were running on the wild side. He had hoped that they were staying clear of riding the owlhoot trail. He blamed Luke for Mike's devilish-ness and felt Luke urged Mike on, but he still did not want some dirty bounty hunter getting his blood-soiled hands on his dead sister's only child. "Well, Salem, I reckon you've earned yourself a five-dollar reward. Here ya go." He passed over a five-dollar greenback and watched thoughtfully as the town loafer rode away.

Whitcomb paused a minute longer to gather his thoughts. He'd sent Luke over toward Spring Creek to see if any cows had dropped any calves that hadn't been

69

branded yet. He knew the lazy Luke was probably taking it easy under the shade of a cottonwood tree near the creek, but he should not be too difficult to find. Whitcomb called out to the cowboy who was slapping dust off after eating a faceful of corral dirt thanks to the bucking bronco.

"Tyler, let that jughead cool off awhile. I want you to ride over to Spring Creek and tell Luke I want to see him, pronto. Then you round up any cows and unbranded calves you see and drive 'em back here to the holdin' pen. I wanna git 'em all branded before we move the herd to the winter range."

"Gotcha, boss. You know where Luke is?"

"Probably sleepin' in the shade of the biggest cottonwood tree on the creek. Don't worry, you'll find him, I reckon. Tell him to git his sorry ass back here mucho pronto, ya savvy?"

"Unnerstand, Mr. Whitcomb." The slender cowboy crawled between two planks of the corral and lithely clambered up on a paint horse tied to the top rail. With a wave of his hand he loped his cow pony out of the ranch yard and down the road toward Spring Creek, which crossed the rutted road halfway between the ranch house and the Salt Lake Road, four miles to the south.

Tyler came to the ford that crossed the creek and turned his pony east, toward a big cottonwood about a quarter of a mile off the roadway. Just as Harvey Whitcomb had predicted, Luke Graham was sprawled out on his back under the shade, his hat pulled over his eyes and snoring like a lumberjack sawing logs. Swinging off his horse, Tyler walked up to the sleeping Luke and nudged him in the side with the toe of his worn boot. "Wake up, Sleepin' Beauty, Mr. Whitcomb wants you back to the ranch."

Graham jumped in startled surprise, then angrily swiped a hand at the offending boot. "Damn you, Tyler. I oughta stomp yur head in. I was havin' a fine dream and you go and ruin it. What the hell do ya want?"

"Your uncle wants you back at the house, pronto. He sounded like he meant business to me. If I was you, I'd skedaddle on back there."

Graham worried a thumbnail for a moment. "I wonder what's up. Well, I guess I'd better saddle up." He quickly put the saddle on his bay and trotted away, without saying anything more to Tyler, who watched him go with a disgusted frown on his boyish face. He patted the nose of his cow pony. "A worthless skunk, if you ask me, hoss. I

71

guess we'd best git to roundin' up any cows we can find. It's gonna take the rest of the afternoon and I shore don't want to miss supper. Cookie's making stew and corn bread."

Luke rode into his uncle's front yard just as Whitcomb stepped out of the front door. "Ya wanted to see me, Uncle Harv?"

"Luke, what'd you and Mike git into over to Reno?"

"Nothin', Uncle Harv. Honest. Nothin' a'tall."

"Then why the hell is a bounty hunter headed this way with a paper for you?"

"I don't know, Uncle Harv. It must be a mistake. How'd you know one's a-comin' out here?"

"Salem Rice was loafin' outside the sheriff's office and heard him talkin' to Sheriff Russell. Salem beat a quick path out here so's I'd git the word and pay him five bucks' reward." Whitcomb fixed a stern glare at Luke. "You done somethin' stupid, ain't ya, son? Ya might as well tell me, I'm gonna git the full report as soon as the lawman arrives anyway."

"I swear, Uncle Harv. It's gotta be a mistake. They musta got me confused with some other jasper."

"Ya plan to wait this fella out and turn

yourself in to him?"

"No way, Uncle Harv. Most of them bounty hunters are stone-cold killers. I'm headed fer California, just as soon as I can pack my plunder and git some vittles fer the trail."

"Okay by me, boy. Just don't come back around here until you git this thing straightened out, unnerstand?"

"Fine by me. You'll try and put him off my tail, won't ya?"

"I'll do what I can, but you best put some long hours on the trail. These men are like bulldogs once they git after a man fer money. Don't mess around, just put plenty of miles twixt here and you, pronto."

"Don't you fret, Uncle, I'm gonna do jus' that. Let me git some grub from Cookie and grab my stuff. I'll be long gone in half an hour."

Luke was as good as his word and rode his pony away from his uncle's ranch in half an hour, using the trail out the back pasture that was a roundabout way back to the road to Reno. The only thing was, he did not trust his uncle to put the bounty hunter on the wrong trail, so he was going to cut north and east to see the little Mex gal who worked in the cantina at Tuscarora, then drop down to Elko and then south to

Arizona Territory. He'd hide out there until the heat died down and he could ease over into California by way of the Fremont Trail. The prospect of seeing Lupe again made him smile in anticipation. He was whistling a tuneless melody as he rode away from his uncle's ranch for the last time.

CHAPTER 6
FLUSHED OUT OF HIDING

The sun was halfway down its afternoon slide to darkness as Marty turned off the Salt Lake road and headed north following the marked wagon trail to the ranch of Harvey Whitcomb. He mulled over what he would find at the end of his ride. Speaking softly to Pacer, he outlined his options. Somehow, talking to the faithful horse helped him to resolve his dilemmas.

"I doubt if we're gonna be able to just ride in and take Graham out with us, old hoss. His uncle may think blood's thicker than obeying the law. We'd best talk about there being some doubt as to his guilt and urge Whitcomb to send the boy back to clear things up. At least that may give us half a chance on getting outa the place alive, once we state our intentions. You agree?"

Pacer continued to plod along across the powdery, gray-black dust that seemed to cover everything in northern Nevada. The land was gently rolling, leading toward snowcapped mountains many miles to the north. Grass was sparse, although a green swath of short-grass grew in a valley to his right, irrigated by a winding stream that cut through the middle of the valley. Marty estimated he was still two miles from the green row of cottonwoods, which traced the cool water that flowed from the far mountains. He licked his dry lips in anticipation. "A cool drink will taste mighty good, won't it, Pacer? Come on, let's get a move on."

They were almost to the stream when Marty spotted the rider hazing six cows toward the rutted, dirt road he was following. The cowboy was far enough away to allow Marty time to get a refreshing drink and let Pacer swallow a few mouthfuls before he tied him to a shady spot under one of the trees next to the creek. "I'll let you have some more once you cool down a mite, Pacer, my friend."

The cowboy expertly hazed the cows and their calves to a shallow spot where they could bury their noses in the cool water. He lithely swung off his horse and grabbed a quick drink for himself. Wiping his mouth with the back of his hand, he gave Marty a friendly grin. "Howdy, stranger. A hot day to be out and about. You headed for the

Lazy W Ranch?"

"Afternoon. Yep, I reckon so. You work for Harvey Whitcomb?"

"That I do. Name's Tyler Percel."

"Pleased to meetcha, Tyler. I'm Marty Keller. I'm hoping to find Luke Graham when I get to the ranch."

"Well, I suppose you'll do that. I sent him there not three hours ago. Whatcha want with Luke anyways?"

Marty made a quick decision. "Luke's got himself in big trouble, Tyler. I'm out here to arrest him. You okay with that?"

Tyler wiped the inside brim of his stained hat while he digested the statement. "I reckon so. I ride fer Mr. Whitcomb, not his no-account nephew. Anyways, I'm pretty certain the no-good horse's ass stole thirty dollars from me the last time he lit out. If Luke's crossed the line, I say let him take his medicine fer it."

"It's bad news, Tyler. Luke killed a man and robbed a stage."

"Sounds like the no-account buzzard. I'm sorry fer Mr. Whitcomb, though. His boy, Mike, run off with Luke last year, 'bout this time. I shore hope he weren't a part of the goin's-on."

"Far as I know, Luke's the only one with a paper out on him. Well, I'd best get on over to the ranch and see if I can convince Mr. Whitcomb to let me have Luke without any trouble."

"Harvey Whitcomb's a fair and honest man, Mr. Keller. I reckon he'll do the right thing. I shore hate it fer his sake, though."

Marty took his leave and rode on until he topped a low rise and spotted the main ranch house and several barns and outbuildings at the bottom of the slope. A stocky man with snow-white hair sat in a rocker on the front stoop, eyeing his approach. Marty headed Pacer directly toward the porch, until he was directly in front of the man rocking.

"Howdy. Mr. Whitcomb?"

"That's me. And you're?"

"Name's Keller. Deputy sheriff from Reno. I'm lookin' for Luke Graham. He anywhere hereabouts?"

"May I ask why you're lookin' fer my nephew?"

"I've got a warrant for him, Mr. Whitcomb. Murder and stage robbery."

Whitcomb lowered his gaze and slowly shook his head. "Damn that boy. He's sure enough gone and done it now."

"I'm not certain the charge is cut-and-dried, Mr. Whitcomb. That's why I hope you'll tell him to come on in with me and get it straightened out."

Whitcomb looked back up at Marty, defiance showing on his worn face. "He ain't here, Deputy. He lit a shuck fer Salt Lake this morning. Said he was gonna visit some friends there and then go on to Omaha and see his kin there. Sorry."

"He still riding the bay?"

"Yep. Luke's had that hoss since he was in school. He won't go far without the animal under him, I reckon."

"Well, I'd best get back on the trail. Thank you, Mr. Whitcomb. If Luke shows up here again, urge him to head back to Reno and turn himself in. Save himself a lot of grief."

"I'll do it, Deputy. But I don't expect to see the boy agin, to be honest." Whitcomb hesitated, and then looked up at Marty, naked worry evident on his face. "Any other men listed on yur warrant?"

"Nope, just Luke."

Whitcomb nodded, relief flooding his countenance. "Good enough. Try and take Luke alive, will ya?"

"I always try, Mr. Whitcomb. The choice is theirs."

Marty rode out of the yard and ascended the small rise. At the top he looked over his shoulder toward the ranch. Whitcomb had not moved, nor taken his eyes off Marty's back. "Looks like Whitcomb's giving the boy a running start, Pacer. Said he's been gone half a day and we know it's more likely just a couple of hours. I wonder if someone let him know I was headed his way."

He ran into Tyler a mile down the road, still pushing the cattle toward the ranch house.

"Howdy, Tyler."

"Howdy, Mr. Keller. I didn't figger to see ya so soon."

"Whitcomb said Luke was off to Salt Lake and then on east. I guess I just missed him." Marty paused and offered Tyler one of his small cigars, lighting both from a sulfur match he struck by whipping it across the leg of his cord pants.

"Too bad. Ya missin' him, I mean." Tyler glanced around, ensuring that nobody was observing their discussion. "Iffen ya was to ask me, I'd say no way is Luke headed to Salt Lake. He shore didn't ride past here, which he would do iffen he was gonna take the road to Salt Lake. 'Sides, he hates them Lambs of God with a passion. He's more likely headed fer Californnie. But iffen I was to really guess, I'd bet he heads over to Tuscarora first, to visit a spell with Lupe, one of Juan Morales' whores. Luke thinks Lupe has her cap set on him. I think it's more likely his purse, but it ain't none of my business, either way. From there, he can drop down and catch the train at the way station at Elko and ride on out to Californnie in style. Probably on my money."

"How would a fellow find this Tuscarora, if he was of a mind to look there?"

"Follow Spring Creek there until ya come across the road, about twenty miles or so. Then head northeast until ya git there. There ain't nothin' else around there but Tuscarora, so you'll find it easy enough." Tyler flipped the butt of his cigar into the dust at his horse's feet. "Of course, I shore would deny ever havin' this here conversation with ya, iffen ya don't mind. Well, I suppose I'd best get these slab-sided mavericks on down to the ranch afore suppertime. Be seein' ya, Mr. Keller."

"Thank you, Tyler. Take care."

Marty followed Tyler's instructions. If Graham had made a run straight for Salt Lake City, he still would not be trailing far behind. The winding creek led north and east and he finally came upon a rutted roadway that led due north. Not long after he headed up the road, he came upon a faded road sign proclaiming, TUSCARORA, 30 MILES.

"Looks like we're headed the right direction, Pacer, old pal. The thing is, shall we ride after dark, or make ourselves a camp? What's that? Ride on? Whatever you say, big fella. Giddyup, then, let's get there as quickly as we can."

Marty had not traveled two more miles before he cut a fresh trail headed the same direction as he was. "Wonder if these are Graham's tracks we're followin', Pacer, old pal. Step lively, hoss. We wanna get to Tuscarora before he gets settled in too tight to dig out."

Luke Graham rode into the once booming town as the sun slipped behind the Santa Rosa Mountains to the west. He put his tired pony in the local livery and hustled over to the cantina where Lupe worked. She ran into his arms as soon as she saw him, showering him with kisses of welcome.

"It's beeen so long, Lukie, baby. I thought you had forgotten Lupe."

"No way, sweetie pie. I've been working over by Carson City. Just got back, and came right here to see my little Lupe."

"You come upstairs with me?"

"In a minute, baby. First, I need a beer and a few hands of poker, so I can give you what you really deserve." With the little whore snuggled into his side, Luke moved to a table where several rough, worn, dirt-encrusted miners were playing cards. His card skill was such that the poor miners scarcely had a chance against him, and he had taken them for twenty dollars in as many minutes. Then he bought a bottle of tequila and escorted Lupe up to the tiny bedroom on the second floor, where she toiled on her back for her daily bread. They quickly settled under the sweat-stained, soiled linens, where he proceeded to have his pleasure with both the woman and the bottle. Time passed quickly for the busy pair of star-crossed lovers.

Even though Pacer did pick up the pace, Marty did not ride into the decaying mining town of Tuscarora until after nine p.m. Most of the shops were closed, only the town's three saloons still open for business. Marty stopped at the first he came to and walked through scarred batwing doors into the smoky saloon. It was nearly wall-to-wall with drinkers and gamblers.

The bar was crudely constructed from raw wooden planks fashioned together on sturdy legs sawn from the trunk of a three-foot-diameter pine tree. Marty ordered a short beer and snapped a fifty-cent piece on the rough surface. "Looks like you're pretty busy tonight."

The barkeep, round in face and body, plucked the coin and dropped it into a gallon can sitting on a shelf back of the bar. "Yep, most nights we stay busy. With the mines peterin' out, we're 'bout all there's left to do in Tuscarora. You want change or will you be needin' another?"

Marty's experienced gaze took in the crowd of miners, merchants, and a sprinkling of cowboys. "Keep it. I'm lookin' for a fellow named Luke Graham. I hear he has eyes for a crib gal named Lupe. She work here?"

"Naw, we don't have any whores here. Gamblin's our thing. The gal you're thinkin' of most likely works for Morales, down at the Cantina Rojo. He's got mostly Mex gals workin' his cribs. It's at the end of the street. Ya can't miss it, the doors are painted red, jus' like the name says."

Marty put a ten-dollar gold coin on the bar. "I'm also lookin' for a fellow who only has three fingers on his left hand. Tall, slender, with black hair, dark eyes. Rides with a Mexican sidekick and goes by the name of Alva Hulett. Ever run across him?"

The money vanished so fast, it seemed as if it had never been there. The bartender scratched his left cheek and thought for a moment. "Nope, can't say as I ever did. He may have crossed this way, but I never noticed him if he did. You a lawman?"

Marty gave the bartender a wan look and said nothing. The bartender nodded in understanding and swiped at the bar top with a rag, moving toward a beckoning customer farther on down the bar. Marty took a final sip of the beer and put the half-empty glass back on the bar. He slowly walked out of the saloon and grabbed Pacer's reins, before walking down the side of the only street in the town toward the red door cantina at the far end.

The stucco-walled building was three stories tall, by far the most imposing building in the town. The second and third floors had balconies running completely around the structure and the flat roof had a three-foot-high parapet around it. It looked as if it was ready to stand off an assault by marauding Indians at any moment. Marty made a mental note of the lack of a sheriff's office or jail as he walked toward the cantina.

Tying Pacer's reins to the end of a nearby hitching post, Marty eased his pistol out and back into its holster. Taking a deep breath, he walked past twin lanterns that highlighted the red wooden doors of the establishment and walked into the cantina, pausing inside to allow his eyes to adjust to the dim lighting of the interior.

Two musicians in festive Mexican vaquero costumes were playing a spirited Latin love ballad, while numerous men drank or gambled at the faro and roulette tables along the back wall. Several tables of card-players filled the front portion of the build-ing. Weary-looking, mostly Hispanic women circulated among the men, listlessly caging drinks or offering pleasures of the flesh to any who would pay their price.

Marty moved over until he was belly-up to the bar. A hard-looking Mexican bar-tender with a narrow-style mustache worked his way down the bar toward him, serving tequila and beer to patrons as he progressed. When he reached Marty, he paused, waiting for Marty's order. *"Qué desea usted?"*

"Cervesa, por favor."

The beer was served and the barkeeper moved on, leaving Marty to casually scan around the hazy, smoke-filled interior of the cantina. He saw no one who matched Gra-ham's description, either at the gaming tables or at the card tables. He motioned to the bartender, who worked his way back to Marty. *"Uno más?"* He motioned to the half-empty glass in front of Marty.

"No, thank you. I'm looking for a gal,

name of Lupe. I heard she was very nice. She working tonight?"

"Oh, *sí*. She upstairs now. Wait a few moments and she weel be back down."

"Dang, I hoped to beat ole Luke here. I guess he got in ahead of me, didn't he, the sly dog?"

The bartender gave Marty a friendlier grin. "You friends with Luke? *Sí*, he beat you here by three hours. He has Lupe in her room for more than two hours now. He weel be down soon, I think. Then you can enjoy her charms. Another beer while you wait?"

Marty grinned back and nodded, happy to be as close as he was. He could wait a few more minutes, he supposed. He decided that he would try and take Graham quiet-like and then get him out of town. They could stop for the night once away from the immediate help of any friends Luke might have in the dissolute town.

Marty sipped at his beer and watched the stairway leading down from the row of rooms up above the gaming floor. Eventually one of the doors opened and a young man and woman swaggered toward the stairway, arms around each other. The man matched the description of Luke, and wore a pistol belt and holster decorated with silver Mexican conches. They laughed at a private joke and then started down the stairs. That was Marty's cue to push away from the bar and move slowly toward the foot of the stairs, his hand hovering close to his holstered pistol.

Luke Graham paused as his wild side suddenly rang a warning. He quickly scanned the room below. His neck hairs were as stiff as a cat's whiskers. Someone or something posed a threat to him down there. What was it?

Marty pushed past a laughing pair of drunken men and looked up. His gaze caught Luke's. Marty ducked his head down, wondering if his intent stare had alarmed Luke.

Had it ever! Luke recognized the deputy he had seen in Reno, the one who was also a bounty hunter. He wildly looked around. Should he draw and shoot, run back up the stairs, or try and brazen his way past the deputy? Marty kept moving toward the stairs, forcing Luke's hand. Grabbing Lupe by her long black mane, he drew and triggered a quick shot at the tall lawman moving his way.

Lupe screamed in pain as Luke jerked her head back, her weight falling against Luke's side, spoiling his shot, which hit the floor at

Marty's feet. Marty shoved a drinker aside and turned over a card table, drawing his pistol and pointing it at the two people slowly making their way back up the stairs, Luke hiding behind the struggling Lupe.

"Give it up, Graham. You're not gonna get away, even using the gal as a shield. Throw away your gun and come on down here with your hands up."

Luke fired again, his bullet slamming into the tabletop. Marty poked his pistol around the side and sought an opportunity to nick Luke without hurting the girl. Luke pulled her to the top of the stairs and into the room they had just vacated. He slung Lupe onto her bed and quickly crawled out the window onto the balcony. Dropping to the packed dirt of the side alley, he grabbed the first horse he saw and thundered into the darkness, headed for the railroad stop at Elko, sixty miles to the southeast.

Marty was up the stairs as soon as the door closed and burst into the room just as Luke's horse galloped away. He climbed through the same window and ran around to the front of the cantina, where he dropped to the street and jumped on Pacer's sturdy back. He was galloping after the fleeing outlaw before the dust from Luke's flight had drifted back to the packed dirt of the street.

A three-quarter moon poked its silver rim over the eastern horizon as Marty settled into his saddle. He was confident that Pacer had enough in him to catch up with any horse taken by the escaping outlaw. He looked down. The silvery dust was broken up by the black hoofprints of the horse ahead. He could have followed Luke's trail if he had been a blind man.

Chapter 7
Another Outlaw
Bites the Dust

Luke spurred his tiring horse again. The animal was obviously old and of poor quality. Luke knew the laboring animal would not last much longer at the speed he was pushing him. Cursing his bad luck, he looked for an opportunity to stop and ambush the law dog on his trail. By the silvery moonlight, he had seen the solitary rider closing the gap on him at the top of the last hill. The lawman was certainly mounted on a better horse than the one Luke had stolen.

Off to the west, perhaps a quarter mile from the dusty road, was an outcropping of large boulders that had over the millenniums fallen from a sheer sandstone cliff. Jerking his reins, Luke turned his horse toward the shelter of the rocks. He could hide among them and pick off the lawman when he rode up. At the least, he could rest his horse and light out again once the moon set, hopefully before dawn cast enough light for his pursuer to follow his tracks.

Marty spotted where Luke turned off the road. He pulled Pacer to a quick halt and surveyed the rocks in the distance. He caught a quick glimpse of Luke as the fleeing outlaw rode into the maze of sandstone. Marty was not crazy enough to ride into an obvious ambush. He climbed off Pacer's back and loosened the cinch of his saddle. He reached into his saddlebags and pulled out a sack of oats. Once he fed Pacer, he poured some water into his hat and let the horse have a short drink.

With the moon shining so brightly on the silvery sand of the high Nevada desert, there was no way Luke could get out of the trap he had put himself into without Marty seeing him. Marty took a sip of water for himself and walked off the road until he came to a small mesquite plant growing through the parched earth. He tied Pacer's reins to it and made himself comfortable against a small boulder, which made a tolerable backrest. He was patient and willing to wait for Luke to come out of the rock pile. The desperate fugitive was not going anywhere as long as the moon cast its silver glow over the desert.

Marty lay quietly as the hours passed and

Luke Graham stayed secreted behind his fortress. The moon progressed across the southern sky. As it dipped beneath the western mountains, Marty leaped to his feet and quietly rode away from the rock pile, anxious to beat Graham away from the area and to get ahead of the fleeing outlaw. Marty galloped across the desert to the top of a low rise a mile to the south of the cliff and pulled up. He had not crossed the road, so he was certain Luke did not know he was now ahead in the chase.

Luke suffered in vain waiting for Marty to come closer to his ambush, but the wily bounty hunter seemed satisfied to sit by the road, perhaps hoping Luke would make some sort of move against him. That was not in Luke's plans. He settled himself against a large boulder where he had a view toward the road, determined to outlast the persistent law dog who was pursuing him. Startled, he roused himself from an unintentional light doze. The moon was down and the sun was still below the eastern horizon. He saddled his nag and slipped out the far side of the boulders. Walking his horse slowly, he made his way to the road and then turned south toward Elko.

Marty tied Pacer off the roadway a hundred feet. In the darkness, Graham would not see the animal as he rode up. Pacer was too well trained to make noise, so Marty settled behind a large cactus bush to await his prey. He hoped that Graham would not deviate from his previous direction of flight in the early morning darkness.

His patience was rewarded when he heard the soft footsteps of a horse working its way up the slope toward him. Luke was riding slowly, directly toward him. Marty pulled his pistol and crouched by the side of the road, keeping his breath slow and even as he awaited the coming confrontation.

The sky lightened a shade against the dark earth. From his perspective, Marty was able to see Graham's silhouette long before there was any chance of Luke spotting him. If anything, he blended into the cactus. When Luke was within a few feet, Marty abruptly stood up, his six-gun pointed at the dark mass of rider and horse.

"That's far enough, Graham. Get your hands up right now."

The sudden movement and sound startled the horse. It reared straight up like a horse half its age. Luke was pitched off the back end of the terrified animal and hit the ground like a sack of flour. Even so, he somehow struggled to his knees and managed to grab his pistol and fire a shot at

Marty. His luck was bad and the bullet sped aimlessly into the darkness. Marty's shot was an instant later and his aim was true. He hit the unfortunate Luke high in the right shoulder, spinning him to the ground.

Luke's fight was over. He lay in a heap, moaning in pain. Marty hurried up to the downed outlaw to check him for hideouts and then pulled off Luke's belt and holster. He tossed them next to the pistol lying in the middle of the road, faintly visible under the rapidly lightening sky.

"Oh, oh, my arm. You broke my arm."

"Shut up, boy. You had your chance. I told you to back off, but you had to try and buck long odds. Hold still now, so I can see just how bad you're hit." Marty flared a sulfur match and checked the damage. "You're lucky, Luke. It looks like the bullet passed clear through without hitting bone. Let me get the wound plugged and you'll live to stand trial for your crimes."

Luke squinted up at Marty through pain-filled eyes. "You're Keller, ain't ya? Damn my luck. If it weren't bad, I wouldn't have none."

"Tell that to the man you killed. You're lucky to be alive, fella. I was aiming for your center, not your wing. Now be quiet and let me work."

By the time Marty finished, it was light enough to see clearly. Marty gathered Luke's weapon and horse and then made a campfire from dried mesquite branches, scattered in abundance on the parched soil. He brewed up a pot of coffee and helped the wounded Luke to sip some from his tin cup. Then he had a full measure before hoisting his whining prisoner back on the stolen horse and embarking on down the trail to Elko.

"Ain't ya gonna take me to Tuscarora? It's only twenty miles back thattaway. It's near forty to Elko. I need tendin' by a sawbones."

"Sorry, bub. You'll have to make do. I reckon you've got too many friends in Tuscarora. We'll see what's available in Elko. If not there, you'll make it to Reno on the train, I betcha."

"But it hurts." Luke moaned piteously. "I'm hurtin' real bad."

"I suspect that guard you killed during the stage holdup would trade places with you, whaddya think?"

With him bitterly complaining with every mile, Marty escorted Luke into Elko the next afternoon, just before the westbound train was scheduled to leave. He stopped at a sign proclaiming a doctor was available for business and watched as the old sawbones swabbed out the wound and cauterized it with a hot iron. Luke fainted, even though he had taken a healthy swallow of laudanum.

"Any chance I can get him on the westbound train, Doc?"

The rummy-eyed old physician shook his head. "Nope. You'll have to wait until Tuesday's train. He's gonna have to rest up some. You can get him a bed at Stella's place. She'll make you up some beef broth to replace some of the blood he's lost."

Marty nodded glumly and waited until Luke regained consciousness. He helped Luke over to the small rooming house across the street from the doctor's office. He obtained a room for the both of them and as soon as the middle-aged Stella had Luke carefully tucked in bed, chained Luke's good arm to the bedstead with his wrist cuffs. Luke cussed bitterly, but shut his mouth after Marty gave him a healthy smack upside his head. "No cussin' in front of the lady, Luke. Mind your manners, hear?"

Luke sullenly nodded his understanding, so Marty gave a quick smile to Stella. "I hope he'll behave, Stella. If not, smack him on the noggin, or give me a call. I think I'll wash up and grab a bite to eat. Don't let him get a hold of any type of knife or such. He may look harmless, but he's a killer and he wants to get away worse than anything else in this world. Don't get careless around him, understand?"

Stella nodded and followed Marty out of the room. "Doc Winters wants me to make him some broth. I'll wait until you come back to take it to him. You say you'll be gone Tuesday?"

"Yes'm. I'll be in the room with him tonight and I'll stay close tomorrow, so you needn't worry. As long as you stay away from him, he'll not bother you."

Marty took Pacer and Luke's stolen claybank to the livery to be fed and cared for. He got a promise from the stable boy to return the claybank to Tuscarora as soon as practicable for a five-dollar gold piece. Marty then grabbed a quick meal at the local beanery and returned to the boardinghouse. He bade good-bye to a relieved Stella on Tuesday afternoon, doubling her normal rental rate, and got Pacer and Luke on the westbound to Reno.

He was in the boomtown by early the next morning. He had Luke locked up in the cell next to the fugitive McNeal, the outlaw who had brought Marty to Reno in the first place. Longabaugh was getting around without any problem and Marty treated him to a big breakfast at the Chinaman's Café.

Jesse saluted Marty with his coffee cup. "I'm pleased you brought Graham in alive, Marty."

"Actually, Jesse, it was more luck on his part than skill on mine. He drew down on me and I snapped a quick shot back. If I'd have hit him where I meant to, we'd be plantin' him on boot hill about now."

"Well, I reckon it's good fer yur reputation to bring one in alive now and then."

"I'd bring 'em all in that way, if they'd let me, Jesse. I take no pleasure in killin' 'em. There's only two men on my death watch and you know who they are."

"Hear anything about them up Elko way?"

"Nope, not a thing. I'll find 'em, though, come hell or high water, I'll find 'em someday." Marty thoughtfully sipped. "You get off a telegram for me to the law in Carson City claiming the reward for Luke Graham?"

"Right after I finish this here nice breakfast you've been so generous to buy fer me."

"In the meanwhile, I reckon I'll lollygag around town and then get some rest. You want to go out shootin' with me tomorrow?"

"Why not? It's a good way to keep my

hand in. Now I reckon I'd best get some work done." Jesse grinned at Marty. "You oughta git yourself a bath, if you git my meanin'."

"Why, thank you, pard. I was wonderin' if I'd got enough fragrance on me to make you notice. I reckon I'll do just that. Then I'm gonna take a long nap, safe in the knowin' that you're out there protecting the town and me while I relax."

The two friends parted at the door. Marty did enjoy both a long, hot bath and a day's sleep. He came out of the hotel just as the sun was dipping low in the west, stretched, and ambled toward the café, where he planned to attack a thick fried steak and potatoes. He waved at Jesse walking toward him across the street, a piece of paper in his hand. Marty waited until Jesse crossed over and came up to him.

"Afternoon, Jesse. I'm about to get a big steak at the café. You interested?"

"Might as well, Marty. I got a reply from the sheriff in Carson City about your reward."

"Oh?"

"Yeah, it's sorta funny."

"How's that?"

"Here, have a look for yourself."

Marty quickly read the yellow sheet of

paper containing the telegram's response for his reward. He looked up at Jesse with a frown. "They want me to bring Graham all the way in to Carson City? That's different. I wonder what's goin' on."

"I can't rightly say, Marty. Never had that request before. Let's mull it over while doin' justice to that steak you was talkin' about."

Over their meal the two lawmen considered the reason behind the strange order to deliver the outlaw. Always before, Marty had only to find the nearest sheriff and receive a verification of capture to collect any reward.

"One nice thing about it," Jesse announced, "I needed to get McNeal to Carson City anyways. Now you can deliver 'em both for me."

"Now, hold on, Jesse. Dadgummit, I hadn't planned on traipsin' around the countryside trying to deliver outlaws to somewhere else."

"I'll get you a delivery fee. It'll pay for your time and expense of deliverin' 'em down to Carson City. I don't see no way you're gonna get any reward money without doin' like the telegram says, Marty. They got ya stuck twixt a hoof and a horseshoe."

"When do you think I could get under way? I hate to waste my time and money just hanging around Reno."

101

"I'll have the sawbones check out Graham tomorrow. He's most likely about recovered from the rigors or yur bringin' him in all shot up like ya did."

The rest of the meal Marty grumbled in frustration about the demand made by the law in Carson City. He saw no way of refusing without perhaps losing the reward money on Graham. He needed the funds to continue his quest, and he resigned himself to the additional burden.

Marty was at the jail the next morning to hear for himself what the doctor had to say about Graham's ability to make the trip on down to Carson City. The silver-haired sawbones was adamant. "Two more days of rest fer him, Sheriff. I can't allow any travelin' by the prisoner prior to then. I'll come on by Wednesday and certify him for release Thursday mornin'."

Jesse rolled his eyes and looked over at Marty. "There ya have it, Marty. I'll order out a wagon and supplies for ya to leave Thursday morning."

"I'll collect the both of 'em at seven, Jesse. I wanna be in Reno before dark on Friday."

Jesse turned his gaze to his deputy, a lanky, light-haired man with a large nose and receding chin. "You heard the man, George. Have a wagon outside the office at seven on Thursday mornin'. Have two days' water and rations packed and tell the smithy to bolt a pair of rings to the wagon bed. That way Marty can chain 'em down so they won't be no trouble on the trail."

"Gotcha, Sheriff. I'll be there." The deputy ambled out the door, followed by the doctor.

"Damn," Marty snorted again for the hundredth time. "This sure burns my hide. I was plannin' on leaving for California as soon as the reward money arrived."

"You can cross over from Carson City. There's the Mormon Pass that comes out at the south end of Lake Tahoe. It's a right pretty trip, believe me. You end up in Hangtown and it's only a day's ride on to Sacramento from there."

"Well, I guess I'd better check on Pacer and pick up some supplies for the road. I'll see you for dinner tonight?"

"Same time, same place, old chum. Now git goin'. I got a ton of paperwork piled up to finish before my noon meetin' with the city council."

CHAPTER 8
UNWELCOME NEWS

Vern Barton was standing in the shade of his porch, talking with Charlie Call, when he paused to watch a galloping rider burst out of the tree line and head directly toward him as if the rider were running from a mad longhorn. As the rider pulled his sweating, panting horse to a sliding stop and swung off the saddle, Vern wondered if he was going to be run down by the hurrying rider. He held up his hands in a defensive posture. "Hold on there, Slim. What the hell's got you so riled up?"

"Boss, I was in Reno to git my saddle fixed when I saw some hombre bring Luke Graham offa the train and march him over to the sheriff's office. Luke was all bandaged up like he'd been shot."

Vern pursed his lips and stroked his bushy mustache with his forefinger. "Damn the luck, that's unwelcome news. I shoulda sent you out to take care of him before, Charlie.

Mike and Sailor screwed it up but good."

Charlie nodded but kept his mouth shut. He had been on the receiving end of Vern's blowups in the past. He would prefer to avoid another if he could. Unfortunately, it occurred to him that maybe everything had been going too smoothly lately. He had the perfect job and wanted it to stay that way. He could indulge in his larcenous desires, had plenty of spending money, and Vern left him alone to run the ranch as he saw fit, as long as there were no problems.

Vern nodded at Slim. "Thanks fer the info, Slim. Get on over to the corral and take care of yur hoss. It looks like you 'bout ran him to death gittin' here."

"Sure enough, boss. I'll grab a bite from Cookie while I'm at it. I rode outa Reno without gittin' any noon chow."

Vern turned away from Slim and looked toward the blue mountains to the west. "Charlie, where's Mike and Sailor?"

"I've got 'em watchin' the stage depot in Carson City, boss. You told me to keep an eye on it in case O'Brian tries to sneak out a run to Virginia City, remember?"

"Of course. Maybe it's just as well we don't involve them in this. Send Slim back to Reno. Tell him to find out what he can about Luke. I'll bet they try and take him to Carson City to stand trial, don't you? Maybe we can free him up when they do, if not before."

"We maybe oughta wait until they move Luke, boss. That Sheriff Longabaugh is a pretty tough nut and the jail is right in the middle of town. It might cost us some men to ride in and bust Luke out."

Vern scuffed the dirt at his feet with the toe of his boot. "Yu're probably right, Charlie. But we gotta make certain Luke don't git to Carson City and spill the beans about us to the law."

Charlie nodded in agreement. "I gotcha, boss. Let's see what Slim finds out first. Then you can decide what ya want me to do."

Vern and Charlie walked over to the kitchen, where they saw Slim wolfing down a bowl of stew from the leftover noon meal. The two outlaws sat down on either side of him and accepted a cup of coffee from the diminutive Cookie.

"Slim, I want you to go back to Reno and nose around. Find out what the law plans on doing with Luke Graham and when. We're gonna have to get him outa their hands, one way or t'other." Vern sipped his coffee and waited for Slim's reply.

"Can do, boss. The jail in Reno sits next

to an alley. I reckon I could sneak back there tonight and have a gabber with Luke. Hopefully he knows what's goin' on."

"Ya don't think he's dyin' from his wound, do ya?" Charlie asked from across the table.

"Naw, the bandage was all around his arm, best as I could see." Slim shoved the last of his meal into his mouth and chewed noisily, then washed it down with a gulp of coffee.

"Could ya get a clean shot at Luke from the alley?" Vern asked. He looked at Slim to gauge his reaction.

"Maybe, I ain't certain. It'd be the easiest way, wouldn't it?"

"And worth a hunnerd dollars to me," Vern replied. "That don't cause you no heartburn, does it?"

"Nope. I ain't a chum of Luke nohow. I'll give it a try. There's an alley behind the jail and the only cell in the jail has a window that looks out over the alley. I was in there once fer fightin' and bein' snoot-faced in public. It's way high on the back wall, but a body could reach it iffen he stood on the bunk. If I could git Luke to stand on somethin' and look out the window, I could plug him easy. If I can't, I'll find out all I can and git back here so's we can try somethin' else."

"And, Slim," Vern cautioned, "we don't want this gittin' out to any of the boys, so keep yur mouth shut, okay?"

"Fer a hunnerd dollars, boss, my mouth is sewed plumb shut tight."

Charlie escorted Slim to the barn to pick up Slim's horse for the return to Reno. "Don't take stupid chances, Slim. I don't need you in the hoosegow either. Iffen ya can't git Luke at the jail, we'll git him on the road to Carson City. They're bound to have to take him there, since that's where the reward was registered. All we gotta do is find out when they're goin'."

"Understand, Charlie. You can count on me. Just make sure I git a chance to earn that hunnerd dollars."

Charlie slapped Slim on the back. "Ya can count on it, Slim. Now git a-goin' and use yur head fer somethin' more than just a hat rack."

Slim made the four-hour trip back to Reno counting the ways he was going to spend the hundred dollars he would earn for shutting up Luke Graham permanently. He did not like the loudmouthed outlaw anyway, so it was no big loss, at least as far as Slim was concerned.

Slim's bay was still tired from the quick trip to the ranch, three hours of hard riding from Reno. Slim let the weary horse set his own pace and continued to fantasize about pleasurable things, like the new Chinese gal at Ruby's Cathouse in Virginia City.

He arrived in Reno after sundown, and enjoyed the next hour wetting his parched throat and filling his belly at the Emporium Hotel's café, his favorite eating establishment in the booming railroad town. After an enjoyable after-dinner whiskey at the Palace Saloon, he walked past the sheriff's office and ducked into the alley behind the lockup area of the jail. A barred window was set into the adobe wall about ten feet off the ground.

Slim tossed small pebbles at the bars until he saw a pair of hands wrap themselves around two of the bars and a dark shape of the top half of a man's head was visible through the bars. "Who's out there?" a soft voice inquired.

"It's Slim Pickett. That you, Luke?"

"Naw, Luke's got a bum arm. He can't pull his-self up. I'm in the same cell with him. Just a second." The man disappeared and then returned in a few moments. "Luke says he knows ya. Whaddya want?"

Slim cursed his bad luck. It was obvious he would not have a chance to plug Luke at the window. "Tell Luke that Vern is gonna git him out. Does he know if they're gonna take him to Reno to stand trial?"

"Yeah," the voice whispered back. "Me and him are goin' down to Carson City with Keller, the bounty hunter, on Thursday mornin'. We're supposed to leave around seven o'clock."

"You gonna ride horses?"

"Naw, they got a wagon fer us to ride in, with a ringbolt to chain us to the floorboard. Bring a hacksaw when you come fer us. And don't forgit to bring horses. We'll not want to walk out there."

"Okay. You tell Luke that Vern said not to say nothin', he's gonna git him outa jail."

"Luke and me understand. We'll keep our mouths shut fer the time bein'. You just be sure you break us free afore we git to Carson City. They got a solid jail there. And tell Vern that Luke says he's got a lot he could say iffen he was of a mind to."

"I'll do it. You two just rest easy. We'll see ya on the road to Carson City Thursday. Do ya know if any other deputies are goin' along on the trip as guards?"

"I heard the sheriff talkin' to the bounty hunter. 'Pears he's takin' us alone."

The head dropped away from the window. Slim walked out of the alley and headed back to the Palace, where he drank and played cards for a couple of hours, then went to the livery and curled up in the hayloft next to several other sleepers. He rode back to the ranch early the next morning and reported on his conversation with the jailed men.

"Talks mighty tough, don't he? Especially fer a man who got hisself caught within a week of goin' on a wanted poster." Vern worried his mustache, as he was want to do when he was agitated. "Two of 'em, huh?" Vern mused. "Do ya think this other fella would be any help once we spring the ambush?"

"I think so, but if they're chained to a ringbolt in the floorboard, there ain't much they'll be able to do," Slim answered. "One thing fer certain, though. If we can't break 'em free, they'll make fine targets, chained in the wagon like they'll be."

"I expect you'll be able to knock off the deputy and free 'em without that. But iffen ya can't git to 'em, do jus' that."

Slim stabled his horse and spent the rest of the day relaxing in the shade. He huddled with Vern and Charlie after supper, while they discussed the best way to ambush the lawman and his prisoners.

"There's a good spot to hit the fella just after he crosses the dry wash at the top of

Low Creek Ridge. You know where I mean, Slim? Where the road cuts through the dry wash at the top of the hill."

"Yeah, I think so. We can ride out there tomorrow and have a look at it. There's high ground up the rise, ain't there?"

"Yep. We'll have good cover too. There's plenty of trees growin' there. Big pines, so there won't be no ground clutter to get in the way of our aimin'."

"The two of ya be enough fer the job?" Vern asked.

Charlie shook his head. "I don't think so, Vern. I think I'd better ask Joaquin to come along. There might be someone ridin' along with the lawman. Three of us'll make the odds a lot better."

"And cost me more money," Vern grumbled. "Still, best to be certain, rather than sorry. Will he keep his trap shut about it?"

"There ain't no doubt about that," Charlie reassured the outlaw leader. "He's pretty quiet around the boys anyways. I'll make sure he knows to keep his yapper shut. Ya know," he observed, "Luke didn't make much in the way of friends while he was here."

Vern nodded. "Make certain Joaquin understands that I want a tight lid on what

112

we're a-doin'," he answered. "Okay, that's it. You two go out there tomorrow and check over the spot where ya want to set up. I don't want no slipups on this. We git Luke or we shut him up. Permanently."

The next day Charlie and Slim scouted the proposed ambush site. It was even better than they had hoped. The high ground looked down on the road, which cut its way through the loamy soil at the top of the rise, ensuring that the wagon would be moving slowly. The towering pine trees provided plenty of cover, and three men spread out in a line would make it almost impossible for one man to escape their fire, should their initial shots fail to knock him out of the saddle. "If we wait till he just comes outa the draw, we'll be all over him afore he can even think about drawin' his six-gun." Charlie chortled in satisfaction.

The two outlaws rode back to the ranch and met with Joaquin after supper. Smoking a thin cigar while drawing with a slender stick in the dust by the bunkhouse, Charlie put the hard-eyed Mexican gun hand into the picture. Slim chimed in with his comments as Charlie finished his explanation.

"We'll space out enough that we should be able to cover anything the deputy tries, if we don't git 'em on the first volley. Ya ain't got no problem pluggin' Luke iffen we can't git him freed, do ya?" Charlie puffed on his slender cigar while he watched Joaquin's expression and awaited his answer.

"Hell, Charlie," Joaquin answered in his heavily accented English, "I'd keel a half dozen just like Lukie for a hunnerd dollars."

CHAPTER 9
DEADLY AMBUSH

Marty walked out of Sheriff Jesse Long-abaugh's office followed by a shackled Luke Graham sharing a leg chain with McNeal, who was cuffed just as securely. Jesse followed, squinting as he stepped into the bright sunlight. Jesse's deputy was already in the wagon bed, ready to attach the leg irons to the two ringbolts mounted into the reinforced floor of the wagon.

The two prisoners sullenly climbed into the back of the wagon and sat down, one on either side of the two ringbolts. The outlaws were quickly secured and the wagon was ready for travel. Marty tied Pacer's reins to the rear of the wagon and stepped back on the boardwalk to shake Jesse's hand.

"Thanks for all your help, Jesse. I certainly appreciate it." Marty offered his hand.

"Take care of yourself, Marty." Jesse pumped Marty's hand up and down. "You were a big help to me and I'm grateful. You just stay on the road all the way to Carson City. There's a good campsite at Mormon Station, and you should git there just before sundown. When you git to Reno, tell Sheriff Schrader I said to cut you some slack, you ain't near as bad as your reputation makes ya out to be. That note you're carrying for me oughta help you out a mite."

"I appreciate it, Jesse. Thanks again for everything." Marty climbed up onto the wagon and settled into the driver's seat. He checked the pair of shackled men sitting glumly on the wagon floor behind him, their faces reflecting the misery they were experiencing. "You jaspers ready to ride? Hold on, here we go." He slapped the reins against the rumps of the two horses hitched to the wagon tongue. "Giddyup, you two. We're got a long haul this day, so start movin'." He drove the wagon with his prisoners out of Reno, turning to wave at Jesse at the end of Main Street.

Luke started complaining about the uncomfortable ride before they had gone a quarter mile down the road. "Damn it, Deputy, slow down a mite. We ain't sitttin' on a seat like you are. This here wagon bottom is tossin' us around like salt in a shaker. My butt's already sore as a boil."

Marty called out over his shoulder at

Luke, "Mister, let me make something perfectly clear. I don't give a good gosh damn if your guts shake clear out your ass. You keep your mouth shut or I'm gonna chain you behind this here wagon and you can walk to Carson City. You catch my drift?"

"Well, hell, don't git so uppity. I was jus' tryin' to ask politelike fer some paddin' to sit on. Do ya have any objections to us usin' our bedrolls as cushions?"

Marty chucked the reins against the rumps of the team again. "Do whatever you like. Just shut your mouth and keep it shut. I don't want to spend my day listening to you two skunks."

For the next several hours there was relative quiet between the two outlaws and Marty, which was just as he preferred it. He had no desire to chum it up with either of the two. Instead, he thought about his next move in his search for Alva Hulett and Sanchez, the two remaining killers of his family that were still alive.

From time to time he glanced back at his cargo, but the two killers were sitting quietly, morosely watching the scenery past by, sitting on their bedrolls and leaning against the sides of the wagon bed, bouncing and rocking with the wagon as it traversed the rocky, rutted roadway.

Marty's bottom was not used to the wooden seat of the wagon, so he stopped and put his bedroll under him as a cushion. As they started up again, he sighed and looked at Graham. "Your idea was a good one. This bedroll makes a decent cushion for sitting."

McNeal spoke up for the first time since they left the jail at Reno. "I need to water the lizards and I'm gittin' hungry. We gonna stop soon?"

"Just as soon as we reach that stand of trees up ahead. Hold your horses till then."

As soon as they entered the shade of the towering pines, Marty stopped the wagon. He unlocked McNeal and allowed him to relieve himself before chaining him to one of the spokes of the rear wheel. Graham whined about his own needs the entire time, but Marty was careful to expose himself to only one risk at a time. Graham remained chained to the wagon bed until the stocky McNeal was secured to the wagon's rear wheel. Then he allowed Graham his turn. As soon as he had Graham chained to the front wheel, he made a quick meal of fried pork and bread slices, gave each man a long drink, allowed each one more stop in the trees, and then resumed his journey.

During the noontime break, Marty devoted the majority of his time rubbing Pacer's leg, grateful that the big horse seemed to have recovered from his leg injury. McNeal spoke up as soon as they were under way again.

"Your horse got a bad leg?"

"I hope *had* is a better word. Got it chasin' you down to Reno from Utah. The smithy in Reno seems to have fixed him up right proper."

"He's too nice a hoss to have to put down. I'm glad. I only ran 'cause I heerd you always kilt yur man once you catched him."

"Not true. I always try to take my man alive. Like ole Luke here. I coulda shot him deader'n a stomped polecat, but I didn't. He certainly tried to do that to me."

"Well, you got my word I ain't gonna cause ya no trouble twix here and Carson City," McNeal announced.

"That's right, McNeal, you aren't. But you're gonna ride the whole way chained to that ringbolt anyway, so don't get your hopes up. Your word doesn't mean much since you killed that man in Utah and stole his horse."

McNeal slumped back and stared at the mountains to the west, silently cursing his fate. Luke Graham wisely stayed silent, content to wait for his friends to spring the trap that would free him and McNeal. If the bounty hunter was still alive when he got free, he'd have his revenge then. He pictured himself wearing the fancy Colt pistols that Marty had slung on his hips. He also planned to be riding the fancy horse docilely walking behind the wagon, and for good measure he would kick dirt in Marty's dead face if he could not have the pleasure of killing him personally.

The afternoon was a repeat of the morning, hard riding on a bumpy road with very little conversation between Marty and his two prisoners. The sun was halfway down the western horizon when the wagon and its human cargo reached the cut made by spring runoffs across the road. Up in the trees, carefully spaced so they could cover any contingency, Joaquin, Charlie, and Slim waited for the opportune time to spring their deadly ambush. The trees grew almost to the roadside and the hill sloped up from the road, so they had the high ground advantage and good cover. Keller did not stand a chance, in the eyes of all three killers.

"You fellas wait till I open up," Charlie instructed as they picked their ambush positions. "I wanna git him just as the wagon slows to cross the stream. If I miss, which I won't, you two blast him offa the wagon. If for some reason he ain't kilt right off, take care of Luke and the other guy. Got it?"

"*Sí,*" Joaquin answered. "I weel have a bead on him from the moment I see him. I weel fire as soon as you do. One of us is certain to git heem."

The three killers waited in the shade of the tall pines, each engrossed with his own thoughts, contemplating how he would spend the bonus Vern would give them for freeing or killing Luke Graham.

As their target came into view, each man settled behind his chosen spot, carefully aiming at the driver of the wagon. A feral grin crossed the hardened face of Joaquin. He was about to make some easy money.

Marty chucked the reins as the team faltered at the bottom of the cut across the roadway. "Come on now, horses, pull together." He leaned forward to check the roadway below the wheels for soft sand or deep mud. Just at that moment, a chunk of hot lead blew his hat off his head, clipping a lock of dark hair along with it. Marty did not hear the report of the rifle, but he threw himself from the seat of the wagon, on the far side from where the shot had come, as instinctively as jumping back from a coiled

121

rattlesnake.

He pulled his six-gun and peered up the wooded slope. Two other bullets cut air beside his head, while another punched through the side of the wagon seat like a hot knife through butter. Marty dropped to his belly and crawled under the wagon to the edge of the cut and risked another quick glance. Seeing movement upslope about forty yards away, he snapped two quick shots with his .44 in the general direction and scooted to Pacer, still tied to the rear of the wagon. Marty needed his rifle to stand off the men shooting at him. He stayed low, but worked his Winchester repeater out of its saddle holster. Knowing he would make himself a target if he tried to get the big Sharps on the far side of the horse, he scooted back to the edge of the roadway and poked his rifle over the top.

Two bullets kicked up dirt beside his head, so he dropped low and moved a few feet to the right. Peering through a clump of bunchgrass, he spotted movement and quickly fired at the target, knocking bark off the side of a big ponderosa pine next to Charlie's head. The outlaw leader ducked back behind the thick trunk of the tree, cursing his bad luck at firing at the lawman just as he dropped his head. He chided himself for not taking a body shot instead of trying to punch one through the target's skull.

"Joaquin, Slim," he shouted. "Take 'em out, the lawman's got cover and a rifle now. He's pinned me down."

The two outlaws quickly aimed at the two men chained to the wagon. Graham was sitting with his back to the hill, twisting his head over his shoulder to see what was happening. McNeal was facing the hill and his chest was exposed to the deadly fire from above the wagon's location. Joaquin's shot hit the back of Luke Graham's head, snapping it forward and spraying McNeal with blood and tissue. Almost simultaneously, Slim's shot hit McNeal squarely in the chest, just above a button. A dark stain quickly spread over the mortally wounded man's chest, and he slumped over.

Marty saw the smoke from Joaquin's rifle and spaced three quick shots at the tree behind which the outlaw was hiding. One was lucky, judging from a sudden scream of pain. A bullet had cut skin and muscle just under Joaquin's armpit. That was enough for Charlie. "Let's go, boys," he called, and slipped back farther into the trees without waiting to see if they heard or needed his assistance.

Marty snapped a hurried shot at one of the retreating outlaws, but the man dodged so quickly into a cluster of trees that he doubted that he hit him. He waited a few tense moments but saw nothing else. He faintly heard the hoofbeats of galloping horses. Slowly, he rose and carefully scanned the area. He saw nothing suspicious. He quickly checked to ensure that Pacer was not injured by the flying lead, then crawled into the back of the wagon.

Luke was long gone from this earth, but McNeal was laboriously breathing, bright blood still seeping out of his wound, staining the dried wood of the wagon a dark crimson. Marty took his kerchief and pushed it against the wound. "Damn," he muttered. "If this jasper was as dead as he's gonna be soon, I could follow those yahoos, maybe pay them back for their little surprise." He looked wistfully up the slope of the hill toward where the men had disappeared. "Later," he vowed, and returned his attention to the wounded McNeal. Tying the blood-soaked kerchief to the wound with a strip of blanket he cut from McNeal's bedroll, he made the unconscious outlaw as comfortable as possible. Climbing back on the wagon seat, his rifle resting on his thighs, he whipped the team of horses, determined to reach Mormon Station as quickly as the horses could make it. Perhaps he could turn over the wounded man there and get back to the trail of the ambushers before dark.

Even pushing the tired horses as fast as he dared, Marty took an hour to reach the little trading post/way station that was Mormon Station. He slid the wagon to a dust-cloud stop right in front of the door to the low-roofed, wood and stone building. A young boy of about fifteen opened the door and peered at Marty, a questioning look on his freckled face. "What's the hurry, Mister?"

"I've got a wounded man here. Your pa or ma around?"

"Nope. They rode into Carson City this mornin'. Won't be back till tomorrow. I'm in charge. Maybe I can help ya."

"Help me carry this man inside. He's taken a bullet in the chest and is bleedin' bad. We've got to get it stopped."

Together they got the wounded McNeal on a low cot in a small bedroom just off the main storeroom of the station. Marty carefully took the compression bandage away from the bullet hole to inspect the wound. "What's your name?" he asked the wide-eyed boy standing beside him.

"Ezekiel," the boy answered. "I will pray

to God this man will live, but it don't look likely. He's shot real bad." The boy touched Marty's arm. "Who are you, Mister?"

"A deputy out of Reno. Call me Marty. I was taking this fella and another to Carson City for trial when we were ambushed back the trail a ways." He wiped the fresh blood from the angry-looking entry hole in Mc-Neal's chest. The bullet had not exited the man, so it needed to be extracted, if he were to live. "Zeke, you need to make me a pot of boiling water, right away."

"Yessir, Marty. I'll get right on it."

Marty held the wad of blanket against the wound until Ezekiel returned with a cast-iron pot of hot water. He washed McNeal's wound and his right hand, gritting his teeth at the pain of the hot water. Carefully, he pushed his forefinger into the wound, feeling for the bullet, although he had no idea what he would use to pull it out when he found it.

"Damn," he muttered, "I don't feel it. It musta hit a bone or something and bounced away. Well, Zeke, all we can do is bind him up and get him on to Carson City. A doctor will have to finish the job, I can't do it."

Together they tightly wrapped a fresh bandage over the wound and carried Mc-Neal back out to the wagon. Zeke made a bed out of both bedrolls, cushioning Mc-Neal to protect him from the inevitable jouncing as best they could. Marty considered McNeal lucky that he was still unconscious. The trip into Carson City would be an agonizing one if he were to regain consciousness. He scarcely glanced at the wrapped form of Luke. The cowardly murderer was past helping anyway.

After McNeal was settled, Marty walked back into the store and bought himself a new sombrero. His old one lay in the dust by the road at the ambush site, ruined by the bullet that had punched through it. "Thanks for your help, Zeke. You're man enough to take care of this place anytime, by my reckoning."

Marty pushed his team hard and they rode into Carson City just before midnight. He called out to the first man he passed, "Where's the doc's office?"

The man pointed down the road. "Down there about two blocks. Doc Jenkins."

"Thanks," Marty answered. He snapped the reins and drove quickly to the small home and office. He hammered on the door until an elderly man in spectacles opened it, holding a burning lamp in an arthritic hand.

"What's the ruckus?"

"Gunshot, Doc. He's bleedin' bad. Happened about five hours ago, just before Mormon Station."

"Give me a hand and we'll git him to the examining table inside. I can't do nothin' out here in the dark."

As he helped the doctor lift McNeal out of the wagon to carry him inside the examining room, the prisoner shuddered and breathed his last. They laid the body on the doctor's examining table. The old physician listened for a heartbeat with a scarred wooden ear horn. "Not a peep. He's a goner, I'm afraid."

"Damn, damn, damn," Marty grumbled. "All for nothing. And now, if that's rain I smell in the air, the tracks will be gone tomorrow. I think I'll stay out of Nevada for a spell. There's nothing here for me." He sighed and climbed into the wagon. He now had to find the livery and get out of the rain. "Just be my luck that it'll snow on me next," he grumbled as he chucked the reins. "First, check in with the sheriff, then get to the stable."

CHAPTER 10
THE DUDE FROM CINCINNATI

Marty stepped out of the sheriff's office into a steadily falling rain. He had spent an hour giving the crusty old law dog his story of the ambush for the second time. "Dang it, not a prayer of finding any tracks now."

He turned to the sheriff, who had followed Marty to the door, savoring the cool breeze of damp air. "Sheriff, any idea when I can pick up the reward on Graham? I'd like to get going as quickly as possible."

Sheriff Schrader shook his head, the curly white hairs nearly brushing the collar of his sweat-stained shirt. "Nope. Malcolm O'Brian, owner of the local cartage company, put it up. I'll check with him tomorrow and tell him you got the man named in the wanted poster. I reckon it'll take a day or two. He's had a run of bad luck lately, holdups and the destruction of several of his stagecoaches and freight wagons. I'll let ya know. After readin' Jesse's letter, I suppose I'd best let ya hang out a spell in Carson City, much as I dislike most bounty hunters."

"Thanks, Sheriff. You're all heart. Suppose I can find a room at the hotel this late at night?"

"Come on, I'll walk ya over. Harry, the night clerk, won't say no to ya iffen I'm along."

Schrader was as good as his word. Marty was quickly issued a room key and deposited at the foot of the stairs by the sheriff, who shook his hand, perhaps so Harry would see. "Stop by tomorrow afternoon, Keller. I'll have yur information by then." He turned to leave and spoke over his shoulder. "Night. I'll have my night jailor take yur hoss and the wagon to the stable fer ya."

"Marvelous. Good night, Sheriff, and thanks for your help."

Marty quickly put his few belongings from his saddlebags in the scarred dresser, then settled back on the worn bed, falling asleep to the soft drumming of raindrops on the balcony outside his window. He slept soundly, not stirring until the sun was clear of the horizon. Marty took a quick turn around the central part of Carson City, then ate a leisurely breakfast at the Two Bit Café. After his second cup of coffee, he ambled over to the livery, where he was assured that Pacer was receiving first-class attention from the clubfooted stable worker.

"That's one handsome hoss, Mister," the stable hand announced as he mucked the stall of one of the pair of horses that had pulled Marty's wagon from Reno.

Marty softly stroked Pacer's velvety nose. "Yes. He's that and more. I don't think I'd be able to get along without him, now that we've become friends."

"Ya wan' I should double up his oats ration? Only cost ya an extra dime a feedin.'"

"Good idea. Do it." He patted Pacer's muscular neck. "Hear that, big fella? You're gonna be eatin' mighty good for a spell. Make up for those tough stretches we've come across on the trail lately."

Marty finished up his morning by walking beyond the town limits to a sheltered alcove beside a cold running stream that flowed out of the mountains to the east of the town. For a couple of hours, he practiced his fast draw and then carefully cleaned his pistols. He meant to clean both his rifles as soon as he returned to the stables. They might have gotten wet during the rain the previous night.

After finishing his chores, he had a sandwich of cold cuts at the Silver Bird Saloon, nursing a beer while he casually questioned the two barkeepers on whether they had ever run across Alva Hulett and Sanchez. He decided to spread a few dollars where he hoped they might be of the most help to him in his search. He slowly strolled to the sheriff's office, pausing to buy himself another shirt at the dry goods store just across the street. "Ever run across a three-fingered man named Hulett?" he asked the one-armed clerk while the slender man wrapped his shirt in brown paper and tied it shut.

"Nope, can't say I did. Why'd ya ask?"

"He's wanted for murder. You ever see a tall, skinny, dark-haired man with only three fingers on his left hand, you be sure and tell Sheriff Schrader."

"I'll do that. Here's yur shirt. Thanks fer yur business. Have a nice day."

Marty tucked the wrapped package under his arm and walked to the sheriff's office and through the opened door to where he found Schrader sitting with his boots on his desk, idly cleaning his fingernails with a small penknife.

"Mornin', Keller. Looks like it's turnin' out to be a nice day, don't it?"

"That it does, Sheriff. Any word on my reward?"

"I spoke to Malcolm O'Brian about it this mornin'. He wants to see ya when ya got a minute."

"Did he say what it was about?"

"Nope. I reckon he's got money troubles, iffen I was to guess. He may wanta negotiate some about the reward."

"Whatever he wants, it sounds like bad news, doesn't it?"

"Can't say, fer certain. The reward was put up by a private citizen, so I ain't got no say-so about yur gettin' it. Malcolm's a fair man, though. Stop by and see what he says."

Marty frowned as he digested the news. He suspected he was about to get a serious reaming and he did not have a clue what to do about it. "Where will I find this O'Brian?"

"Walk south to the edge of town, to Seventh Street. Turn right and you'll see the stable and corrals for his horses and mules. He's got a freight office there and lives over it, so you ought to find him close by." Schrader paused, then continued. "Watch out fer his daughter, Colleen. She's got a tongue sharper'n a tomcat's claws. Don't give her no excuse to tie in to ya. You'll come out with yur ears bloody."

"Thanks, Sheriff. I just spent a considerable amount of time with a woman like that.

It was not the best of experiences."

Marty stepped out of the office and started toward O'Brian's office. He mentally prepared himself for bad news. "It would come at a time when I really need to fill up my poke," he mumbled to himself.

Marty paused at the end of the street to watch the Sacramento stage clatter in, accompanied by a rolling cloud of dust and the snorting of tired mules. A dusty driver swung off the top and opened the side door of the red and yellow painted stage. "Carson City, folks. All out, it's the end of the line."

Marty's mouth dropped in astonishment. A young man, barely into his twenties, of medium height and sturdy of build, light brown hair, and a fair enough face that had not seen much of the outdoors, was the first out of the stage. He hit the dust of the street and stretched, looking around, his brown eyes sparkling in lively interest at the sights of the town. It was his dress that caused people to stop in their tracks.

His pants were skintight doeskin, with fringe running up the seams. His feet were tucked into Texas-style boots that reached nearly to the bend of his knees. His shirt was softly tanned doeskin, with six-inch fringe running along both arms and a riot

134

of beadwork trimmed the upper chest. A twenty-gallon white hat covered his head, its crown rising eight inches above the brim and the brim itself as wide as a small Mexican sombrero. A new pistol rested in its new holster and belt, strapped around the man's waist. There were new, shiny brass bullets filling the belt loops and a fancy scabbard held a long bowie knife on the opposite side of the holster.

The young man could not have more proclaimed his status as a fresh-faced dude from back East if he had worn a sign around his neck. Oblivious of the pedestrians' gawking stares and chuckles, he grabbed the valise that was swung down by the guard and stepped onto the wooden sidewalk. Seeing Marty close at hand, the dude walked up to him, a friendly grin on his face.

"Hello, sir. My name's Carson Block. Could you direct me to the establishment of Malcolm O'Brian, owner of the Washoe Mountain stage line?"

"Howdy, Mr. Block. I'm Marty Keller. I was headed that way myself. Care to walk along with me?"

"Most kind of you, sir. I'm a stranger here and Mr. O'Brian is my uncle, although I've never met him. I'm going to be working for him."

"You don't say. Ever been in the West before?" Marty started on toward the O'Brian office, young Block tagging along, swinging the filled valise in one hand.

"No, sir. This is my first trip west of Ohio. I was raised in Cincinnati. I just graduated from Harvard College in Boston. My job with Uncle Malcolm will be my first since I graduated. And please, Mr. Keller. Call me Carson."

"Okay, Carson. Harvard College. Congratulations. I'm a VMI man myself, class of 'sixty-one.

"Oh? Then you must have been involved in the war? Were you a, er, a Reb?"

"I fought for the South during the late unpleasantness, so yes, I was a Rebel, I suppose."

"I missed most of it, although I did deploy with the State Militia when the villain John Hunt Morgan brought his cutthroats into Ohio in 'sixty-three. Did a lot of marching, but very little of anything else. My feet were sore for a month afterwards."

Marty chuckled. "In the South, John Hunt Morgan is considered a hero. Best not call him a cutthroat, at least until you know who you are talking to."

Carson laughed good-naturedly. "I'll have to remember that, Mr. Keller. Up in Boston, we sort of saw everything from our side only, the Union side, I mean."

"A lot of the men out here came from the South, where they think of the war as a victory of power over right. They lost all they had and are startin' over, but they still look with pride on the cause they fought for. Best not to say anything that might inflame some repressed passions."

"I'll remember that, Mr. Keller."

"Call me Marty, Carson. I keep thinkin' you're speaking to my father, when you say mister."

"Thank you, Marty." The youth paused, then spoke again. "People seem to be, um, amused, or perhaps *startled* when they look at me. Is it my clothes?"

"They are a bit gaudy for the average working-class cowboy, I think, Carson. You'll notice most men out here wear denim pants and cotton work shirts."

"Dang, I had these clothes made for me in Cincinnati. They looked quite impressive when I tried them on."

"They're impressive all right, but a little too much for folks around here, I'm afraid. If you'd like to buy something less noticeable, you can get all the stuff you need at the dry goods store as soon as you get settled in. Do you have a place to stay yet?

With the boom on from all the mining towns around the area, rooms are in short supply."

"I think Uncle Malcolm has a place for me."

"Well then, you're in luck."

Carson walked along beside Marty, taking in the scene of the town, looking around in avid interest. Suddenly he turned to Marty. "Do you work for my uncle Malcolm, Marty?"

"Nope, I just have some business with your uncle that we have to work out together. I just got in from Reno last night, myself."

They passed the open doors of a saloon, filled with men busily drinking and gambling the morning hours away. Four men staggered out, well into their cups, singing some drunken ditty in painful harmony.

They stopped abruptly at the sight of the fancy-dressed dude in front of them, the last man stumbling into the one to his front. "My God, Jimmy, you see what I see?" The first man spoke loudly, humor and disdain both evident in his voice. "Lookie at the little dude. Hey, dude, where'd you crawl in from?" He laughed at his own witticism.

"Looks like he just got off his mama's teat," another of the men said, laughing at his coarse humor.

A third grabbed Carson and swung him around, to face his four tormentors, who were all anticipating the coming thumping they were going to inflict on the hapless stranger.

Marty suppressed a groan of despair. It was inevitable that Carson's dress was going to create an incident among the rough-hewn miners and cowboys of the town. Marty did not mind taking on a quartet of drunks, but he hated to get all mussed up so early in the day. "Gentlemen, my friend and I were not bothering you. Please allow us to proceed on our way and you go on yours."

The biggest drunk laughed and took a mighty swing at Marty's head. The donnybrook was on.

CHAPTER 11
CARSON SHINES

Marty deftly eluded the wild swing of the pugnacious drunk. The man spun on his feet until his back was facing Marty, who promptly gave him a hard shove into his startled comrades. The swinger and another man went flying into the street, all tangled up with each other. If he had had the time, Marty would have laughed at the pair. Unfortunately, the two remaining antagonists bored in on him and Carson, swinging wildly.

Marty blocked the fist of one opponent, and followed it with a hard left to the man's unshaven jaw. The stunned man fell hard on his butt, right where he stood. Marty spun to take on the other attacker only to see Carson give him a vicious left to the solar plexus followed by a hard uppercut to the jaw. The man flailed back, tripping over Marty's opponent, and sprawled on his back at the edge of the boardwalk.

By this time the other two drunks had untangled themselves and regained their footing. Both angled toward Marty, their fists cocked, intent on taking him out first. A doeskin blur flashed past Marty, ramming head-on into the first man, the momentum carrying both into the street. Carson was first to his feet and immediately began hammering hard lefts and rights against the man's jaw and head. He took a couple of blows in return from the hard-rock miner, but gave them back fivefold.

Marty moved easily on the balls of his feet toward his man, seeing the first signs of doubt and concern in his opponent's eyes. A couple of hard rights to the face put the man down to stay, blood spurting from his broken nose with every breath.

Another man leaped on Marty's back, pummeling his neck and head with hammer blows. Marty bucked the man off, swinging him headfirst onto the dirt of the street, where he lay stunned, gasping to catch his breath. His adrenaline flowing, the fighting bounty hunter ducked under the rush of the last man in the group, tripping him as the out-of-control drunk went stumbling past. Marty was on the man before he could push himself up and drove two hard blows into the back of his neck, rendering him hors de combat without another swing. Marty swung off the downed man in time to see Carson give his sparring partner a classic one-two with his left and right fists. The man staggered back against the hitching rail, flipped over it, and lay unconscious on the street, out of the fight.

Both men surveyed their opponents, but the fight was gone from all and they were content to lie where they fell.

"Not bad, Carson. Where'd you learn to fight like that?"

"Oh, I took boxing lessons while I was at Harvard. I had a scrape or two with sailors when slumming with my friends along the wharfs of Boston. They made these fellows seem almost tame in comparison." He looked at the four downed antagonists. "You took three to my one, it seems. I need to be praising you."

A crowd had gathered during the fight, and now slowly started to disperse back into the saloon or continue on their way. A short fellow with a thinning cover of gray hair and a tobacco-stained walrus mustache on his face limped up and spoke to Marty. "Both you boys did a right smart job on those yahoos. Would you allow me to buy you a drink?" His eyes danced in lively amusement as he looked at the four downed fighters.

Marty wiped the back of his hand across his mustache. "A cool beer would taste right soothing, I reckon. Thank you, sir. We accept." He clapped Carson on the shoulder. "You learn how to drink beer back in Boston?"

"You bet."

The two victorious fighters followed their host inside the bar and to a small table by the roulette wheel.

The old man took a seat and offered chairs to Marty and Carson. He stuck out a gnarled paw and introduced himself. "I'm Squint Richards. Had me a run-in with Lebo Ledbetter there myself a while back. He laid a few hard licks on me, fer certain. I'm glad to see him git his'n." Squint shook Marty's and Carson's hands, while Marty introduced himself and Carson to the old-timer.

"Mabel, three beers, darlin'," Squint shouted to a passing bar girl. The three men waited in silence until the beers arrived and each swallowed a goodly portion.

"Mighty tasty," Marty announced, wiping the foam off his lip with the back of his hand. "Trading fisticuffs with those boys gave me a powerful thirst. Thanks, Squint."

"My pleasure, Marty. Why'd Lebo sic hisself onto ya anyways?"

"He and his friends took exception to my friend's clothing," Marty answered.

Upon Carson's hearing Marty say "friend," his youthful face broke into a wide grin. He sat more upright in his chair and attempted to look as manly as he felt.

"Well, I shore can sympathize with 'em on that. Where'd you git them duds anyways, Carson?"

Carson looked down ruefully at his prized outfit. "I had it made for me in Cincinnati. At the time I thought it was pretty nice, but now I'm not so sure. I saw a dry goods store just down the block, Marty. Maybe I ought to buy that new shirt before I meet Uncle Malcolm."

"Did I heer ya say Malcolm? Air ya a kin to Malcolm O'Brian by any chance?"

Carson nodded. "Yes, I'm going to work for Uncle Malcolm at his stage line."

Squint slapped his knee. "Why, hell's bells, boy. I work fer Malcolm too. I'm jus' about his bestest stage driver."

Carson chuckled. "Looks like we're all going to see Uncle Malcolm. Marty here has business with him too."

Squint favored Marty with a one-eyed stare. "Do tell. What was yur name agin, Marty?"

"Keller."

"Marty Keller. The man who brought in Luke Graham. The famous bounty hunter? Of course. I was on the stage that Luke held up and kilt poor ole Dave Gunther. Dave left a widder and baby girl. Damn Luke's hide." Squint finished off his beer and motioned for another. "You brought Luke in, dead, I heer."

"That's right. Three men, hidden in ambush, killed him about five miles from Mormon Station. They shot him down like a dog, never giving him a chance."

"I can't say I'm overly sorry," Squint announced. "Poor ole Dan never had no chance either. And he's also the coyote who shot me and throwed me offa the road at Graveyard Pass." Squint looked again at Marty. "That what you're about with Malcolm? Gonna help him fight off them outlaws that are tryin' to destroy his business?"

"I wouldn't say that. We have a small business matter to work out."

"Well, I fer one hope you can stay and lend a hand. Malcolm's a all-right fella and he deserves all the help he can git." Squint smiled at Carson. "Work on 'im, boy. He may be the answer to all our troubles."

Carson was looking at Marty with a strange, worshipful glow in his eyes. "Marty

145

Keller, the Man Killer? That's you? I read about you in the *Cincinnati Inquirer.*"

"I prefer not to be called that, Carson. I don't agree that I'm just a bounty killer for the law."

"But it is you? You are the famous bounty hunter?"

"Yes. I hunt men for the bounties placed on them. I always try to bring them in alive, believe me."

"I reckon most reputations are a mite exaggerated," Squint agreed. "Any man who steps up agin a desperado with a gun in his hand has my full appreciation."

"Mine too," Carson quickly agreed. "Marty, will you teach me how to use my pistol?" he pleaded.

"Ya mean ya can't use that there shooter of yurs?" Squint asked.

"Well, I can shoot it fairly well if I take my time and aim carefully. I certainly can't draw and fire quickly and hit anything beyond a few feet in front of me." He drew himself up proudly. "I am a rather fair shot with a rifle, however."

Marty gave the youth a wry grin. "That may be enough, Carson. A fast six-gun usually gets its owner in more trouble than it gets him out of."

Carson turned to Squint. "What do you

146

think, Mr. Nelson?"

"I ain't certain you'll thank him, sonny, iffen he makes you lightnin' fast with yur pistol. What you ain't got you never try and use. Still, to be fair, Marty, iffen the boy is gonna work fer Malcolm and take a chance of gittin' his arse shot off, he needs every tool in his box, includin' a fast and accurate six-gun."

"If I stay around a spell, I'll try and pass on some useful tricks. That fair enough?" He favored Carson with a warm smile.

"Thanks, Marty. I'll try and be a quick study. Now I suppose I'd best get me some new clothes and present myself to Uncle Malcolm."

"I'll tag along with you two iffen ya don't mind," Squint announced.

The three new acquaintances headed out of the saloon to discover the four drunken fighters were long gone from where they had recently decorated the dirt at the entrance to the saloon. Carson quickly bought and donned a blue linen work shirt and gray whipcord pants, placing his gaudy doeskin duds in a bundle of wrapped butcher paper, hidden from the sight of any other obnoxious ne'er-do-wells spoiling to pick on an eastern dude.

Together the three walked on toward the

147

O'Brian stables and wagon barn, two blocks south of Jack's Bar, where Marty and Carson had had their street brawl and met up with Squint Richards. A young woman and an older man stood in the front yard, talking with the driver of the recently arrived stage, who was still sitting in the driver's box, a whip in his right hand.

As they walked up, the man spoke to the driver. "Take the stage around back and unhitch the horses, L.J. I'll be there directly." The stage driver nodded and got the six-mule team in motion, slowly pulling the stage toward the rear of the bigger of two barns. The man turned toward Marty and the others, a warm smile creasing his worn face.

"Squint, you ole mossy back. Good to see you up and about. How you feelin'?"

"Doin' jus' fine, Malcolm. I was over to Jack's Bar and run into a couple of fellas headed yur way. Thought I'd tag along and say howdy."

The girl, who was eyeing Marty and Carson with interest, moved to Squint and gave him a quick hug. "Welcome back, Squint. Glad you're doing better. How's your leg?"

"Thankee, Miss Colleen, it's doin' jus' fine. Folks, this here is Marty Keller, and his pard is Carson Block. Malcolm, Carson here says yu're his uncle."

O'Brian's eyes changed expression as Marty offered his hand. Malcolm took it and spoke softly. "Would you give me a few minutes to properly greet my nephew, Mr. Keller? Then we'll talk."

"Certainly, Mr. O'Brian. Take your time." Marty stepped back and allowed Carson to edge closer.

"Carson, welcome to Nevada," Mr. O'Brian said, and offered his hand. "Your pa and ma are doing well, I hope?"

"Thank you, Uncle Malcolm. Yes, they're fine and send you their regards."

"This is my daughter, Colleen, Carson. I suppose you two are sort of cousins, some way or another."

"Hello." Carson's voice was suddenly very shy and tentative as he took the offered hand of the pretty, redheaded Colleen. "Pleased to meet you."

"What on earth happened to your face?" the impulsive Colleen inquired. "You've been in a fight, already?"

"And a doozy it were too," Squint chimed in. "Marty and Carson took on Lebo Ledbetter and three of his drunken pals. Wiped him good and proper. Left all four in the dirt outside Jack's place."

"You don't say," Malcolm exclaimed.

"Yep. I was about to jump in myself, only they didn't need my help to handle 'em. Anyhow, that's how the boy got his scrapes."

"Come on, Carson," Colleen ordered. "We've got to get some beef on that eye before it swells up shut."

"Aw, I'm all right," Carson offered.

"Nonsense," Colleen answered. "Come on and no back talk. Shame on the both of you. Fighting like common riffraff in broad daylight. You both ought to be ashamed."

"Forgive my daughter," Malcolm apologized. "She tends to speak her mind."

"You watch out, Malcolm," Squint laughed. "She'll have that boy collared and hog-tied afore he knows it."

"If so, my sympathies are for him. She's a handful and that's a fact." Malcolm looked at Marty. "The sheriff said you'd be along. Can we talk, Mr. Keller?"

"Sure, I reckon so."

"Come on in my office. I've got a bottle of good stuff there. No need to bake in the sun while we discuss our business."

"Can I join ya, Malcolm?"

"Squint, when'd you ever pass up a chance for a drink? Sure, come on. That is, if it's all right with you, Mr. Keller?"

"Certainly. And please, call me Marty. I

have a feeling we're going to be on a first-
name basis before this is over anyway."

CHAPTER 12
FATEFUL PROPOSITION

O'Brian led the two men inside the office. Marty could hear Colleen's muffled voice talking to Carson somewhere close by, perhaps inside the inner office. O'Brian poured Squint and himself a drink of sipping whiskey; Marty took a pass on the alcohol. "I avoid strong spirits for the most part, Mr. O'Brian, but thank you for the offer."

Marty waited patiently until the other two had savored their drinks. Realizing he could put it off no longer, O'Brian put down his tumbler and, clasping his hands together, faced Marty. "You did a good thing, bringing in Luke Graham like you did. I'd hoped to talk with him, once he was captured, but obviously his cohorts had other plans for him."

O'Brian twisted his hands together, clearly uncomfortable with what he had to say. "I truly meant to pay the reward for his capture when I had the posters printed, I honestly did. Did the sheriff tell you about my troubles with the outlaw gang Luke Graham belonged to?"

Marty shook his head. "Not really. He mentioned you'd had a run of holdups and such lately, culminating with the robbery and killing of one of your guards."

O'Brian launched into a detailed report of all that had happened the past few weeks, and the desperate financial straits he was currently saddled with. "So you can see," he summarized, "I had the reward money, but the last robbery and wrecking of my stage just about wiped me out. I had to buy another stage, and that took the last of my brother-in-law's loan to the company. I only got that by promising to give young Carson a job."

Marty nodded in sympathy. "You've had a spate of bad luck, no doubt about it. Well, you can't squeeze blood out of a turnip. I reckon I'll just write off Luke to doing what's right and hit the trail. I've got to pick up some spending money pretty quick."

"No, wait." Malcolm held up a meaty paw. "Don't go jus' yet. I want to make you a proposition. I think it has a good chance of making you a lot more money than you'd get bringing Luke back to Carson City. Will

153

you listen?"

"It never hurts to listen, Malcolm."

"One of the reasons I wanted Squint here was to back up what I'm about to say. Marty, this county is about to have a boom that will make the last look like a piker. There's so much silver and gold in the Comstock that it'll make yur jaw drop. I'm in a position to make a million dollars with my freight and stage line when that happens. The only reason it ain't started yet is that the man I'm sort of aligned with, a fellow named George Hearst, has his two most profitable mines closed down. One caused by a fire of a very suspicious nature and the other flooded when a drift crossed into an underground river. Once he gets back into production, I'll start makin' plenty of money from his contracts."

"I got to agree, Marty," Squint chimed in. "Once George Hearst gits to producin' agin, Malcolm will be ten times as busy as he is now."

Carson and Colleen burst into the room, Carson holding a small slab of red meat against his bruised eye. "Papa, I'm gonna show Carson his room, okay?" Colleen said.

"Sure, honey, go ahead."

Carson looked at Marty, his eyes beseeching. "You'll be here when I get back, won't you, Marty?"

"I reckon so, Carson."

The young man gave a happy grin and followed Colleen out of the office. Malcolm watched the two depart, a wistful expression on his face. Then he returned his gaze toward Marty. "Where was I? Oh yeah. Anyways, Hearst and another big mine owner by the name of Ransom Stoddard are in a power struggle for control of the Comstock. Stoddard has bought up the only other freighting company, over to Reno. He won't give any business to Hearst, claims he has to use all the equipment to haul for himself. Stoddard is probably behind my troubles, but there's no proof."

O'Brian had to pace the floor he was so agitated. "Hearst has convinced most of the other mine owners to use my freight wagons, but I gotta deliver or they'll move to Stoddard's company, as much as they would prefer not to. The key will be some large water pumps Hearst has ordered from back East. They'll clean out the flooded mine no problem. The thing is, I gotta deliver 'em from Reno at the railhead to Virginia City to the mine. The Comstock and the Little Bill are, according to Hearst, close to hitting the mother lode of silver. He's certain that he'll hit the jackpot within days of getting his mines in production again. Until then, he's as strapped for cash as I am, so I can't count on him for extra funds."

"All right, Malcolm. Now, how does all this affect me?"

"Believe me, Marty. I'm gonna make a million dollars once things shake out, if I can just stay in business. I'd like for you to come to work for me, as my security head, so to speak. I'll give you five percent of my business if you'll do it. If you can get this wave of violence against me stopped, you'll end up much better off than any reward you might get huntin' some other wanted outlaw."

"Malcolm, I can't take your offer, although I thank you for it. It's way too much. You can hire a dozen guns for a lot less."

"Yes, but they'd want pay as we go, and I can't do that. You'll be riskin' yur life and takin' yur pay on a promise. I just maybe can give you enough cash to stay in beans and a cot at the hotel, nothing more. As for it bein' too much, I'd rather have ninety-five percent of somethin' good as opposed to a hunnerd percent of nothin'. Which is what I'll have iffen we can't get this thing cleared up so I can service the mines in Virginia City."

Marty dropped his gaze to his thumb,

worrying a hangnail that was breaking off at the cuticle. "I don't know, Malcolm. I need to think about this some."

"I understand. Take your time. It's a big risk. Just know that I'll back you up to the best of my ability."

"Me too," Squint chimed in. "I owe them rats some payback."

"Marty," Malcolm cautioned, "don't kid yourself — you'll mostly be on your own. Me and Squint together wouldn't make half a gun hand."

"I understand. You'd be surprised what good men can do once they put their mind to it. It's just not what I do. Like I say, let me think on it some."

"Good enough. Why don't you let me know tomorrow? Meanwhile, I got to get the stage ready to head out to Sacramento, so if you'll excuse me."

"Of course. I'll stop by tomorrow and let you know my decision."

Marty returned to his hotel, and lingered over a cup of coffee before leisurely walking over to the livery stable and checking on Pacer. Satisfied, Marty stopped by several places where he thought he could get an accurate appraisal of Malcolm O'Brian's character, business prospects, and honesty. The responses were all positive and laudatory. It appeared O'Brian was a good person and a respected businessman.

Marty passed the day in these labors and as darkness slipped across the western slopes, walked to the Bluebird Café to eat his supper. As he ordered from a harried waiter, Carson Block entered the café and moved to Marty's table.

"May I join you, Marty?"

"Certainly, Carson. You all settled in?"

"Yes. They put me in a small cabin next to the stage barn. It's quite comfortable, if a little primitive. Come on by after supper and have a look."

"Thanks. You ready to order?"

"You bet. I could eat a horse."

"Better watch out what you wish for, Carson. It may come true."

They savored the meal, talking about Boston, the West, and Colleen O'Brian. They finished their coffee, walked out of the café, and slowly strolled to the O'Brians' stage barn, relishing the coolness of the evening. As they passed Jack's Bar, where they had had their encounter with Lebo Ledbetter earlier, a man burst out of the batwing doors and blocked their path. He was scruffy looking and his clothing was badly soiled. Judging from the smell, he could also have used a long bath. He glared at the two men with smoldering dark eyes and snarled a warning, "You two. You two kilt a friend of mine, Luke Graham. If you know what's good fer ya, you'll be out of town before sunset tomorrow, else I'm gonna call ya out and fill yur rotten hide full of holes."

The man lurched back inside the bar, leaving Marty and Carson shocked by the sudden, deadly warning. "Well," Carson blurted out, "what was that all about?"

"I think you've been tarred with the same brush that was meant for me. You certainly didn't have anything to do with Luke Graham. I'm sorry, Carson. Maybe you'd better distance yourself from me a little. At least until we know if that fella is all bluff or if he means what he says."

"Not a chance, Marty. I'm proud to call you my friend and I am not about to run from some drunken scalawag."

Marty nodded, but he was not so convinced Carson was ready to be involved in a possible shoot-out with a hardened gunman, which the unknown man probably was. "Let's get on with our business, Carson. No need to let the drunken rants of someone neither of us ever met ruin our plans. You were gonna show me your new home."

"Well, come on, let's get it done, then." Carson picked up the pace and led Marty to his new living quarters.

The little one-room cabin was attached to the rear wall of the stage barn, a cavernous building where O'Brian stored his stagecoaches and freight wagons, and where they were maintained. Inside, it was cozy, with cedar paneling on the walls, a small bed in the corner of the only room. There was an iron Franklin-style stove in one corner, and a horsehair couch and an overstuffed chair facing the stove. A small side table and armoire were the only other items of furniture in the room.

"A fine place, Carson," Marty complimented. "You'll be right comfortable here."

Carson beamed. It was important to him that he had Marty's approval. "Thanks, Marty. I think so too. Malcolm says I'll be working with the mules and horses for a while. I told him I wanted to try driving eventually. If you go to work for him as security chief, I wanna work with you. Do you think I can?"

"Carson, if I do this thing for your uncle, it's gonna be damned dangerous. These outlaws have shown they have no compunction agaist killing in order to get what they want. You've got a long life ahead of you.

You don't want to bleed it out on some dusty road in the next few weeks."

"Aw, I don't worry about that."

"Yes, that's why I'm doing it for you. I will promise you, if I decide to stay, I'll work with you to make you proficient with your pistol and rifle, so you can hold your own. When I see that you're ready, I'll consider using you as my partner."

"Thanks, Marty. I'll look forward to it."

Colleen dropped the curtain covering the window in the front room of the apartment over the office. "That Marty Keller person is in the little house with Carson. Dad, are you certain you want somebody like that as a part owner of our company? I mean, after all, he's just a common fast-gun killer."

"Colleen, honey, I'm pretty certain that Keller is anything but common. Don't forget, according to Sheriff Schrader, he was once a Texas Ranger. And he's damned good with his gun. Outlaws shake when his name is mentioned."

"Since when do you put any stock in anything Sheriff Schrader has to say?"

"Keller is the sort of thing Schrader would know about. It's his business. I like what I saw of him, honey. If he gets himself killed, God forbid, he will have done it for money

161

and I won't have any guilt, or maybe just a little. Better him than someone we know and really care for."

"Well, there is that, I suppose. I'm going to keep my eyes on him, I promise you."

"I thought you had them all filled up with Carson. It certainly looked that way this afternoon."

"Oh, Dad. You're so silly sometimes."

"We'll see, daughter. We'll see."

Marty finally got away from Carson without hurting the young man's feelings. He was anxious to get back to Jack's Bar and make inquiries. He wanted to see what the man who had threatened them was all about. At this time in his career as a bounty hunter, he never discounted a threat against his life. His mission was to survive until he found the two men who still had to pay for his family's death.

Marty entered the smoky interior of the saloon, quickly scanning the room for his antagonist. The place was jammed with customers, but Marty did not see the man in question. He moved to the bar and waited until the bartender, a brawny man with a bulbous nose and fleshy lips, moved in front of him.

"What's yur pleasure, buddy?" the barkeeper asked with a deep bass voice.

"A fellow was just in here. Dark hair, dark eyes, needed a shave. Short, wearing a black shirt and a white kerchief. You remember seeing him?"

"I might have," the bartender replied, his eyes passing over Marty to the rest of the room. "I think I know who you mean. I don't see 'im now, though."

"What was his name?"

"Let me think." The bartender scratched at his lip. "What was his name?"

Marty passed a five-dollar gold piece across the scarred bar, which the bartender quickly made disappear.

"Oh yeah. Brazos Dreesen, is his name. A shiftless no-account, comes in from time to time. I think he works on a ranch somewhere around Virginia City." The barkeep wiped the place in front of Marty. "Need a beer? Otherwise I gotta serve my other customers."

"Yeah, bring me one. Where might I find this Dreesen fella?"

"I can't help ya there. Like I say, he only stops by from time to time."

"Well, if he comes in again tonight or tomorrow, tell him I'm here and staying here. Tell him to think about what he's threatening, and if he pushes me too much,

I'll kill him deader than a skunk caught in a buffalo stampede." Marty looked around the room but saw no sign of Lebo Ledbetter. "Does Dreesen hang out with Lebo Ledbetter?"

"Yeah, I see them in here together, now and then."

"Well, give 'em both the same message." And with that, Marty finished his beer, slapped on his hat, and stalked out of the bar.

CHAPTER 13
NIGHT FIGHT

Vern Barton and Charlie Call rode their horses into Reno shortly after ten in the morning. As soon as Charlie told Vern that they had finished the assignment, Vern began to worry that Luke might have mentioned his name before his death. The outlaw leader felt that he needed to know exactly what was being said about the death of Luke Graham and if there was any connection to him or his ranch. He did not trust the secondhand information he usually heard from his informants.

Their first stop was Sheriff Schrader's office, where Vern claimed that Luke had once worked for him, leaving many months earlier, and he was just curious about what had happened. Schrader had no reason not to believe Vern and thus told the ranch owner and outlaw what he knew, which was very little other than that Luke had been killed by unknown assailants while being delivered to jail by a bounty hunter.

"Any chance this bounty hunter kilt poor ole Luke or the other person?" Vern inquired.

"I doubt it, Mr. Barton. If he had done it, why'd he try so hard to git the other one, a wanted killer named McNeal, into the doc's before the fella died?"

"Well, you know these bounty hunters. They got no respect for human life. Money's their only thing."

"You may be right, but I don't think Keller's the one. Hell, Malcolm O'Brian tells me he's tryin' to hire Keller to be his security chief to stop them spate of robberies agin his stages and freight wagons."

"Ya don't say. Sort of a new twist to things, ain't it?"

"Well, I suppose Malcolm's gittin' a mite desperate. He's just about on the ropes, there's been so much robbin' and such agin him lately."

"Um, too bad. Well, Sheriff, I suppose I'd better get on with my business, I wanna get back to the ranch afore dark."

The two men left the office and walked away toward Jack's Bar, both silent, each engaged with his own private thoughts. Sheriff Schrader thought to himself, *That Charlie Call is a cold one. Never says nothin', never smiles. Makes a man right uncomfortable to be around him. I wonder if he's wanted by the law somewhere.*

Vern and Charlie turned into the saloon, where they encountered Lebo Ledbetter, Brazos, and Luke's cousin Red Mike. The three men were seated around a green felt-covered gaming table, their heads together, engaged in intense conversation. Their eyes widened in surprise when they saw Barton and Call walking toward them.

"Howdy, boys," Vern greeted the three. "Gettin' a head start on today's drinkin'?"

"Nope," Mike answered. "We was talkin' about the skunk that brought in Luke Graham. He kilt him as sure as I'm sittin' here, damn cold-blooded murderer."

"Yu're right about that, Mike," Vern answered, seizing an opportunity. "I was jus' talkin' with the sheriff. He's pretty certain the bounty hunter who brought him in did it, but he ain't got no proof. It's a pure shame, since Luke was chained to the wagon he was in and couldn't defend hisself or nothin'."

Mike seemed to have overlooked the fact that Vern had ordered Luke's dispatch with just as little regard for Luke's chances only days earlier. "Well, we're gonna make it right. Brazos and me will be takin' him

167

down tonight, iffen he don't light out afore then. We'd 'a done it last night but I was too filled up with rotgut to help Brazos out."

"A good idea, Mike. I'm proud of you boys for bein' so loyal to poor ole Luke. Still, this Keller is a stone-cold killer. Lebo, if you and some of yur friends will lend a hand, I'll put a hunnerd dollars in the pot, share and share alike. And another hunnerd to the man who gits Keller."

Lebo's ugly face broke into a wide grin. "By Gawd, I'll take some of that action. Me and some of my friends have a score to settle with that jasper anyhow."

Vern and Charlie sat down. "Well then, let's git ourselves a plan," Vern declared, a confident smirk on his face.

After completing their preparations, Vern and Charlie rode out of Reno. They had not gone a half mile when Vern pulled up and turned to face Call. "Charlie, ya need to ramrod this thing through to the finish. Sneak back into town after dark and hide yurself someplace where you can see what's happenin' and maybe get yurself a shot at Keller. We don't need him helpin' out O'Brian this close to winnin'."

"All right, boss. I'll see ya tomorry."

Meanwhile, Marty ambled over to O'Brian's

office after a hearty breakfast and three cups of fresh, hot coffee at the hotel restaurant. He had mulled over O'Brian's offer, made his decision, and now hoped it was the right one for him. Colleen O'Brian met him at the front door of the office and directed Marty to the stage barn, where her father and Carson were busy supervising the painting of the new stage that Malcolm had purchased from Wells Fargo in Sacramento. They were changing its colors from yellow and Malcolm's livery colors of brown to black and red.

"Howdy, Marty," Malcolm greeted as he walked into the barn. Carson quickly added his greetings, smiling broadly at his hero.

"Morning," Marty answered. "Mr. O'Brian, I reckon I'll take you up on your offer, with three conditions."

"Let's hear 'em."

"One, you'll have to defer to me on all things about security. I call the shots. Two, we don't gamble lives against schedules or money. Three, once I start, we don't quit until it's over. No getting cold feet if it comes to a point where people start to die."

"Those conditions seem fair enough. What do you think, Carson?"

"Seem perfectly sensible to me, Uncle Malcolm. Only thing is, I want to be Marty's assistant."

"No way, Carson," Marty objected. "We're talking about a chance of serious gunplay here. People on our side stand a good chance of being badly hurt or killed. I don't want your blood on my conscience."

"I reckon you'll find you have plenty to do right around here, son. Marty's right. Don't step in over your head, right off the git-go."

Carson was disappointed, but he wisely shut up. There would be another chance to press his case later on. Marty and Malcolm walked out of the barn and over to the corral, where each man rested one foot on the bottom rail of the fence, while watching the mules mill around the enclosure as they continued to talk.

"What do ya want to do first?" Malcolm asked.

"I think I'd like to ride the routes with you. See where the holdups occurred, what sort of places the outlaws have been working their skullduggery from."

"We can do that. Carson told me about the threat against you last night. What do you aim to do about that?"

"All I can do is go on, Malcolm. I can't let anyone put the bluff on me. If they try anything, I'll respond appropriately."

"You're right of course. Still, I'd walk a mite softly tonight. It sure sounded like the yahoo was intent on makin' good his threat."

"No matter what his plan is, I'll be ready," Marty assured O'Brian. "Do you think we can start looking at the routes tomorrow?"

"Sure can. I'll have the stage ready at eight o'clock."

"I was thinking we would just ride horses."

"Let's take the stage. You'll be able to see what it's like for a driver then."

"All right. Let's do it. Who's doing the drivin'?"

"I guess I could ask Squint if he's ready to drive. He's my best driver and may want to get back in harness after his being hurt so bad."

"Good enough. Well, if you'll excuse me, I need to familiarize myself with the layout of the town. Just in case."

Marty took his leave and moseyed around Carson City the rest of the day, seeking the most likely locations for ambush, spots where assailants might run to if flushed out, and routes to and from key points in the town. By the time supper rolled around, Marty felt he was reasonably comfortable with his knowledge of the town.

He ate a light supper, not wanting to fill his gut in case of a stomach wound. He

171

lingered at the café just down the street from the sheriff's office until the sun was dipping behind the mountains to the west. Fingers of red and gold spread across the heavens as the sunset washed the low-lying, fluffy clouds in the evening sky.

Marty puffed an after-dinner cigar as he waited for the cover of darkness. Finally, hitching up his gun belt, he began a slow walk toward Jack's Bar, where he guessed his antagonists were building up their courage to face him.

As he approached Third Street, Squint scooted out of the shadows of an alley next to the saddle and tack shop. Marty almost jerked out his pistols at the unexpected movement but had enough self-control not to draw down on the grizzled stage driver.

"Marty," Squint said softly, "there's three men waitin' fer ya twixt Fifth and Sixth streets. Two on the east side, and one in the alley on the west side. A fella named Red Mike and Brazos are hangin' out by Jack's place, waiting on you to show up. It 'pears they're gonna brace ya in the street and let the hideouts shoot ya in the back."

"Thanks, Squint. Can you get the two on the east off my back?"

"That's my plan. I'm headed fer the roof of Marcy's Millinery Shop. It's got a flat roof and a parapet, just made fer shootin' down on the street. And Carson is coverin' the fella in the westside alley from the doorway of the feed store, directly across the street."

"Damn it, Squint. I didn't want the boy involved in this."

"He insisted on helpin' ya, and I reckon he's got sand enough fer these skunks."

It was too late for Mary to protest any further. "I'll give you five minutes, Squint. Then I'm headed right to 'em. First sign you have that hideout is aiming at me, cut him down. I hope you told Carson the same thing."

"Shore did. Don't worry, we got yur back." Squint slipped away while Marty waited in the shadows.

After the allotted time had passed, Marty continued his walk, moving quickly from shadow to shadow until he was within a hundred feet of the brightly lit opening to Jack's Bar. Then he stepped off the wooden sidewalk to the edge of the street. He stopped just as he was about to enter a pool of light from the dry goods store and saw the two men watching his progress from the boardwalk in front of the saloon doorway.

"You fellas looking for me?" he boldly called out.

The two dark figures immediately stepped away from the wall of the saloon and into the street. "That you, Man Killer?" of the men shouted at Marty. "Step outa the shadows so's we can see yur face when we plug ya."

"Why should I make it easy for you vermin? You want me, come and get me."

Suddenly a rifle blasted a throaty roar from the roof of the millinery shop where Squint was positioned, followed almost immediately by three pistol shots from the doorway to Marty's immediate left. His backups were in action. Marty drew his pistol and blazed away at the two targets in front of him, while they crouched and returned fire at him.

One dark form sprawled backward, while the other took one final shot and sprinted into the darkness of the alley where Squint had said a back shooter was hidden. Marty thumbed off a final shot from his .44 at the fleeing man and then cautiously moved toward the silent form in the street. It was Brazos, laying faceup in the dust, sporting a third eye right between his original two.

Marty turned toward a movement. It was Carson walking toward the alley across the street, a smoking six-gun in his hand. "You okay, Carson?" Marty called out.

"Yeah. I think I hit the fellow hiding in the ally. I saw a glint of light from his rifle as he aimed at your back. I can still see the rifle where he dropped it."

"Be careful, it may be a trap. I'm gonna check the alley across the street. Squint said that two men were in there."

"Gotcha," Carson answered, then continued on, his weapon at the ready.

Marty eased up to the dark alley, his senses on full alert. He heard the ragged breathing, but did not see the downed assailant until he stepped into the blackness and his eyes adjusted. One man sat with his legs outstretched, wedged between a water barrel and the wall of the building, holding a hand tight against his other arm.

Marty stepped close and put the barrel of his pistol against the man's cheek. "How bad you hit?"

The man let out a low moan. "Busted my arm and it's bleedin' like a stuck hawg. I dasen't let go of it fer an instant."

"Stay still and I'll send the doc around. Where'd your buddy run off to?"

"I don't know. Hurry up the doc, will ya? I'm beginnin' to hurt awful bad."

"You're not getting any attention until you tell me where the two men ran off to. Take your time, you're the one that's bleeding to death, not me."

Squint and Carson ran up to Marty. "I got one, didn't I?" Squint questioned. "Good. Carson plugged his dead square. That leaves two, I reckon."

The wounded man groaned again, then gasped out, "We was planning to meet a fella at the church, when this was all done."

"Which one?" Squint queried.

"The Mex church, down at the end of Fifth Street. Now git me the doc, I'm hurtin' bad."

Carson took a close look at the downed man. "This is one of the four we had the fight with the other day, Marty."

"You runnin' with Lebo Ledbetter?"

"Yeah. Lebo said we'd git to share a hunnerd bucks iffen we got ya."

"Who paid you that?"

"I don't know. Lebo never said. It musta been the guy waiting fer us at the church. He's supposed to have the money. He's a pal of Lebo's and Red Mike's."

Marty pursed his lips. Somebody wanted him dead pretty badly. Was it just for Luke Graham or perhaps for helping the O'Brians? He stood and directed. "Carson, you run get the doctor and then guard this jasper. We may want to ask him some more questions after we take care of the two left."

"Can't I come with you?"

"Nope, you've gotta watch this fellow. He may be able to tell us more, later. Go on now. If you see the sheriff, tell him we're trying to corner the rest at the Mexican Church at the end of Fifth Street."

Marty inserted fresh cartridges into the cylinder of his pistol. "Come on, Squint. We have us some rats to flush."

CHAPTER 14
A MAN-SIZED RAT HUNT

Marty and Squint carefully eased down the darkened alley. Marty glanced back at Squint, trailing a few feet behind him, his rifle at the ready. "Squint, you have a pistol?"

"Naw, this here Winchester is all the firepower I can handle. Never got comfortable with them there six-guns nohow."

At the far end of the alley, Marty slowly eased his head out until he could see across the street. He saw nobody, although several of the rough houses along the street still had the glow of lamps spilling out of windows. "Squint, which way to the church?"

Squint pointed to Marty's left. "Thataway, to the end of the block. The street dead-ends at the church."

Farther on down the street, the stucco building that was the church stood in massive silence, its walls reflecting a muted gray in the silvery light of the half-moon shining overhead. Marty saw no sign of anyone waiting for them, but it was a perfect location for an ambush. He and Squint would be easy targets if they just charged up to the front doors.

Marty ducked back into the dark alley. "I don't see anything. Doesn't mean they're not up in the bell tower waiting for us to show ourselves. I'll slip across the street and you stay on this side. When I signal you, we'll make our way toward the church together. Stay close to the side of the buildings. No need to give them an easy shot at us."

"Gotcha, Marty."

Just as Marty steeled himself to dash across the street, both men heard heavy footsteps hurrying down the alley from the main street behind them. Both men spun around, their weapons at the ready.

It was Sheriff Schrader, puffing hard after a long run from his office, three blocks away. "Hold on now," he spit out between gasps of breath. "What's goin' on here?"

Charlie Call could not hide his disgust when Lebo Ledbetter finished his report on the ambush of Keller. "Damnit, Red Mike. I thought you said this Lebo jasper and his friends were the real stuff. Sounds like they couldn't finish off a tied-down rabbit."

"It was a series of bad breaks, Charlie. Someone was up on the roof across from me and Gates. He winged Gates with the first shot and pinned me down so I couldn't git a shot at Keller. Someone else plugged Wes across the street, and Keller shot Brazos down in the street. I don't know how he missed Lebo. Lebo ducked into the alley and me and him hurried here. Maybe we can git 'em here iffen they come after us."

Charlie quickly considered his options. "Lebo, git yur ass up in the belfry and keep a sharp lookout. Keller and whoever is with him will probably come after us right away. Me and Red Mike will set up an ambush down here, if they git inside the church."

Lebo looked nervously at the bigger Call. "Well, don't you two sneak out on me. I'll never git down from up there if you two was to run and leave me to face them alone."

"You don't worry about that. You jus' git up there and keep yur eyes peeled."

As Lebo hurried up the winding stairway to the top of the belfry, Charlie's lips curled in a half smirk. His horse was tied outside and he planned to light a shuck out of the confines of the church at the first opportunity.

Charlie pointed to a dark corner across from where he stood in the sanctuary close to the back door of the church. He wanted to stay by his escape route. "Red Mike, you git settled over there, and I'll set up here. We'll have 'em in a cross fire iffen they do break into the church."

As the cousin of Luke Graham scurried away to his hiding place, Marty and Squint were finishing their explanation to the Carson City sheriff about the ambush and shoot-out.

"I don't like it when someone settles their differences on my streets, Keller. Ya shoulda come straight to me. I'da run Brazos and Lebo outa town."

Marty thought to himself that he'd rather face the varmints in town than out in the countryside where they would have many more ambush sites available. "I'll remember that, Sheriff," he answered stoically. "Now that we've got 'em cornered, you want to flush 'em out, don't you?"

"Yep. You two are temporary deputies, just to make it legal."

Once again, the men heard someone running toward them through the dark ally. All three men crouched with their weapons at the ready. It was Carson Block. He slid to a stop, his eyes widening at the sight of three grim shooters looking at him, ready to fire.

"Don't shoot," he whispered as loud as he dared. "It's me, Carson."

"Carson," Marty growled, "didn't I tell you to get the doc and stay with that wounded fellow?"

"I did, honest. When we got back, the fella was dead as a doornail."

"What?"

"Yeah," Carson answered. "The doctor said it musta been shock or a clot from the wound. I thought I'd better get here and back you and Squint up." He glanced at the form of Sheriff Schrader.

"This is Sheriff Schrader, Carson," Marty told the young man. "He's gonna help us root those last fellas out of the church." Marty looked at Schrader. "How do you want to handle it, Sheriff?"

"What was you and Squint plannin'?"

Marty relayed his plan for assaulting the old church building. The old sheriff nodded his approval. "Sounds good. Squint, you and I will go down this way. Keller, you and the boy cross over to the other side of the street and cover us fer a spell. Then we'll take cover and do the same fer you two." The sheriff risked a quick glance at the church at the end of the street. "When we git to the front doors, we'll go in together.

We'll take the left side and you take the right."

"Right. Come on, Carson." Marty dashed across the street, Carson on his heels. As they reached the boardwalk, a shot boomed from the church, barely missing Marty and scoring the side of an adobe wall of a private home.

"Damn," Marty grunted shakily, "that was close." The scar cut into the adobe by the bullet angled downward by maybe twenty degrees. "Someone's in the belfry," he told Carson. "Stay in the shadows." Marty eased into the cover of a recessed doorway and peeked around the jam toward the belfry of the church. All was dark and quiet.

"Squint," he called softly across the street. "There's a shooter in the belfry. Put a couple of rifle shots off the bell and see if it forces him to duck down until Carson and I make the cover of the next house up the street."

"Gotcha, Marty. Stand by, here goes." Squint opened up with his Winchester, slowly banging shots off the bell and tower opening.

"Come on, Carson, follow me." Marty ran to the next house in line on his side of the street, ducking behind its solid bulk without drawing any return shots from the tower. A half-filled water barrel sat next to the corner of the house. "Help me, Carson," Marty whispered as he struggled to roll it out away from the wall until it presented a shield from gunfire from the church.

"Carson," Marty instructed, "get behind this water barrel and keep your rifle on the opening in the belfry. If you see any movement, open up."

Across the street, Squint and Sheriff Schrader were still at the opening of the alley, straining to see them in the darkness. Marty softly called out, "Squint, you and Carson stay where you are and cover the sheriff and me while we make our way to the front of the church."

"Gotcha, Marty," Squint called back. "Carson, I'll start, you wait till I'm empty. Then you fire whilst I'm reloading my rifle. We oughta be able to keep the varmints pinned down until Marty and the sheriff is at the front door."

"You ready, Sheriff?" Marty called over.

"Yep. Let's git the dance started."

"Squint, open up," Marty shouted.

Squint fired at the opening of the belfry and was rewarded with a resounding *bong!* when his bullet hit the large bronze bell from the belfry. He fired again about three seconds later, without the same results, but Marty knew whoever was hiding up there was certainly not going to risk sticking his head up to shoot at either him or the sheriff.

He raced straight down the sidewalk to the edge of the churchyard and then to the slight protection of the small canopy over the front door. Squint and Carson were still steadily banging away at the opening of the belfry above him. He waited until Sheriff Schrader ran to the other side of the door and then allowed the puffing lawman a few seconds to catch his breath.

Finally, Marty whispered, "You ready, Sheriff?"

"Yep. Let's do her."

Marty pushed open both of the double doors and darted inside, immediately turning to the right. Two men at the rear of the church fired at the open doorway, from both sides of the building. The bullets missed their targets and slammed into the stucco wall behind him. Sheriff Schrader crouched behind the last pew on his side, keeping his head below the top of the backrest.

"Lebo Ledbetter, you in here?" the sheriff shouted.

The only reply was a flurry of gunfire from the two men hidden at the front of the church. The sharp crack of a rifle echoed above him. Someone was still in the belfry, trading shots with Squint and Carson.

"Sheriff," Marty whispered over to the lawman, "there's still one in the belfry."

"I heerd him," Schrader answered, and then raised his head and gun over the pew and fired three quick shots at the location of Red Mike, who was squatting below the statue of the Virgin of Guadalupe reloading his empty six-gun. The movement saved his life, as Schrader put his bullets where he had just been standing.

Charlie Call quickly fired at Schrader, but his bullets went wide. Marty returned fire immediately, his bullets slamming into the back of the pew where Call was hiding, causing Charlie to duck back down to cover. Call grimaced. Things were not going right and getting worse by the minute.

He plotted a quick exit from the church by the door behind him. He knew that if he could reach his horse, he was clear, since those at the front of the church would have to return to wherever they had tied their horses before they could pursue him. He would be long gone and untraceable by then.

Charlie had long ago found a way to enter and exit Carson City that would disguise his route away from the town.

During a sudden lull in the firing inside the church, a loud shriek of pain penetrated the quiet of the main sanctuary. A rifle fell clattering down the circular steps leading up to the belfry followed by a limp body that thumped and rolled down the stairway like a sack of potatoes, finally sprawling on the wooden floor of the sanctuary.

In the shocked seconds following the fall of Ledbetter, Marty darted halfway down the side of the building to the confessional box, which protected him from the man on his side of the church and gave him a better vantage point to fire on Red Mike, who was opposite from him at the front of the building.

As the unfortunate outlaw rose to shoot toward Sheriff Schrader, he exposed his head and upper body to Marty's view and fire. Aiming carefully, Marty shot Red Mike in the top of his left shoulder, but Red Mike was unlucky this time. The bullet hit his shoulder bone and glanced upward, cutting out of the shoulder and hitting the outlaw under the left ear. Ranging upward, it came out above Red Mike's right ear. The impact of Marty's bullet caused Mike to stand, and Sheriff Schrader put two bullets into his chest, dropping the outlaw on his back, dead before he hit the floor.

Charlie Call crouched low and scooted for the back door. His movement caught Schrader's eye and the sheriff zeroed his pistol in on the retreating outlaw's back. The hammer of his pistol fell on an empty cylinder and the next two clicks of the hammer were just as futile. By then Call was out the door, running as fast as his excited legs would propel him to his pony, which started running while he was holding the saddle horn. With an acrobatic leap, he slammed both feet into the dirt of the street and using the momentum of the running horse, flipped into the saddle. His horse's hoofbeats were fading away before Marty and the sheriff made it outside the church.

"That jasper was ready to run from the time this all started," Schrader complained. "The cowardly sumbitch never even tried to see iffen his henchmen was still alive."

Squint and Carson were just easing their way into the front of the church when Marty and Schrader came back inside from the rear. "I think we got the varmit up in the balcony," Squint announced. "Can we be any help in here?"

"Nope," Schrader answered. "Two down and one on the run, like the devil was chasin' him."

Squint went over to the limp body by the

stairs. "Lebo Ledbetter. I reckon I had the last laugh after all."

Marty checked Red Mike's still form at the front of the church. "This one's a cooked goose as well. You know him, Squint, Sheriff?"

He rolled over Red Mike's dead body; its face grimaced as if the dying outlaw had viewed the hot reaches of hell before his soul departed this life.

"Nope," both answered.

"I seem to remember seein' him around town a time or two," Schrader announced. "I'll have some of the bartenders and tradesfolk have a look at him once the coroner has him all laid out. Maybe someone will come up with a name."

"What about Brazos or those other two jaspers back on Main Street?" Marty questioned. "Know them and who they might have worked for?"

"Two of 'em ran with Lebo and are, to the best of my knowledge, just town loafers, earning a few bucks here and there from temporary work, and Brazos seemed to be around town all the time. I don't think he had a job, but I'll ask around."

"Our bad luck, I reckon," Marty grumped. Then he turned to Squint and Carson. "You two did mighty fine work tonight. Thank

189

you both." The looks on their faces were answer enough.

CHAPTER 15
A TRIP TO VIRGINNIE CITY

The next morning, Marty felt relaxed and refreshed after a massive breakfast to make up for the very light supper the night before, and a sound sleep, once he had calmed down from the nervous energy coursing through his veins from the shoot-out. He ambled toward the O'Brian office, whistling a nameless tune. Colleen O'Brian was waiting for him, her lips pinched in anger, obviously carrying a full head of steam and about to blow.

"Mr. Keller," she practically snarled, her green eyes flashing in anger, "what on God's green earth were you thinking, taking a nice, inexperienced Eastern dude like Carson Block on a shoot-out with vicious outlaws? Don't you know he could have been killed? It's bad enough that Squint was involved, but Carson?"

Marty retreated in the face of the enraged young woman, his hands up and palms out in surrender. "Whoa there, Colleen. I swear to you, I was as surprised as you when I found out Carson had dealt himself in. I told him to steer clear, but he chose otherwise. And to be honest, I'm grateful he did. Thanks to him and Squint, I'm still walkin' around this morning."

"Well, I declare, you just aren't listening, are you? I want you to swear that you'll never involve Carson in anything like this again, no matter what the provocation. Do you understand me?"

"Don't you think Carson ought to have some say in this?"

"Daddy, fire this gunslinger this instant, do you hear me?" She stamped one of her dainty feet to emphasize her point.

Malcolm walked out of his office, a wry grin making its way across his face. "Colleen, dear, go out to the mule barn and see if Carson needs any help deciding which mules need new horseshoes. Be off now, that's a good darlin'."

Colleen glared at both men for an instant; then, her lips pressed tightly in indignation, she spun on her heel, flaring out her dress like an opened umbrella and stomping out of the office. Malcolm waited until Colleen had left before saying any more. Then he apologized to Marty. "You gotta give her a little slack, Marty. She's really taken by young Carson. I often wondered if she was ever gonna find someone to give her affections to. Looks like she finally has. If you can forgive her fer her outburst, I'll try to convince her to ease off on her rantin'. She ain't really lookin' at things with an objective mind."

Marty laughed. "As long as she doesn't take after me with a meat cleaver, I reckon I can, Malcolm. I'll stay out of her way until she cools off a mite."

"I'm mighty happy none of you was hurt last night. What do you think should be our next move?"

"Well," Marty mused, "it's clear the shootout last night was more than just some saddle bum defending the honor of a chum. Someone doesn't want me working for you. They're ready to kill me to make sure I don't. Let's take a look at your routes, and the places where you've been attacked. We need to work out a plan that gives us the edge, instead of the lawbreakers."

"You want that I should ride up to Virginnie City with ya?"

"Certainly."

"Good enough. I've got a load of mail and such that needs deliverin' anyways. The thing is, if we git hit again, I'm afraid it'll be the end of my business."

"We won't advertise what we're doing. When we're ready, we'll simply drive out of town. I can't believe the outlaws are just standing around waiting for a stage to ride by."

"I hope you're right, laddie. A lot depends on it." Malcolm opened the door, "Come on, let's get my last good stagecoach hitched up. You ever drive a six-team mule stage?"

"Nope."

"I'll send for Squint. Iffen he's well enough to fight gunslingers, he oughta be able to drive us up to Virginnie City." Malcolm locked the door to the office behind Marty. "Meanwhile, I'll git the mail that's collected in the post office."

Malcolm sent Colleen off to find Squint while he hurried to get the past-due mail. Marty and Carson awaited Squint's arrival before trying to hitch up the lines to a six-mule team.

"I'm pretty sure I can do it," Marty commented, "but we may as well have an expert show us the first time."

"I want to go with you, Marty," Carson suddenly announced.

"You certain, Carson? There's liable to be trouble. You sure you're ready to jump in feetfirst in this fight?"

"I'm ready. I told Colleen to keep her nose out of my affairs. I'm ready to pull my own weight with Uncle Malcolm's troubles. She's madder than blazes at me now, but I don't care."

"It's just that she likes you, Carson. You're lucky, she's a real beauty."

"Maybe so, but she's got to understand that I'm my own man and I don't need her clackin' at me about everything."

Marty just smiled. The trials of true love were many and varied. He knew better than to get involved. Each man had to experience it on his own. About then Squint walked into the mule barn, Malcolm right behind him carrying a large canvas sack filled with what had to be the delayed mail for Virginia City.

The skinny, bowlegged stage driver did not take long to harness up the mules to the gleaming, freshly painted stage in the red and black of the O'Brian livery. Marty opened the doors and stood to the side as Squint walked the mules out of the cavernous barn. The handsome stage shone impressively in the morning sunlight.

"Carson, if you're going with us, I want you to get your rifle and ride inside the coach with Mr. O'Brian. I'm gonna ride up on top with Squint where I can see the ground from his perspective. Malcolm, you get a rifle too. If we do get jumped by outlaws, we need to pour fire at them hot and heavy."

Colleen stood on the front stoop of the office as Squint pulled the stage up in front. He called down to her, "Anything else fer Virginnie City, missy?"

"Nothing, Squint. Good luck. Papa, you keep your head down if someone starts firing at you." She glared up at Marty. "I'm depending on you to make certain nothing happens to Carson, Mr. Keller."

"Colleen," Carson shouted from inside the coach. "What'd I tell you?"

With a disdainful sniff, she spun on her heel and walked back inside the office. Marty grinned at Squint. "Okay, old-timer. Get these mules to moving. Let's go to Virginia City."

Vern Barton could not sit still as he listened to Charlie Call describe the shoot-out. "Damnit, Charlie. Whatta I pay you fightin' wages fer anyways? How could you let things get in such a confounded mess?" He pounded his fist into the palm of his hand.

"It were Red Mike's fault, Mr. Barton. He forgot to check out the ambush site to make sure Keller didn't have no backup. When it turned out he did, Red Mike panicked and ran fer the church instead of making certain he plugged Keller first."

"What if he ain't dead? He can tell a lot to hurt us."

"Believe me, Mr. Barton, he's dead. He took one in the head and several in the brisket. He ain't talkin' to nobody, you can count on it."

"And Brazos? He's dead as well?"

"Red Mike said he was. I never saw him."

"You need to git a couple of new men into Carson City right away. We've got O'Brian dancin' on a hot skillet and I don't want to let him off." He glared at Call. "Next time I send you out to git someone, you better do it right, or don't come back."

"Yessir, Mr. Barton, I unnerstand."

"You'd better send someone into Reno with a message. I want Sam and Waco to be especially vigilant. Those pumps are due in from Pittsburgh any time now and they can't make it on to Virginia City. We have to stop 'em, no matter what."

"I'll do it right away, Mr. Barton. Now, if you'll excuse me, I'd like to git a bite of breakfast. I rode all night to make certain nobody was followin' me."

Barton waved his second in command away with a flick of his hand. He worried about Keller. Was the bounty hunter that good or was he just lucky? Barton wondered if he needed to tell Mr. Stoddard about Keller. He decided not to risk incurring the wrath of the mine owner. His stock with the man was not too high at the moment as it was.

Barton wandered over to the corral. He wondered when O'Brian was going to resume his stage runs. The demands for service must be increasing daily. He meant to hit the next and every other stage running to or from Virginia City until the O'Brians quit in defeat.

The first part of the drive to Virginia City was pleasant and uneventful. The six-mule team settled into a ground-eating trot. Marty estimated they were doing better than five miles an hour. After two hours the road started to climb into the mountains, which lay to the east and north of Carson City. The stage slowed as the mules strained to pull the coach up the winding and switchback roadway to the summit.

Squint kept up a continuous dialogue with his mules, cussing them and cajoling them with equal fervor. Marty kept a log of times to reach various points along the road, continuously watching for both outlaws and likely ambush positions. Finally, the coach and its passengers reached the top of the pass, now referred to as Stagecoach Graveyard by most everyone in the area.

"This is the spot where those skunks shot me and kilt Dave," Squint announced, looking around with a wary expression on his weathered face.

"Pull up, Squint. I want to look around."

"Dang, Marty, don't ya think we oughta get on outa here? There might be some more of 'em hang-in' around."

"I don't think so. I imagine they don't even know we've left Carson City yet."

"Well, how is it you think they knowed when to hit us like they did?"

"I've been thinking about that very subject. I think that they've had someone in town, watching the stages. When you pull out, the spies skedaddle to wherever the rest of the outlaws are holed up and then the outlaws head here to spring their ambush."

"Do tell." Squint pulled the stage over to the edge of the road nearest the side of the mountain and looped the lines around the braking handle next to his seat. Marty and Squint climbed off the stage while Carson and Malcolm stepped out of the interior.

Marty rocked up on his toes, stretching the kinks out of his back. He rubbed his bottom, grinning wryly at Squint. "I've got to admit, that driver's seat is becoming mighty hard right now."

"Anything wrong?" Malcolm asked as he exited the coach.

"Nope," Marty answered. "I just wanted to look over this area for a few minutes."

"Have a look." Squint pointed. "Here's where them skunks threw me over the cliff and pushed Dave and the stage right over me." He led the way to the edge of the road and pointed at the scrubby bush growing out of the side of the steep slope. "That's what was twixt me and eternity." He pointed downward.

"My gosh, Almighty," Carson announced breathlessly. "Look at all those wrecked stages and wagons down there." He shuddered. "I'd certainly hate to have been in one of them when they went over the side."

Malcolm barely glanced down before returning to the coach. "I'm just grateful only one man did go over. You want to see anything else, Marty?"

"Yes, I want to see if we can find where the outlaws hid themselves before and during the ambushes." He scrambled up the rocky slope toward the tree line, which had been cut back from the roadway a dozen feet or so by the engineers. Carson was right

200

behind him, but Squint and Malcolm had a more difficult and slower assent into the cover of the trees.

About a hundred feet above the roadway they came upon a small clearing on a flat protrusion from the slope. Numerous cigar butts, a small rag, perhaps used to clean a weapon, and an empty can of peaches in syrup, now beginning to rust from the rains, were strewn around the area. Marty bent down and picked up an empty Winchester .44-40 cartridge and rolled it in his fingers as he surveyed the scene.

"You know, it's been my experience that most crooks are lazy and unimaginative. They've used this place more than once. I'd wager they'll come back here again the next time they set up an ambush. It's the sorta thing that we can use against them." He started down toward the coach, the others following.

"Malcolm, I need to hire some fighting men. Preferably ex-soldiers, tough and reasonably trustworthy. Will you think some on that when we get back to Carson City?"

"Marty, I don't see how I can pay 'em."

"I'll pay them out of my own pocket if I have to. I'm beginning to formulate a plan and I think we'll have a good use for them."

Carson spoke up as they slid down the

steep slope toward the road. "I've not been in the army, but I'm ready to sign on with you."

"You've proven to me that you're man enough to ride by my side," Marty answered. He grinned. "Just don't tell Colleen that I agreed."

"Dang it, Marty," Carson sputtered, but the laughter of the others shut him up before he could say any more.

Malcolm and Carson climbed back into the coach and Marty and Squint took their places on top. The mule skinner snapped the lines against the rumps of the mules and they were under way again. The rest of the trip was uneventful although they passed several steep inclines where an ambush could have easily been sprung. Marty kept his eyes busy scanning the cover for danger, while Squint cussed the mules every mile of the trip. Carson had his rifle out and was carefully watching his side of the road as well. Marty nodded in satisfaction. The boy was definitely beginning to prove himself a worthy ally.

Finally, about seven hours after they left Carson City, the stage crested a small hill and the mining boomtown of Virginia City lay before them. The main street cut across the flattened hilltop, and was lined with buildings constructed of logs or cut planks. On either side of the main street ran several side streets, most fronted with houses made of canvas or logs, green lumber, or creek stone, mortared with mud. Beyond the three dirt streets that ran north to south, most of the buildings and homes were scattered haphazardly about the hillsides, which sloped away on either side of the plateau upon which the town was built.

The buildings on Main Street held stores, shops, hotels, a theater, and several offices of mining companies, but saloons and bawdy houses made up most of the buildings. All seemed open for business and business was apparently good.

The stage clattered down the main street to a large livery barn at the north end of the town, where Squint pulled the stage to a stop. A grizzled man with white hair and chin whiskers walked out, his thumbs hooked in his suspenders.

"Why, hallo thar, Squint. I weren't expectin' a stage arrival today. How ya feelin'? I heerd about yur bad luck."

"I'm good, Louie. How's things in Ginnie City?"

"About the same, I reckon. The fire's still burnin' in the Comstock. Ain't been an ounce of gold or silver taken outa there in a month now. George Hearst was by a couple a' days ago. He's lookin' fer them pumps to pump out the Little Bill Mine. Any word on 'em?"

"Ain't heerd a thing, Louie. Mr. O'Brian's in the coach. You can ask him."

"Do tell." Louie hurried to the door of the coach and opened it for Malcolm and Carson. "How do, Mr. O'Brian? Nice to see ya agin."

"Thanks, Louie. I heard what you said. I reckon the first thing to get done is to see Mr. Hearst and let him know what's goin' on." Malcolm turned to Marty. "You may as well come along, Marty. He'll wanna look you over anyways."

CHAPTER 16
MEET GEORGE HEARST

Marty turned to Squint. "Squint, you and Carson get the mail delivered and pick up any that needs to be delivered to Carson City. I'm going with Malcolm for a spell."

"What'll we do after that?" Carson asked.

"Have Squint show you around Virginia City. It's a real, live boomtown. I doubt you've seen one before, have you?"

Carson's eyes brightened at the invitation. "Say, that's a good idea. Where do you want us to meet up with you and when?"

Malcolm spoke up. "Meet us at the hotel dining room about seven." He pointed at a three-story structure across the street. "Over there." A prominently displayed and brightly painted sign proclaimed VIRGINIA HOTEL.

"I'll invite Mr. Hearst to join us for supper, if he ain't already et yet." Malcolm motioned to Marty. "Come on, Marty, we'll start at his office. Iffen he ain't in one of his mines, he'll probably be there."

Malcolm led Marty across the street, past the hotel to a nondescript, two-story building, which held second-story offices above a land investment company that took up the entire first floor. The building had a brick facade, but the sides were raw lumber, whitewashed to hide their greenness. Sap had oozed out of the freshly cut, nondried lumber, giving the wood a rippled texture.

Malcolm led the way up the interior stairs to a door with a half panel of frosted glass that proclaimed COMSTOCK MINING COMPANY. Beneath it, painted in smaller letters, read GEO. HEARST, OWNER AND PRESIDENT. Malcolm stuck his head inside the office. A male clerk was sorting papers on a large desk at the far end of the room. "Mr. Hearst in, James?"

"Oh, hello, Mr. O'Brian. Nope, I think he's over at the Silver Dollar, playing faro. He said he was feeling lucky today."

"Come on, Marty, I know where that is."

As they exited the building, Marty made an observation. "Seems like Mr. Hearst has enough money to gamble, doesn't it?"

"To be honest, Marty, I doubt it. But let me tell you, it's almost like magic. When he gets that lucky feelin' he's unbeatable. I've seen him do the same thing before. Believe me, you're gonna be amazed. He'll come outa there with a wad of money that'd choke a horse."

"If that's true, I wish some of it would rub off on me."

"Me too. Unfortunately, it don't seem to work that way."

"The Silver Dollar Saloon is down the street that way. Follow me."

Malcolm swung open the twin batwing doors of the saloon and stepped through, followed by Marty. The place was filled with miners killing time and spending their money until their next shift underground. Malcolm looked around and then gestured with his thumb. "There he be, at the far table." He pushed his way through the crowded room, stepping around both men and gaming tables, Marty in tow.

As they reached the faro table, Marty got a good look at George Hearst. The mine owner was tall, lean, and worn, his dark hair and full beard liberally sprinkled with gray. His dark eyes were intense and his whole focus was on the cards being rolled over by the dealer.

The dealer, short, bald, and overweight, intoned the play in a calm, almost bored manner. "Queen is the winner. Congratulations, Mr. Hearst, you are a winner." He pushed over a pile of chips, which Hearst added to a much larger one. The dealer urged the players, "Place your bets, gentlemen."

Malcolm put a restraining hand on Marty's arm. "I don't think we'll interrupt the game right now, Marty. George really doesn't like to split his attention when he's gambling."

Marty smiled and nodded in agreement. "I understand. It's fun to watch a winner at work."

Hearst played on, losing some and winning more. Suddenly, a drunken miner shoved his way to the playing table and slapped down several bills, scattering some of Hearst's chips across the table. "Say," he slurred in a drunken tone, "this table is hot. Let me git in on the action."

The dealer quickly gathered Hearst's chips and put them back in front of the offended gambler. "Sorry, Mr. Hearst," the dealer said softly to Hearst.

"Not your fault, Joe. Cash me out, if you please."

The dealer quickly complied and Hearst stuffed the money in his inside coat pocket and turned away from the table. "Come on, Phil." He spotted Malcolm and Marty. "Why, hello there, Malcolm. Didn't expect to see you here. You bring a stage in?"

"Sure did, George. We need to talk. Had your supper yet?"

"Have any trouble?"

"Nope, and that's another reason I wanted to see you."

"All right, let's talk. I'd like for my chief engineer, Phillip Diedesheimer, to join us for dinner if it's all right. I'm buying. I just won big at the tables. I don't know if you saw or not."

"Fine, George. I want to introduce you to my new head of security, Marty Keller, as well. Marty, meet George Hearst. He's gonna be the richest man in the Comstock someday."

Marty shook the offered hand. Hearst had a grip as hard as the rock he dug the silver ore from, and his engineer's was even harder, if that was possible.

"Pleased to meet you, Mr. Hearst, Mr. Diede. . . ."

The mining engineer smiled. "Please to call me Phil. No von can say my last name, except Herr Hearst."

"You just over here from Germany, Phil?" Marty gave him a friendly smile.

"Ya, about two years now."

"I spent the winter a couple a years ago in a gold mine in California. Drilled a lot of holes, but didn't find much yellow stuff."

"I hired Phil to figure out some way of improving my timbering process in the mines," George Hearst broke in. "He says he has an idea. Come on, let's go eat. I'm starved. Where do you want to eat, Malcolm?"

"I promised my driver and nephew that we'd meet at the dining room at the Virginia. That all right with you?"

"Sure. Their food is as good as any in town, I guess."

The four men were silent as they made their way to the hotel. The boardwalks were crowded with pedestrians, mostly miners, but some businessmen and a few ladies of the evening getting ready to start their trade for the night. They trooped into the café and were shown seats at one of the tables to the rear. All four ordered the special, roast beef and potatoes, then settled back to await their meal.

As they waited, a nondescript man with slicked-back, thinning blond hair and a wispy mustache sauntered by on his way out. He glanced at the four and slightly nodded his head in greeting. Flashing a shallow smile, he moved on, his walk purposeful. The smile never reached his eyes, Marty noticed.

"Who was that?" he questioned.

"That's Ranson Stoddard, owns the Gould and Curry Mines. He's an ambitious bastard. He's made several inquiries about buying my two best mines, the Comstock and the Little Bill. I have a suspicion he's behind the problems I've been having. I just can't prove it, unfortunately."

"You talking about the fire in your mine shaft?" Marty asked.

"That and other things. Coupled by the fact that I can't get any freight in from the railhead at Reno except through Malcolm here. And someone seems intent on driving him out of business."

"Marty's gonna help me with that, George. He's makin' plans right now."

"Oh?" Hearst looked expectantly.

"I don't have anything exotic in mind, Mr. Hearst. Just to have more men, and more guns, and then put them out of business, permanently."

"Sounds good to me. Them pumps, Malcolm. Any word on when they're gonna arrive?"

"Nope, not yet. Any day now, I suppose."

The food arrived and the four men dug in, not saying much until they were working on their after-dinner coffees.

"Mighty good chow, for a change," Hearst announced. "Now, Malcolm, what can I do for you?"

"I need some money, George, not much. Just enough to hire a fightin' crew for Marty here. You make any money at the faro table tonight?"

"Better than five thousand." Hearst chuckled. "Didn't think I'd be losin' it so quickly, though."

"I don't need it all. Maybe a couple of thousand?"

"All right. Anything else?" He looked at Marty.

"I just had an idea. Mr. Hearst, Malcolm tells me you're pretty well connected in San Francisco. That right?"

"I guess so."

"You have enough clout to get something from the army?"

"Well, I know General Thomas, the commander of the Western Pacific. His headquarters is at the Presidio, in San Francisco. What did you have in mind?"

"Is that Pap Thomas, the Rock of Chickamauga?"

"The very same."

"My outfit went up against him during the late war. He's a tough fighter." Marty paused for a second, then returned to his train of thought. "I want to borrow a Gatling gun."

"What?"

Marty nodded. "A Gatling gun. Is there a better way to put a lot of lead into some bad guys who are well hidden and have the drop on you?"

"I don't know." Hearst looked around, as if to see if anyone was listening. "I've certainly got some contacts who might help." He smiled. "If some of them knew just how deep I'm in the hole here in Virginia City, they might not be so chummy with me."

"Try, it might be the difference between winning and losing this fight."

"All right, I will. I'll go to San Francisco tomorrow. If General Thomas will loan me one, shall I bring it to Carson City?"

"No, to Reno, but don't let anyone know what you're traveling with."

"I'll give it my best shot. I'm skating on thin ice now, believe me."

"You get your mines up, it's a different story, though, right?"

"Absolutely. We're almost there, in both of my shut-down mines. The glory holes are close, I can smell it, every time I go down in the shafts." Hearst sighed. "But first, I've gotta have those pumps and get the water out of the Little Bill and put out the fire in the Comstock."

"How do you get a fire in a mine, Mr. Hearst?" Carson asked.

"It had to be on purpose," Hearst answered. "We had a big pile of cut logs positioned on the bottom level to build timber bracing. Suddenly, it was on fire. The smoke and flames have spread to upper levels until a man can't get in there to put it out without suffocating. It's a mess."

"Why not do 'em both at the same time?" Marty asked.

"What do you mean?"

"I was just thinking, you're gonna pump out the Little Bill with your new pumps, why not just pump the water over to the other mine, flood it, and put out the fire, then pump it out? Malcolm says those new pumps are big and move a lot of water very quickly."

"By damn, that's a good idea. Phil, we have enough hose to pump water from the Little Bill over to the Comstock?"

"I can certainly order enough tomorrow, Herr Hearst." Phil smiled heartily at Marty. "Dat vas a good idear, Herr Marty."

"If it works," Hearst gushed, "I'll give you a thousand in bonus, just for thinking of it." He stood. "This calls for a drink. Come on into the bar, I'm treating." He led the way out of the café, running into Squint and

Carson at the doorway.

"George, here's my driver and nephew. May they join us?"

"The more the merrier," Hearst answered. He took a seat at one of the tables and motioned for the waiter to head his way.

After the introduction, Hearst turned his attention back to Phil. "Now, Phil, what was it you wanted to talk to me about?"

"The shoring, Herr Hearst. I tink I haf figgered it out." Phil took a piece of paper and started drawing. "De shafts are in bad rock. It slab off, very bad."

Hearst broke in. "If we can get the shoring problem solved, it will save countless lives and enormous amounts of time and energy."

Phil laid the paper in front of them. It looked liked a line drawing of a honeycomb.

"It looks like a, a, what?" Hearst asked.

"A honeycomb," Marty guessed. "One of the strongest structures in nature. We studied them in natural physics at VMI when I was in college."

"Dat it is. A honeycomb. Many times stronger dan vhat ve use now. It vill vork, I know it."

"If it does, we're gonna need a lot of timber," Hearst observed. "Much more than ever before."

"The mountains are full of trees," Marty ventured. "Virgin lumber by the hectares. If it works, it will be worth it."

"By Jehovah," Hearst gushed, "this has been a most profitable exchange. Solutions to my problems one after the other. By damn, I'm feelin' lucky again. I'm gonna go back and take some more money from the Silver Dollar. Any of you want to come along?"

Marty and the others bowed out and excused themselves. As they walked back to the stage barn, Malcolm was quiet. "Do you think George can get a Gatling gun?" he asked Marty.

"If he can, and we can mount it on a wagon to accompany the stage or freight wagons, we'll have one nasty surprise for our outlaw tormentors the next time they hit us."

"By dang, I'd shore like to be thar when that happens," Squint growled.

"First things first. Let's go on to Reno tomorrow and then on back to Carson City. I want to start putting my army together."

"You ever see a Gatling gun shoot, Marty?" Carson asked.

"Once, in a demonstration at Fort Reno, in Wyoming Territory. It was fearsome."

"I can't wait to try it," Carson bubbled in

youthful anticipation.

They settled in for the night on new-mown hay just delivered by a local farmer. Surrounded by the others, Marty relaxed and slept soundly. The next morning as the sun was rising, they rode out of Virginia City for Reno. The route was once again steep and winding until they cleared the mountain, then an easy ride into Reno. After delivering the mail for Reno and picking up the deliveries for Carson City, they hit the road again the next morning. It was a quiet trip. As Carson City came into view, Malcolm sighed and spoke to Carson, who was sitting across from him.

"A successful run. I needed to get that mail delivered. The contract is about the only thing between me and complete ruin."

Atop the rocking stage, Marty smiled grimly at Squint. "A safe run, my friend. Just the first of many, if things go the way I have them planned."

"How often do plans go the way ya lay 'em out?" was all Squint had to say.

CHAPTER 17
PLANS ARE MADE

The trip convinced Marty that he had enough knowledge about the outlaws' operation to start finalizing his plans to thwart their nefarious game, whatever its purpose.

He walked with Malcolm toward the local café at noontime the next day. "Malcolm, I need fighting men. Do you have any ideas?"

"I have one man in mind: Johnny Harper. He was a captain in Hood's Mounted Texas Dragoons. Lost his arm at Nashville, and came out here a year ago. Has been clerking at Dwyer's Dry Goods Store since his claim didn't pan out. He's a good man and hasn't had the best of breaks since he's arrived. If you can overlook his missing arm, I think he'd be a good man for your little army."

"I don't know, Malcolm. Missing an arm?"

"I saw him whale the tar out of a miner half agin his size who'd insulted his wife. He didn't need two hands then. He's a stand-up man, fer a fact."

"Well, it won't hurt to talk to him, I guess. Lead on."

Malcolm escorted Marty to the dry goods store and held the door open for him to step through. The interior was somewhat dimmer and a golden ray of sunshine from a transom above the door revealed sparkling motes of dust floating in the air.

The one-armed clerk stood behind a sales counter in the midst of selling some work clothing to a burly miner. Malcolm waited patiently until the sale was complete, then stepped to the counter. "Hello, Johnny. How goes yur day?"

"Why, hello there, Malcolm. Fine, thank you. What can I do for you?"

Marty critically gauged the man. He was slender, medium height, with broad shoulders and a steady gaze. He was dark enough that Marty wondered if there might be Mex blood in him, not that it mattered. His brown eyes were direct and frank, and the man had an appealing habit of looking at you when he spoke.

"Johnny, this is a friend, Marty Keller. I've engaged him to help me rid myself of the outlaw gang that's been plaguing my stage and freight operations. Marty, this is Johnny Harper."

The handshake of Harper was iron hard.

"My pleasure, Mr. Keller. Will you be needing some clothing?"

"No thanks, Johnny. May I call you Johnny?"

"Of course."

"What I need is a small number of fighting men to act as a reaction force when I go up against the outlaws. Malcolm thinks you might be interested in being one of them."

Almost subconsciously, Johnny rubbed the stump of this left arm with his right hand, advertising his handicap. "You certain about that, Mr. Keller?"

"Call me Marty. Yes, I am. I was thinking, if you were interested, you would be my second in command and in charge of their training. I'm gonna be pretty busy with other aspects of my plan and I might not have enough time to see to all the details. I was thinking about a salary of two hundred a month and a month's bonus when the job's done."

Harper sighed. "The money sure sounds good. But I can't quit my job here, Marty. I've got a wife to take care of."

"I don't want you to. I want to get men who are already working, so there are no questions asked about how they manage to survive. You'll train them after work and on Sundays. Do you think you could find me eight to ten more good men? Able to ride hard, hold their own in a fight, be a good shot with rifle and pistol, and willing to put their life on the line for a hundred a month plus the bonus when it's done?"

"That's what a good miner makes now, and he has to work twelve hours a day, six days a week. Hard, backbreaking work too. How long you think it'll take to bring this operation to a head?"

"I'm guessing a month, no more than two."

"I know a lot of men who are scratching around town trying to get enough to grubstake themselves for a winter of prospecting. If I find some, they might not be working."

Marty nodded. "Malcolm, could they do some stuff around your place, to placate any questions about their source of money?"

"How am I gonna pay 'em?"

"Use some of the money from Hearst. That'll get 'em by the first month. After that, if it goes any longer, I'll tap my bank in Texas to stake you."

"All right, whatever you say."

"All right, Johnny. Get started. Get the best men you can, and remember no polecats who'll sell us out at the first opportunity."

"I meet a lot of men in my business. I already think I have most of what you'll need. What do you want me to do once I hire 'em?"

"Sunday morning, we'll meet about ten o'clock. Where's a good spot, Malcolm? Someplace to shoot and not arouse curiosity?"

Malcolm scratched his chin whiskers for a moment. "Up the Carson Creek Road. About a mile and a half outa town. There's a steep clay bank that comes right down to the edge of the creek. Be a good place to shoot into."

Johnny spoke up. "I know the place. The creek's a good thirty feet wide there. And the ground to the south is open and flat for a couple a' hundred yards. Be an ideal spot for both rifle and pistol practice."

"It's done, then. Have our little army out there then, Johnny. Malcolm and I will be out to look 'em over."

"What if the men I hire don't have rifles, or maybe even pistols?"

"Then we'll outfit them. They can pay us back with their bonus money."

"I'll let you know when I've completed hiring my men. See you Sunday."

"I'm going to be out of town awhile, so if I'm not there, just inform Malcolm."

222

"Where you goin', Marty?"

"I want to ride back to where the outlaws attacked the stage. Maybe I'll learn a little about them. I'll be back Friday night. In the meantime, I want you to plan on making a stage run Monday. I've got an idea for getting to Virginia City without being bothered by the holdup men."

Marty and Malcolm returned to the freight office. "I've got a good feeling about Johnny," Marty suddenly said. "He'll give me a well-trained reaction force if I'm any judge of men."

"I've liked him since I met him, over a year ago. When you plan on leavin' fer yur scoutin' trip?"

"Just as soon as I can put together some supplies."

Carson overheard the statement. "Where you going, Marty?"

"I want to check out the land around the stage routes to Virginia City and on to Reno."

"Marty, I want to go too. Will you allow me to accompany you?"

"Malcolm, can you spare Carson for a spell?"

"I reckon so. You boys better be careful, though. Don't get sucked in by the same men you're after."

"We're just gonna poke around. We'll make special pains not to get involved in anything over our heads." Marty paused, then looked at Malcolm. "What's it gonna take in wagons and mules to deliver the pumps to George Hearst from Reno?"

Malcolm thought for a moment. "About eight wagons and sixty-four mules."

"Do you have that much equipment?"

"Nope. Up in Reno I've got four wagons and twenty-six mules."

"And down here?"

"Two wagons and twelve mules."

"Then you're short two wagons and twenty-eight mules. How were you gonna handle that?"

"I sorta planned on makin' two trips."

"Never gonna work. We'll take everything the first haul. Anyone else in Reno have any wagons and mules we might use?"

"Clem Atkinson has several wagons and plenty of mules. But he's under personal contract to the Stoddard Mining Company. He isn't allowed to loan or rent me anything."

Marty nodded his head thoughtfully. "Um, looks like I'll have to pay him a visit, once we're ready to make our play."

"He's a decent fellow, Marty. It's just that his hands are tied."

Marty gave Malcolm an enigmatic grin. "That's how I'll leave him then, once the time is right."

Marty and Carson rode out of town by way of the Carson Creek Road. Once they passed the spot where Johnny had spoken about for the Sunday target practice, Marty cut across the landscape until they were headed north on the Virginia City Road. Riding easily, they surveyed the countryside carefully, discussing any locations they thought potentially useful as an ambush site by the outlaws, until they reached the infamous Stagecoach Graveyard Pass.

There, Marty led the way into the trees, to where the outlaws had obviously hidden themselves prior to springing their ambush. He swung down from Pacer's back and led his horse while he searched for a way to enter and exit the area. "I doubt if they rode over the top of the mountain, do you, Carson?"

"It'd be a fearsome climb if they did," Carson answered. "If they had to run away in a hurry, they'd be in a world of trouble."

Marty scuffed at the pine needles covering the ground. "We need some tracks to follow. What do you think? Did they go north, toward Virginia City, or south, back toward Carson City?"

Carson rubbed the back of his neck. "Danged if I can tell."

"Well, think about it. What is your gut reaction?"

Carson paused, then pointed toward the north. "I'd guess north. If they came from the south, they'd have a hard climb up to here. It's easier riding to the north, isn't it? Seems like it to me."

"A good guess," Marty agreed. "Let's continue on to the north, over the top of the pass, and see what we find."

The two men had not ridden a half mile when they ran into the stream that cut across the roadway. It was the very one the outlaws had used to hide their trail after the last holdup. "Let's see if this stream leads anywhere," Marty said. "Keep your eyes open for any sign that men on horseback have come this way." They urged their horses into the sparkling water and rode toward the top of the mountain, still far above them.

After only a few hundred feet, the stream flowed past the side of a large flat expanse of hard stone providing a natural exit from the cold water. Numerous scars on the dark chirt was visible testimony that many horses' hooves had scraped their way across the flintlike stone. Marty slowly led the way across the dark rock to a well-worn path that followed the contour of the hill around to the back or east side of the mountain. Signs of heavy use by mounted men were everywhere. Horse droppings littered the trail, and tree branches that overhung the path were broken or rubbed free of pine needles.

"I'd guess this is the way they got to the back side of the mountain, wouldn't you?" Marty asked his companion.

"Absolutely," Carson agreed.

They came upon a clearing where they could view the countryside to the east. Numerous farms and ranches were scattered in the valley below, and a road was visible, running north to south at the base of the mountain.

"Look out there," Marty said, sweeping his hand across the scene from their vantage point. "At least a dozen places where outlaws could be waiting, within thirty minutes of a perfect ambush site. What would it take to get them the word that a stage or freight convoy was on the way to Virginia City?"

Carson squinted his eyes. "Maybe a lookout? Watching the trail."

Marty shook his head. "I don't think so. That would mean men just sitting in one place for long periods of time. Someone would be bound to notice. Perhaps a look-out in the town? He could blend in with the other men just loafing or between jobs in the mines. A couple of strong horses — what is it, twenty miles to both Virginia City and Carson City from here? And most of the attacks have been between Virginia City and Carson City. A couple between Reno and Virginia City, but none in the opposite direction, and only one between Carson City and Virginia City. Why?"

"Someone wants to keep Virginia City from being supplied, but doesn't care about what goes the other way?"

"Perhaps. And perhaps because they can't get information to the gang in time, I don't know. But I'd bet that if we could follow our outlaws, they'd ride down there to one of those ranches, as sure as I'm sitting here right now. Come on, let's head on down and visit a few of the ones closest to the road down there. See if we run across anything interesting."

At the base of the mountain, they turned right and rode toward a nearby entrance gate. It led to a functional-looking ranch about a mile off the road. The ranch, called the Lazy L, had its main cluster of buildings centered on a small stream that ran toward the east. The owner, Horace Livingston, was nearly sixty and no stranger to hard times and harder work. He was quite friendly and invited Marty and Carson to share the noon meal. Marty instinctively liked the old rancher and after eating told him some of the reason for his visit.

"There's only about six other ranches along what we call the Ranch Road that you might want to visit," Horace replied. "After that, you run on to the Peavine Ranch. It has land all the way to the other side of Virginnie City. Old man Morse has been around here fer nigh onto thirty years now. I doubt if he's harborin' any outlaws on his place."

"Mr. Livingston, if you had to guess, would any of the ranches along the road be a good candidate?"

"I hate to speak bad of anyone, Marty. But since I'm gonna say you held my feet to the fire, the only one that comes to mind is the V bar B. It's under new ownership and the man ain't friendly a'tall, which is plumb foolish iffen you wanna survive as a rancher in these times. But I could be all wrong, so's I don't want you to jump to the wrong conclusion based on my say-so."

"Well, I guess it won't hurt for Carson and me to ride up and see if there's anything amiss. We'll stop at all the ranches until we reach the Peavine Ranch, I reckon. Come on, Carson, we'd best get started if we plan to make it to all six before the sun goes down. Please keep our conversation private, Mr. Livingston, if you would."

"Certainly. Now how 'bout some hot coffee afore you boys hit the road?"

Marty and Carson rode down the road toward the ranch house for the V bar B. "We'll say we're looking for some work to earn a grubstake, Carson. I imagine everyone along here has heard that story before."

The ranch buildings were run-down and badly in need of ordinary maintenance. Marty and Carson stopped at the front steps to the main house, and waited for an invitation to get off their mounts. Several men stepped out of the bunkhouse and watched them with hard eyes. "An unfriendly looking lot, aren't they?" Carson whispered softy.

"Doesn't seem to be much work going on, does there?" Marty replied. He paused as he caught movement out of the corner of his eye.

A man swung open the front door and walked over to the edge of the porch. "Whaddya two saddle bums want?"

CHAPTER 18
SUSPICION

"Howdy." Marty took off his hat. "Mighty warm today, ain't it? Are you the ramrod or owner of this here spread?" Marty slurred his natural Southern drawl to imply his ordinariness.

"I'm the owner. Whaddya want?"

"Name's Mike and this here is Chris. We're look-in' to make a little to build up a grubstake. You got any work fer a few weeks?"

"Nope. Ain't interested in bankrollin' none a' you tenderfoots who think you can find the next bonanza. Hit the trail."

"Sorry to hear that, Mr. . . . ?"

The man sighed in exasperation. "I'm Vernon Barton. I own this ranch and I don't need no help. Make tracks."

"All right if we water our horses, Mr. Barton?"

"Yeah, I reckon. Then don't let the front gate slap ya in the ass on yur way out." He called out to one of the men lounging beside the bunkhouse wall, watching the interplay. "Joaquin, let these two saddle bums water their horses and then escort 'em to the road."

"*Sí, Jefe.*" The Mexican pushed away from the wall and walked toward Marty and Carson. "You heer Señor Barton. Water your hosses and then move on. *Comprende?*"

"Yeah, we're goin'. Don't get your long johns bunched."

"That fellow was certainly an unpleasant sort, wasn't he?" Carson stiffly remarked as they rode down the road away from the ranch turnoff.

"That he was. Unfortunately, it doesn't prove that he's behind all the holdups."

"Well, my daddy used to say, 'Where there's fire, there's smoke,' or something like that."

"Let's reserve judgment until we've visited the rest of the ranches along our route." Marty chucked his spurs lightly into Pacer's side. "Get going, Pacer. We've got a lot of ground to cover before dark."

By the end of the second day, Marty and Carson had interviewed themselves all the way to Virginia City and beyond. The owner of the Peavine Ranch, a crusty old Southern gentleman named Noah Peabody, told them about the same story as Livingston. "I don't know what I can do to help ya, Marty, but whatever it is, you jus' call on me. Nevada's had enough of lawlessness."

On the morning of the third day, they were in Reno, having spent the last night at the Steaming Springs Resort, just outside the town. There they soaked away the soreness from long days in the saddle and slept like logs until well after the sun had risen.

Marty introduced Carson to Sheriff Longabaugh. After sharing lunch with the lawman, they walked over to speak with O'Brian's station manager, a wispy, shrunken old-timer named Tom Dawkins, whose ornate muttonchop whiskers were the most striking feature of his nondescript appearance. "Any word on the arrival of the pumps for Hearst up in Virginia City?" Marty asked after the introductions were complete.

"Nope, Mr. Keller. Nary a word yet. I told Mr. O'Brian that I would send him a telegram just as soon as I heard anything."

"Good. I would hope that nobody else hears about it, else I'd have to come back and find out why. You get my meaning?" He stared coolly at Dawkins while giving a slight hitch to his gun belt.

"Oh, you can be assured of that, Mr.

Keller. I'm completely loyal to Malcolm."

"Excellent. Come on, Carson, let's make the ride from here to Virginia City before it gets too late." The two men left the office, leaving behind a steaming Dawkins, who saw a hundred dollars fly out the window if he failed to alert Ransom Stoddard as soon as he knew anything about the expected pumps. But he also saw the cold eyes of a man killer delivering a warning.

Marty and Carson studied the terrain on the ride from Reno to Virginia City, spending a good deal of time inspecting the site where the freight wagons had been attacked. They found the exact location where the outlaws waited for the unsuspecting freight wagons. "Look at the tracks, Carson. Just like the other place. Headed to the road that goes past the V bar B. I sure wish we could catch them in the act. I know they're the ones, I can smell it." Marty broke off a small twig and put it in his mouth. "The only thing is, the timing is off for an attack on this side of Virginia City. It'd take a man on horseback leaving from Reno longer to get to the ranch and then back here than it would take loaded freight wagons, even going slow."

"So how did they do it?" Carson asked.

"Either they had advanced information on

the time the freight wagons left, or they spotted themselves somewhere in between here and the ranch in advance of the attack."

"I wonder where."

"It had to be somewhere close, since we're only three hours out of Reno." He scanned the valley to the east, where the outlaws came from. "I've got to figure out how to hit them with my reaction force before they shoot up my drivers and Mr. Hearst's wagonload of pumps."

Carson spoke in a hesitant way, as if Marty might belittle his thought. "Marty, I've been thinking on just that."

"Oh?"

"Yes. Here's what I was thinking. When it's time, you let me take some of the reaction force and go where we can watch the approaches to the ambush site. As soon as the outlaws ride past, we'll follow 'em and be in position to jump in once they try anything."

"By gosh, Carson, that's not bad. If you come in behind 'em and I'm in front with the Gatling gun, they'll be facing a lot of firepower from different directions. And if there is a spy in the town alerting the outlaws and you go out well before we leave, he wouldn't know what a surprise is waiting for 'em. A pretty good idea, Carson. Let me think on it some."

They rode on to Virginia City talking about Carson's idea, and how to implement it. As soon as they arrived, Marty checked on George Hearst, but his secretary said the mining magnate had not yet returned from San Francisco. They stayed the night and then rode back to Carson City, as the next day was Sunday and Marty wanted to see what manner of recruits Johnny had hired.

Colleen lassoed Carson away as soon as they arrived in town, flashing a wicked glance at Marty as she marched the grinning young man out of the office. "She's madder than a wet hen that you took him with ya," Malcolm explained. "She always worryin' that he'll git shot by someone you run up agin."

"I'm doin' my best to keep him safe, Malcolm. I like the boy too."

Malcolm gave Marty a huge grin. "I know ya do. So do I. But you know womenfolk. Once they git their mind set on somethin', well, look out iffen you git crossways to it." Malcolm's smile faded as he changed the subject. "Did ya run across anything useful?"

"We did." Marty explained what they had discovered and his belief that the outlaws were headquartered at the V bar B Ranch.

"Any way we can bring the law down on 'em?"

"Not a chance, Malcolm. All I've got is a gut feeling."

"Damn, 'cause I need to make another run to Virginia City. There's money that needs to get to the bank here in Carson City and mail that needs to git to the railroad in Reno. What do you want to do, fill up the coach with some of your new gunfighters?"

"I'd rather not, just yet. The timing's not quite right yet. I do have an idea I'd like to try, though." Marty explained that a lookout was likely in Carson City ready to speed the word to the outlaws once he saw the stage leave town. "I want us to take no passengers. Just me and Squint on top, and Carson and a couple of others in the coach."

"That's not enough, Marty." Malcolm pointed a finger at the map behind him showing the route from Carson City to the mining town. "They can put twenty men up against ya. Maybe more."

"Yes, but I'm gonna surprise 'em. Just as soon as we hit the switchback road to the top of Roberts Pass, I'm gonna stop and wait until dark before I go up and over and on down to Carson City. Do the same thing coming back, maybe."

Marty pointed to the map. "It seems to me that the only way a fella could get to the ranch on the far side of Jefferson Mountain would be to ride hard up the road beside Carson Creek until he could cut cross-country to the road on the backside of the mountain. He'd have very little time to waste, so he'd likely be in a fierce hurry. If we were to watch over the road we might spot him, and maybe find out where he's from."

"A good ideer. Can you go tomorrow? I really need to git the run in right away. The mail contract requires me to make weekly deliveries."

"Monday's the earliest. I need to look at Johnny's recruits tomorrow. Put the word out that the stage is leaving Monday around ten. Allow no passengers. Tell Squint the plan and have him pick the most reliable mules for the team."

"I'll do it, Marty. Almost wish I could go with you, sorta glad I ain't. Going up and down them mountain roads in the dark. It's gonna be hairy, let me tell ya."

"You might be surprised. Mules have better eyesight than humans by a long shot. Hell, it'll be almost like a daylight run for 'em. And the outlaws, who will have spent all day vainly waiting for us to appear, will either have given up and left, or will be reduced to shooting blindly at a sound thundering past."

Malcolm shook his head. "Madness, pure madness. But I gotta make a stage run to Virginia City and that's that. So let's git her done. Where the hell's Squint?" Malcolm walked out the door hollering for his best stage driver.

Marty and Carson rode over to Carson Creek around ten the next morning. They left to the sound of church bells from the local houses of worship and rode into the sound of gunfire. Johnny was there with more than a dozen men, watching as they fired at targets on the far bank of Carson Creek.

"Hello, Mr. Keller."

"Morning, Johnny. Looks like you've assembled a good number of men who are anxious to risk their necks."

"I picked up fifteen. I figgered if any of them were trying to throw smoke about how well they could handle firearms, I'd be able to drop them without having to recruit any more. I know you said to only get ten or so."

"I'm beginning to think we may need a few more. Keep all you deem qualified to serve in our little army."

"Well, they're all looking pretty good. Pat, come over here, please."

A solidly built man, well over six feet tall and weighing more than two hundred and fifty pounds, rose from where he had knelt beside a man on the firing line, and walked to Johnny's side.

"Mr. Keller. This is Pat Quinn, former first sergeant of the Third Brigade, Fifth Division under General Hatch. It was a cavalry division in Scho-field's Corps. Pat is a fine NCO and I sorta wondered if I could assign him as my sergeant, with a twenty-five-dollar increase in pay. If you say no, I'll put him back in the ranks."

"I think it's a good idea. Call the men over, Johnny. I want to talk to them for a minute."

Johnny quickly gathered the men around Marty and Carson. Marty introduced himself and his young friend. He explained the trouble O'Brian was having. "I want you men to understand, this is no game. The outlaws will stop at nothing to halt the freight shipment we have to deliver very shortly. They've killed before, they will again, especially if we get them cornered. I'm not gonna put you in any more jeopardy than humanly possible. But you're gonna have to root these crooks out with hot lead, make no mistake about it. Any of you want out, now's the time."

One man stepped up. "Ross Wilbarger, Mr. Keller. I've got a wife and kids back in Missouri. Maybe I'd better take a pass on this. I certainly need the money, but I'd better not get involved in any gunplay. Any other way I could be of service?"

Marty thought a minute. "I'm gonna need two men to serve as lookouts when we start the ball rolling on this little shindig. Only half as much money, but you won't be expected to do any fighting."

Marty nodded. "Anyone else decide to join Ross here, do it today. After that, it's too late to back out and get any of your money. If nobody volunteers today, Ross, can you find someone trustworthy to join you?"

"My friend Dick Ruud, he'd join me, I think. I've known him since I got here and he's given me no reason to doubt him, ever."

"Good. Well, you fellas better get back to work. Johnny, I want Carson here to stay with you and train some. He needs a refresher in marksmanship and he'll tell you about the plan we're working on, at least as far as what your men will have to do. You need to run a few drills on approach and fanning out behind cover. Johnny, I'll check in with you later this week. Let me know what you think about the men then."

"Will do, Marty."

"Ross, you come see me at the O'Brian freight office about eight o'clock tonight, if you will."

"Sure thing, Mr. Keller."

Marty paused, then looked at the men, still gathered around. "I need a couple of men to make a ride to Virginia City on the stage with me and Carson. Any volunteers? We'll be gone about four days. I'll pay ten bucks a day to whoever goes along."

The ex–sergeant major Quinn immediately stepped forward. "I'm busted, Mr. Keller. Reckon I'll take a hand."

Another man spoke up. "Me too."

"Good, meet the stage at the place where the road crosses that little creek just outside of town. Say about ten o'clock tomorrow. You know where I mean?"

"Sure do," Quinn answered. "We'll be there."

"See you then," Marty answered, then rode away from the training site. He spent the rest of the day going over the trip to Virginia City with Squint and Malcolm. Carson returned from training at about six and flopped into a chair, wiping sweat and dust off his brow. "Whoa, did Johnny and

Pat work us over! You'd think we were all in the army or something."

"Good, that's what I want. What do you think?" Marty asked. "They look like they ready for some gun action?"

"I think so," Carson answered. "I don't think an army unit could be any better. Every man there but me was in either the Union or the Rebel army."

"Confederate, you mean."

"Certainly. Pardon my mistake."

Marty smiled. "Some would take it a lot more seriously than I do, Carson. Well, you'd better get cleaned up if you want to go to supper with Malcolm and Colleen and me. We're leaving in about thirty minutes."

Marty was sitting on the front porch smoking a small cigar when Ross walked up, accompanied by another man, stocky, several years older than Ross but of a very similar modest appearance and demeanor. Ross introduced him as Dick Ruud, as if it were spelled Rude. "Call me Ruud, everyone else does," the man instructed.

"You willing to work with Ross here as a scout for me?" Marty queried, getting right to the point.

"Yep. Ross said you'd pay fifty dollars a month fer the job."

"I will, but make no mistake, it's a job

that will not last longer than a couple of months, probably only one."

"Still, it'll buy us some food fer the winter. Unless we can git on at one of the mines, this winter is gonna be pretty lean."

"You both have horses?" Marty questioned.

"Shore do," Ross answered. "Got 'em stabled in the livery."

"I want you both out on the Carson Creek Road tomorrow at sunup. We're gonna take the stage out and I suspect somebody will ride out that way to inform the outlaws. I want you two to just watch, maybe trail along at a good distance back because I certainly don't want our spy to be alerted that we're wise to him. But see if you can discover where he goes." Marty explained his suspicions about the V bar B Ranch.

"We'll do it, Mr. Keller. You can count on us."

"Good enough. Report back to me on Friday, when I return from Reno."

Marty flipped the burning stub of his cigar into the dirt street and headed for the hotel and his room. He would be up all night tomorrow, so he had better get to sleep. "Looks like we're about to start the dance," he muttered to himself. "And about damned time."

CHAPTER 19
NIGHT RIDE

"Malcolm, let's get ready to go. Bring the stage out where everyone can see us."

"You sure, Marty? That'll just make it that much easier for whoever's watchin' fer the outlaws."

"Exactly. I want those outlaws sitting at the ambush site all day, getting tired and careless, before we rush past them after dark."

"You heard him, Squint. Help me push the stage outside."

Carson stepped out on the porch and then walked over to where the stage was standing, in front of the office, within sight of anyone on the street. Squint was expertly maneuvering two mules at a time into their positions on the lead lines and properly adjusting the collar and harness for each animal.

"I finished cleaning the shotguns, Marty. Do you want me to put them in the coach?"

"Cover 'em with a blanket, Carson. No one needs to know what firepower we're carrying."

"Will do."

Several men, early morning risers, stopped to watch the activity. "You plannin' on takin' the stage to Reno, Malcolm?" one man asked.

"Nope, this stage is goin' to Virginia City, come eight o'clock."

Marty heard someone softly mutter, "Good luck, then," but paid it no mind. He continued to put the mail and other sundry items in the boot or on the top. The last thing he passed up were six sixty-pound bags of grain that he had purchased from the feed store. Once they were away from prying eyes, he planned to make them into a cover for protection from outlaw bullets.

As he finished, he asked Squint, "Squint, did you put that piece of boilerplate on the stage?"

"Yep. It's in the coach. Think we can get it to ride up next to me without fallin' off?"

"That's what the rope is for. We'll figure it out somehow."

"I shore hope I can handle the team with that piece of iron in my lap, and I shore hope it'll stop a rifle bullet that just might have my name on it."

"It'll stop a rifle bullet, believe it. Once we get it tied to the side of the driver's box, I imagine you'll hardly notice it." Squint finished putting his chosen mules in harness and then turned to Malcolm, standing on the porch, along with Colleen. "Well, I guess we'd best be going. So long, Malcolm, Colleen." He gave her a quick grin. "I'll take good care of Carson, I promise."

"You better," she answered, her tone serious. She walked over to say her good-byes to the object of her affections.

"Take care, Marty." Malcolm held out his hand. "Don't git nobody hurt, if you can help it."

"That's my intention, Malcolm." He climbed up in the driver's box, next to Squint. Both men looked down at Carson and Colleen, talking quietly at the side of the coach.

"Git in, Sonny," Squint called out. "It's time to make tracks."

Carson started to turn, but Colleen stopped him long enough to plant a quick buss on his cheek, then hurried to stand beside her father. Squint snapped the lines and the stage rumbled down the street, Squint already shouting and cussing at the mules. Pedestrians walking along the boardwalks stopped to watch, their eyes following it as it left town and everyone wondering if this stage would end up like the others, in pieces, at the bottom of Graveyard Pass.

As soon as they crossed the wooden bridge over the shallow Carson Creek, Pat Quinn and his compadre stepped out of the tree line, each man carrying a small carpetbag packed with things needed on the trip.

The two men quickly clambered into the coach with Carson. Squint snapped the harness lines and got the mules going again. Marty focused his attention on the passing roadway for any sign of trouble, his shotgun cradled in his arms, but the stage arrived at the start of the switchbacks that led to the top of Roberts Pass without incident.

"Pull her in anywhere you can find us a little cover, Squint," Marty instructed. "We'll wait it out here until the sun sets before starting up the mountain."

Squint nodded and pulled the stage off the road and into a small clearing just inside the tree line. He looped the lead lines around the hand brake and sighed. "I shore hope these critters won't hold all the cussin' I done agin them when we start up this road after dark. I'll jus' be along fer the ride, unless the moon's good and bright."

"Let's hope it's not," Marty answered. "I want it plenty dark. So dark the outlaws can't get us in their sights."

Marty swung down from the driver's box and opened the door to the coach. "Might as well get comfortable, boys, we're here fer a spell."

"What's goin' on, Mr. Keller?" Pat Quinn asked, a confused look on his face.

Marty explained his plan to make the run over the top of the pass during the hours of darkness.

"Can them mules see in the dark?" the other man asked, his voice betraying both his Southern roots and his nervousness at the notion of driving blind.

"Sure can," Marty answered. "What's you name, by the way?"

"I'm Del Murphy, Mr. Keller. I was in Logan's Rangers durin' the war."

"From Georgia?" Marty asked.

"Yessir. Fought with Johnson at Stone Mountain and got captured. Spent the rest of the war in the prison camp at Rock Island, up in Illinois. A damned cold place to be in the wintertime."

"So I've heard. Well, Del, let me assure you, and Squint and probably Pat here can tell you, mules can see like it's pure daylight, even on the darkest night. I learned a long time ago to just let them be and they'll get you wherever you want to go."

Pat Quinn nodded his head. "I see where you're goin'. Yu're gonna make a run past them outlaws in the dark. What they can't see they can't hit."

"Yep, and we'll be answering back anything sent our way with double-O buckshot from the shotguns we're gonna carry the rest of the way.

"Squint, you take care of the mules with Del here. Pat, if you'll give Carson and me a hand, we're gonna put some boilerplate up for Squint to hide behind if the shooting starts."

"I wondered what that chunk of tin was for."

With the strong Irishman's help, it did not take long to tie the boilerplate to the side of the driver's box in such a way that Squint was protected from shots fired at him from the side of the road.

Squint climbed up into the driver's box and settled himself so the iron plate was touching his shoulder. "Well, I reckon it'll keep the bees away," he snorted. Then he climbed down and returned to where he had chosen to wait out the day, although Marty noticed that every once in a while he would look at his stage with its dark iron barrier and smile.

The men gathered around a small campfire while they had hot coffee and ate fried ham and beans for supper. Then as the sun dropped into the far ocean west of California, Marty poured the last of his coffee into the tiny fire, raising a puff of smoke and ashes. "It's time. Harness 'em up, Squint. Let's get on the road."

Charlie Call cussed for a solid minute, then threw his cigar into the tiny fire the men had made for their coffee. He was hungry and irritable. None of the outlaws had brought any food assuming they would finish the job before noon and be back at the ranch in time for a late lunch. He slopped the dregs of his coffee into the flames and spoke loud enough for the men to hear. "To hell with it, let's go home. The skunks musta gone some other way, else they'd be here afore now."

The gang started to gather their rifles and saddlebags before heading back to the clearing where they had tied their horses. "Joaquin, go git Miguel and tell him to come on, we're headed fer the ranch." He worried over just how he would explain this to Barton. The outlaw leader was as irritable as a mangy cat lately. Charlie had just climbed onto his horse when Joaquin came running up.

"Senor Call, the stage, she coming. Right now."

"What the hell? You sure 'bout that?"

"Oh, *sí*, she coming. Almost to the top of the pass already."

"Come on, boys," he shouted. "Git back to yur places. If you can't see nuttin', fire at the sound. Hurry, hurry, damn your hides." Charlie grabbed his rifle and ran as quickly as he could in the darkness back to the tree where he had a good view of the road. In the dim moonlight, he could just make out the lighter trace of the roadbed about thirty yards below him.

Just as he got there, the outline of the stage went past, faster than he would have imagined anyone would dare drive it in the darkness. He quickly snapped off three shots at the general location of where the driver would be sitting. Several of his men also fired at the indistinct mass hurtling past. They were answered by what sounded like cannons in the darkness, but it had to be twin-barrel "greeners," being fired from the stagecoach's interior. The whistle of buckshot zipped past, tearing away branches and ripping into the trunks of trees. He could hear the outraged cries of two or three men who had stopped one of the pea-sized lead balls from the shotguns being fired at them. Then it was too late. The stage rolled even deeper into the gloom until only the sound of hoofbeats and squeaking wheels was left, and a descending cloud of dust. Cursing at his bad luck, Charlie fired at the fading sound, hoping one of his bullets might hit something, anything.

As he cursed the fleeing stage, one of his men ran up. "Do ya want us to chase after it, boss?"

"Naw, in the dark we couldn't go fast enough to catch up with it noways. Anybody hit?"

"Yeah, two men got pellets in their legs and Shorty got hit over his right eye. He may lose it iffen we don't git him to the doc in Reno right away."

"Damn. All right, git everyone mounted. We may as well go on back to the ranch. Them skunks got the best of us this time. There'll be another day, I reckon."

As they rode toward the V bar B, Charlie knew he was in for a major ass eating over the unfortunate development. "Next time I'll kill everyone on the damned stage, just see if I don't," he snarled to himself as the discouraged outlaws rode back to their lair.

Squint drove the mules as fast as he dared until they came to a small dip between two low rises in the road, where he stopped the panting mules for a breather. "Whoo-eee," he shouted, "did we ever surprise them owl-hoots!" He struck a match and looked at the outside face of the boilerplate fastened next to him. "Lookie at this here gouge. If-fen I hadn't had this plate fastened next to me, I'd be tradin' my mule whip fer a pair of heavenly wings."

Marty got up from his position behind three of the grain bags. "Anybody inside hurt?" he called out.

Carson climbed out of the coach, followed by Quinn and Del. "No," Carson called back. "One bullet came through the door, but it buried itself in the grain sack."

"Good. Squint, check the mules and make sure none of them got hit."

Soon Squint was back beside the coach, shaking his head. "Nope, looks like they all came through jus' fine."

"Good enough. Let's get on to Virginia City. I'm tired of riding along like a blind man."

"Hells, Marty. We still got twenty miles to go. It'll be two a.m. afore we get thar."

"Well, let's get going. It won't be any earlier the longer we stand around." As he climbed back up on the stage, he thanked his lucky stars nobody had been hurt. An awful lot of lead had come down from the hidden outlaws. There had to be fifteen or twenty of them. "I wonder if we hit any of them?" he asked Squint. "It'd be only luck if we did. Fast as we were going plus the darkness. Only good luck."

Just as Squint had predicted, the clock in the freight office chimed twice as Squint pulled the tired mules to a halt outside. Marty swung down and checked the office. It was empty and locked and he had not thought to ask Malcolm for a key. "All locked up tight, fellas. Let's get the mules taken care of and grab some shut-eye. Pat, if you and Del want to have a drink, it's all right with me, but I want you sober and ready to go early tomorrow morning. We're going on to Reno before the outlaws have a chance to recover."

"I imagine me and Del will grab ourselves a beer afore we call it a night, but don't worry, Mr. Keller. We'll be alert tomorrow."

"All I can ask."

Carson spoke out. "Pat, Squint and I will join you if it's all right with you."

"Hell, if you're all going, so'll I, if nobody objects," Marty broke in.

"Sure. The more the merrier," Quinn answered.

The tired men rousted the mule barn swamper from his cramped quarters off the main building and got the mules taken care of.

"Where can we bunk out?" Marty asked. "There's no chance of us getting a room at the hotels in town this late tonight."

"There's plenty of fresh hay in the loft. Be my guest," the swamper answered.

"We will, but first we're gonna treat ourselves to a cool beer."

"Me, I'm going back to bed. Unless, that is, if you was to be a-buyin'?"

"Be my pleasure," Marty answered. "Come on. Last man to the bar is a hoot owl's fur ball."

Marty had his party on the road to Reno by nine the next morning. They arrived in the town without incident. Marty instructed Squint to get the mules settled and for Pat and Del to stay close to the office while he and Carson checked in with Jesse Long-abaugh. The town sheriff had a good laugh when Marty described the hair-raising ride in the dark and the wild shoot-out with the outlaws.

"They'll be looking for you to try that again, Marty. Probably have torches or a woodpile ready to light up, so they can see you outlined by the fire."

"I didn't think we could try it but one time, Jesse. I've got one more surprise for them this trip. Then we'll have to wait until I'm ready to make the all-out effort against them."

"When will that be?"

"When the pumps George Hearst ordered arrive. If they don't stop us from delivering them to Virginia City, all their effort will have been in vain. They'll be coming out of the woodwork then and we'll have the opportunity to stomp 'em out, permanently."

"By the way, Noah Peabody sent a man in here yesterday to find you. I told him you were on the way, so he may have waited for you."

"How'd you know I was on the way?"

"Malcolm sent me a wire, asking for me to watch out for you. He was worried about you, I guess. You'd best send him one sayin' you're here and all right."

"Guess I'd better."

"While you're doin' that, I'll look around for the Peavine rider. I'll send him over to the freight office if I run across him."

"Thanks, Jesse. Also, put out the word the stage'll be leavin' day after tomorrow to Virginia City."

"You're not . . . ?"

"Nope, but I wouldn't mind if it got to

certain ears that I was. Keep 'em off my back while we take the flatlands route to Carson City."

"Now, why didn't I think of that?"

CHAPTER 20
THE GATLING GUN ARRIVES

Marty sent a quick wire to O'Brian telling him of their safe arrival in Reno. He walked back to the mule barn at the rear of the freight office just in time to find Squint instructing Carson on the finer points of driving a six-team stagecoach.

"You planning on making a driver out of Carson?"

"It's somethin' the boy needs to know iffen he's gonna be in the stagecoach business."

"Do you think I could ride up with Squint when we go back to Carson City, Marty? Maybe get a few miles under my belt handling the team?"

"If it's all right with Squint, it's fine by me. I'm tired of hearing this ole geezer cuss those poor animals anyway. My ears need the relief."

Before Squint could think of an appropriate reply, Jesse Longabaugh walked into the

259

barn with a stranger. The man was short and blocky, with the bowed legs that proclaimed him to be a cowboy most of his life. He walked as though he could straddle a barrel without breaking stride.

"Hello, Marty. Here's that man from the Peavine Ranch. Shorty Royall, meet my friend Marty Keller."

"Howdy, Mr. Keller. Mr. Peabody sent me into town to give ya a message." He offered his hand in greeting.

Marty shook the hand. It was rock solid. "Hello, Shorty. Glad to make your acquaintance. Say hello to Squint, the old-timer, and Carson."

"Howdy, boys." Shorty turned back to Marty. "Mr. Peabody said to tell ya that someone is usin' our easternmost line cabin. Not often, but they left plenty of sign. It'd put them about two miles beyond Virginnie City and twelve miles closer to the Reno Road than from the V bar B Ranch. He said it was probably the gang you been searchin' for."

"Thank Mr. Peabody for the information. It will prove useful. Tell me all about the cabin. Where is it? What's it made of?"

The cowboy finished all of Marty's questions and took his leave. He smiled as he walked out of the barn. He still had time for a cooling drink of beer before he had to start back to the ranch.

Marty walked Jesse back to his office. "Well, old pard, that answers the question how the outlaws can hit the freight wagons en route from here to Virginia City. They get word a shipment is going out, wait at the line shack until their lookout arrives with word the wagons have left town, then move to their ambush site."

The whistle of the arriving eastbound train interrupted their discussion. Jesse steered Marty in the direction of the train station. "I try to meet as many of the arriving trains as I can. I like to take a look at any newcomers to town."

The first person they saw stepping off the passenger car to the station walkway was George Hearst. He stretched his back and then walked to where Marty was. "Hello, Mr. Hearst. You met Sheriff Jesse Long-abaugh?"

Hearst stuck out his hand. "My pleasure, Sheriff." He turned to Marty, a satisfied grin on his bewhiskered face. "I didn't expect to see you here, Marty. A pleasant surprise. Well" — he beamed in satisfaction — "I got it. I got your Gatling gun. And, even better, some more capital from some of my more affluent friends. We got enough to carry us awhile longer."

"Good news, Mr. Hearst. While you were gone, I think I found out who's been behind the rash of attacks on the O'Brians."

"Do I know him?"

"I doubt it. A rancher named Vern Barton. Has a spread on the east side of Jefferson Mountain."

"I do know him, by damn. He's a friend of Ransom Stoddard. I ran into them at the Virginia Hotel dining room one evening. So Stoddard does have something to do with it, huh?"

"And you think Stoddard was behind the fire in your mine, don't you?"

"Think? I know it. The skunk has been trying to get my holding in the Comstock ever since I sank the first shaft." Hearst started toward the freight car just forward of the passenger coaches. "General Thomas was a tough nut to crack, but when I reminded him that he had invested in the Comstock Mine, at my recommendation, he gave in. He also sent us two experts to man the thing."

Hearst beamed as the door to the boxcar swung open and two black soldiers appeared, blinking their eyes in the bright sunlight. "Hop down, Sergeant. We're here."

The two soldiers hopped down and stood

passively, awaiting their next orders. "Marty, this here is Sergeant Henry LeCroix and Corporal Samson Blue, of the twenty-fifth Black Infantry Regiment. They're stationed at the Presidio, under General Thomas. He assures me they are well-qualified experts when it comes to firing the Gatling gun."

Marty shook hands with both soldiers. "Glad to meet you fellas." He turned to Jesse. "Can we get inside, Jesse? I don't want people seeing Mr. Hearst and me with these soldiers and wondering what's going on."

"Good idea. Come on, we can use the freight storage room in the station here." Jesse led the others into a room partially filled with suitcases and wooden crates.

"Sergeant," Marty instructed, "would you and Corporal Blue mind staying out of sight until we can get you back to the freight office? Is the Gatling gun in a crate or something so it can't be noticed?"

"Yes, sir. It's all boxed up. Me and Corporal Blue don't mind lyin' low iffen that's what you wants."

"Thank you. I'll explain what this is all about in a few minutes." Marty turned to Sheriff Longabaugh. "Jesse, would you have the depot agent get the crates holding the gun placed in here with us? Then make certain the agent keeps his mouth shut about what he saw. I don't want anyone alerted to what we're doing."

"Sure, no problem. Where you headed?"

"I'm going to get a covered wagon to pick up the men and gun and get them over to the freight office."

"I'll stick around until you return."

Marty was back in short order, in a covered wagon and accompanied by Carson. Using a little ingenuity, they soon had the gun and men delivered to the freight office. Marty outlined the problems with the outlaws' attacks and some of his plan. "If we can surprise them with your gun, we ought to clean house."

"Yessir, Mr. Keller. Me and Corporal Blue here will blow them outlaws to kingdom come."

"You feel confident that you can handle the gun mounted on a wagon like I envision?"

"Not a problem. Up thar on that wagon, we'll be a mite exposed. Can we make up some sort of cover?"

"A good idea." Marty thought for a second or two, then grabbed a pencil and some paper. He quickly sketched out a crude protective box to surround the gun. "How about something like this?" he asked Sergeant LeCroix.

"I reckon we can make somethin' lik' dat. You can git us some heavy timbers?"

"Not a problem." Marty gave the tall, dark soldier a warrior's smile. "You fellas bring any civilian clothing with you?"

"Nope, alls we's got is the uniforms on our backs."

Marty turned to Carson. "You get these boys some civilian clothes, will you? Put it on the company bill down at the dry goods store." He then faced Clyde, the office manager. "Clyde, you tell anyone who asks, these two are new swampers for the mule barn."

"I shore will, Mr. Keller. They can sleep in the hayloft iffen they want."

"You two be all right there? I'd rather you kept a low profile and didn't raise any questions."

"Yessir," LeCroix answered. "Maybe iffen Mr. Clyde could bring us a bucket of beer once in a while?"

"He'll deliver beer and a hot meal every night, don't worry. You two just stay close, get the wagon fixed up to transport the gun, and stand ready. It won't be long before we're gonna need you and your Gatling gun. The pumps for Virginia City will be here soon, and when they arrive, we put my

265

plan into action."

Marty next headed to the hotel and reported what had happened to George Hearst. The mining magnate nodded his head at the information. "I am exceedingly hopeful you'll get my pumps to me, Mr. Keller. They're all that stands between me and bankruptcy."

"With the gun and the two soldiers, I think we'll go into the fight with a distinct advantage over the outlaws. Then we'll drive them back to where they came from, wipe that out, and hopefully get all the leaders, including your Mr. Stoddard, as well as deliver your pumps."

Hearst smiled, his dark eyes twinkling. "That would certainly make my day, I assure you." He passed over a bank draft. "Here's three thousand in advance for Malcolm O'Brian. You'll give it to him from me?"

"Gladly."

"When are you headed back to Carson City?"

"Tomorrow morning, although we've put out the word we're leaving day after tomorrow, for Virginia City."

"Good idea. Well, I'm gonna get me a bite to eat and then get a good night's sleep before I go back to the mines. Care to join me?"

"Thank you, I'd be happy to."

Marty and Hearst spent the meal talking about mining and the unique problems at the Virginia City mines. Marty listened and learned about hard-rock mining. He quickly brushed over his adventures on the bounty trail, and Hearst picked up on his reluctance to talk about it. He did relay a quick version of the attack on his home that killed his wife and son, the reason for being a bounty hunter.

"You still haven't heard anything about this Hulett fellow or his companion?" Hearst commented.

"Not a word in nearly five years."

"I agree, it's very odd. They must have crawled into a hole somewhere and stayed put."

"They'll come out," Marty answered. "Then I'll find 'em and have my retribution. I'll never stop looking for them until I do."

"If it was my Phoebe and son Willie, I'd feel the same way. I wish you luck, Marty."

With that, the two men parted company, Hearst headed to the bar for a nightcap and Marty to check on his new soldiers, before he bedded down. The next day would be a full one and they had to drive the stage over fifty miles of rough road to get back to Carson City. He walked into the barn to find the two black soldiers sitting on hay bales regaling Carson, Quinn, and Del with stories of their experiences against the Modoc Indians in Northern California.

"Evening, gentlemen," Marty greeted them. "Seems like everyone's here but Squint. Where's he?"

Carson laughed. "He said something about getting a few drinks in him so he could sleep good. Said he'd be back directly."

Marty listened as the tall, muscular, dignified, professional soldier softly spoke of a campaign where his rapid-fire gun made the difference in a long battle with entrenched but cornered Indians in the lava mountains west of Mt. Shasta, almost to the Oregon border.

"Sounds a lot like how I'd like to see our battle going," Marty replied at the end of the story.

Carson eagerly spoke out. "I can't wait to see that danged gun in action. It must be something."

Corporal Blue smiled and spoke in his high, tenor voice. "You'll never forget it, once you git it a-goin'. It really is somethin'."

Marty watched as LeCroix tamped and lit a worn pipe, methodically got it fired up, and then contentedly puffed a few streams of white smoke into the air, the pleasant aroma of pipe tobacco mingling with the acidic odor of horse manure.

"LeCroix," Marty asked, "that's a Louisiana name, isn't it?"

"That it is, sir," the black sergeant answered. "I's the head Negra on a plantation near Baton Rouge, afore the war. Had near four hunnerd mens and womenfolk workin' under me. When the war started, I runned off to New Awlens and jined the Yankee army. After the war was over, I jined the black regiments bein' formed up to fight the Injuns. Been in the army ever since."

LeCroix chuckled and pointed with the stem of his pipe. "Corporal Blue here, he's from Ohio, come from free blacks, and jined the army after the war was over, but he's seen the ole elephant, yessir, he's seen 'em. Chasin' them murderin' Modacs through the lava rocks. He's earned his stripes."

"I'm sure he has," Marty answered. "Do you have any questions on what I want you to build on the gun wagon, Sergeant LeCroix?"

"Nope, we'll build it right, never you fear."

"You stick close to the barn. I'll be back

once the pumps arrive and we'll make our final plans then."

"We'll be here, Mr. Keller. Yessir. We'll git it done."

"I have no doubt, Sergeant. Come on, Carson, let's grab some shut-eye. Tomorrow's gonna be a long day."

Squint drove the stage out of Reno the next morning before the sun came up, giving Marty hope that they had jumped the gun on the outlaws, in case there was any intent to hit them on the way back to Carson City.

The road from Reno south to the new state capital was along the valley floor, and was much easier to traverse than the mountain roads to and from Virginia City. They arrived in Carson City without any problems and Marty released Pat Quinn and Del until they met with the others on Sunday to continue their training for the coming showdown.

Chapter 21
Vern Blows His Stack

Vern Barton was mad. "Damned mad and with good reason," he shouted at a cowed Charlie Call. "Whaddya think I pay ya for? Three trips. Three trips made by the stage and we ain't hit it once."

"I done told ya, boss. We was surprised. I've got some men up on Roberts Pass right now stackin' some brush and logs fer a fire. The next time they try comin' through, we'll be ready. We'll put a pile of burning brush out in the road to outline 'em by its light. Hell, we'll cut 'em to pieces."

"And what about them no-account lookouts in Virginia City and Reno? Neither one got word to us in time to git in position. Whatta they doin'? Lyin' around swillin' liquor on my time?"

"They're ready now, boss. Next time, I'll move some men to the Peavine line shack as soon as I hear a stage is in Reno, ready to head fer the Reno Road and hit 'em as

271

soon as they leave town."

"Damned right ya will. I don't care iffen they gotta camp out a week in the cold. We gotta stop the stage and freight from movin' twix Virginia City and the rest of the world. However, that ain't what's important now. I jus' got word from Mr. Stoddard in Virginnie City that his spy in Pittsburgh says the pumps for Hearst are almost done. He expects 'em to be shipped early next week. That means they'll be in Reno within two weeks, at the latest. We absolutely gotta stop them pumps. Get 'em fer Stoddard if we can, but stop 'em from ever reachin' Hearst, no matter what."

"I unnerstand, boss. I'll have every man at the line shack as soon as ya git word they're in Reno. O'Brian may try to sneak 'em out of town or travel in the dark, but I'll be ready."

"Damned right ya will. Call in the lookouts from Carson City and Virginnie City. I want every man we got on the firin' line when it comes time to hit them freight wagons."

"I gotcha, boss. I'll call the lookouts in right away."

A sinister gleam crossed Barton's dark eyes. "Hold on a second, I'm gittin' an ideer. Keep the lookouts on the job in Carson City. As soon as the pumps arrive, have them git O'Brian's gal. Iffen he's lookin' fer her, he ain't gonna be worryin' about takin' no pumps to the mines. Then we can have Clem Atkinson step in and offer to freight 'em in his wagons. Maybe we can git the pumps without a fight and hide 'em out till Stoddard needs 'em fer his mines."

"You think Hearst would ever use Clem's freight wagons?"

"He would iffen O'Brian was too busy lookin' fer his bratty daughter to bother freightin' the pumps up to the mines as soon as they arrive. Hearst ain't gonna let them things jus' sit at the railroad depot whilst O'Brian looks high and low fer his kid."

"Good idea, boss. I'll ride into Carson City tomorrow and pass the word to Sid and Jack to start workin' on gittin' O'Brian's gal. Where should they put her?"

"Hell, I don't care. Kill her and bury her deep in the woods fer all I give a hoot."

Call shook his head. "I don't know, boss. Killin' a woman. It might bring a passel of law down on us. Maybe we oughta jus' hide her out good fer a week or so. That oughta be long enough."

"Whatever. Jus' so they're lookin' fer her a good long while. There's dozens of old mines up and down the Wasach Range. Park her in one and keep her there. In fact, take two more boys and put 'em in Carson City. I don't wanna take no chances on her slippin' away from our men."

"I'll send Dusty and Rod from Virginia City down to Carson City. Sam and Waco will stay in Reno in case O'Brian does try and ship the pumps. They'll be our eyes on the pumps."

Barton waved his hand dismissively. "Whatever. Jus' so we don't botch this thing up. Things are gonna come to a head real quick-like now. We gotta be ready."

"I gotcha, boss. I'll git right on it." Call slipped out of the house, anxious to get out of Barton's view. He did not need any more of his backside chewed off by the mercurial outlaw leader.

He sent Slim into Virginia City to tell Dusty and Rod to move on down and join up with Sid and Jack in Reno. Then he went out to inspect the few cows the ranch supported, just to stay clear of Vern Barton for a while. The next morning, Charlie headed south on the ranch road toward the Carson Creek road into Carson City while Barton girded his loins and reported to Ransom Stoddard in Virginia City. The outlaw leader had to explain how O'Brian's successful stage run eluded his ambush and why he thought it would make ambushing the freight wagons even easier.

As he rode, he reviewed his plan to upset O'Brian's applecart and grew more heartened every time he did. His ego prevented him from seeing any flaws in a plan he had devised. By the time he explained it to Stoddard, he was so confident that he convinced the scheming mine owner it was infallible.

Stoddard's closing comment was "It's almost time for me to break George Hearst, Vern. Don't let anything stop you. You'll never see the snow fall if you do. Understand?"

Barton swallowed the lump in his throat and nodded. "I won't let ya down, Mr. Stoddard. You can count on it."

He got out of the office before he wet his pants. As he relieved himself in the privy behind Stoddard's building, he cursed himself for being so intimidated by the greedy mine owner. He just couldn't help himself. Great evil triumphed over lesser evil every time.

Charlie arrived in Carson City and quickly met with his two henchmen to lay the groundwork for kidnapping Colleen O'Brian. "Start watchin' her, and git an ideer of any habits she's got that we can use. I seen half a dozen abandoned mines twix the ranch and here. Git her, stash her in one, and watch her like a hawk till I say fer ya to let her go." Call paused until both outlaws' eyes met his. "You two and Dusty and Rod, who're on their way here from Reno, have only one job now. When I tell ya, grab the gal and hold on to her. But I don't want to hear that any of you done anything to her. We don't need that. You be certain Dusty and Ron unnerstand as well. No hanky-panky with the gal. Got it?"

Both men nodded, their faces serious. And both imagined what it would be like to have an attractive gal like Colleen O'Brian subject to their every whim and want. A very desirable image indeed. Both outlaws suppressed a smile of anticipation.

Marty rode out to the training site with Carson and Squint. As the men John Harper was training started their marksmanship exercise, Ross and Ruud rode up. They dismounted and tied their horses with the others, then walked to Marty's side.

"Mornin', Mr. Keller." Ross spoke before Marty could greet the two scouts. "We been keepin' our eyes on that jasper who rode outa town the day you left in the stage. His name's Jack Page, by the way. For a while it was just him and a fella named Sid, who was hangin' around keepin' an eye on the O'Brians. Yesterday, two more fellas rode in and joined up with 'em."

"What are they doing? Just watching?"

" ' Pears so."

"Got any names on the new pair?"

"Nope, not yet. Me and Ruud here has stayed pretty far back, since you said you didn't want us to give them any idea we was a-watchin' 'em."

"That's right. Try and keep an eye on the four of 'em. Let me know if they do anything you consider suspicious."

"We'll do it, Mr. Keller. Is it all right if Ruud and me join in on the target practice?"

"By all means, if you want. Tell Johnny I said it was all right."

Marty stayed at the training site, and by the end of the day was satisfied that the men were as ready as they probably ever would be with the limited time available to train them in the art of moving and shooting, using cover and concealment, and close-quarter fighting. As the day ended, Marty called the men to gather around him, which everyone did, silently awaiting his words.

"Well, it seems to me that Johnny and Pat have got you fellas pretty well prepared for the coming showdown. Today is your last chance to get out. I suspect the little dance we're cooking up is gonna occur pretty quickly. All of you men were in the army, I think. Blue or gray, you know that one thing you had to do in a fight was react immediately when you got the orders from your superiors. If you want to increase your chances of surviving the next fight, listen and obey Johnny and Pat. They've got good experience going for them. I'm confident we can whip this bunch of outlaws, but to do it as safely as possible, you must listen and obey. Is everyone clear on this?"

There was a rumble of "Yessir," "Yep," and "I understand," from the assembled men. Marty grunted, "And everyone is in?"

Again all he heard was affirmatives.

"Good enough, then. Stick close to town. Check in with Johnny twice a day, noontime and around six p.m. I'll get word to you through him when and where I want you."

As the men straggled off, Marty asked Johnny and Pat, as well as his two scouts, to stay behind. "They look pretty good," Marty complimented Johnny and Pat. "You two have done a fine job in a short amount of time. Things are about to come to a head. I want to go over my plans with you fellas, along with Squint and Carson. You'll all have major parts to play in the final outcome to this little barn dance."

Marty picked up a stick and drew a rough outline of the roads between Reno and Virginia City, the location of the V bar B, the Peavine Ranch line shack, and the place where the last freight wagon attack had occurred. "The first part of my plan will be for Carson and you and your men, Johnny, to slip out of town here the day before we are due to leave Reno. I'll telegraph you the exact date once I'm in Reno. Then you'll go to a place where you can watch the road from the Peavine line shack without being seen. You'll have to be able to spot the outlaws once they start up into the mountains. Then you'll trail after them and get into a place where you can ambush the ambushers. When they start the ruckus, you will put a world of hurt on 'em, added to what I'm gonna be sending at them from the wagons. I've got a Gatling gun on loan from the army, which I'll bring as additional fire support."

"Oh me blessed saints," Quinn murmured. "I've seen one a' them bustards in action. It was brutal. I do believe we're gonna make those ladies wish they'd stayed in bed that day."

"Mr. Keller, why don't we just hit them at the line shack, or on the way to the ambush site?" Ruud asked.

"It might be a bit safer if we did," Marty answered, "but I want there to be no mistake, that these are the men who have been ambushing the stage line. We're gonna wipe them out, off the face of the earth. The next bunch to consider doing it will have to think about that if they decide to try any funny business."

"How many men we goin' up against?" Ross asked.

"A good question. I'd imagine twenty to thirty. We'll be outnumbered, but we'll have the surprise on them, if things go as I plan. Like my old commander, Nathan B. Forrest, used to say, 'Put the skeer into 'em, git 'em runnin', and pile it on.' "

Carson jumped in, "And that's what we're gonna do, by gum. Where do you want me, Marty?"

"You'll ride with Johnny and his men. You know where any surviving outlaws may run to, in case something happens to me."

"Heck, I wanted to go with you."

"Orders, Carson. You wouldn't disobey me in front of the others, would you?"

"Of course not, Marty. I'll go where you think I can do the most good."

"That's the spirit. Johnny, Carson knows my entire plan and has ridden with me on the backside of the mountains. He knows the location of the ranch, the outlaws' last ambush site, and the trails to get there. Use him to your best advantage."

"What about me?" Squint asked.

"I wanted you to drive the wagon carrying the Gatling gun. It'll likely draw a lot of fire from the outlaws, so we'll make you another iron box like we did for the stage."

"I'm yur man, Marty. I'll enjoy givin' some payback fer my leg and shoulder."

"What about us?" Ruud asked next.

"Yeah," Ross echoed. "We don't wanna git left outa the fun."

"I thought you both wanted to avoid any gunplay?"

"Well, I sorta have changed my mind. I want in."

"Me too."

"Good, because I've got plenty for you both. You'll be the scouts for the reaction force. You'll have to watch for the outlaw gang and warn Johnny and his men as they approach. If they run, you'll have to trail 'em until the rest of us can catch up with you."

Marty looked at his pocket watch. "Well, it's about suppertime. Interest you fellas in a meal, on me?"

Everyone agreed except Carson. "Sorry,

Marty. I'm eating with Colleen and her father."

"Can't say that I blame you for that. Get on with you. Don't want her after my hide for your being late."

"Now, Marty," he protested, "you don't have to fret about her. She knows I'm in good hands when I'm with you."

As he rode away, Marty chuckled. "That boy doesn't know it, but she's measurin' him for his wedding suit or I'm a ring-tailed coon."

Squint laughed. "He may as well snort and shout for a spell, 'cause he's headed fer the sedate life of matrimony, just like you says."

On Monday, Marty drew several rough maps showing the locations of the V bar B and the ambush sites, as well as the trails in and out of the mountains, for he wanted Carson and Johnny to have no doubt where they were supposed to be, no matter the situation.

The next afternoon, he stopped by O'Brian's office about three. "Hello, Mr. O'Brian. Where's Carson? I want to talk to him."

"Him and Colleen are out ridin'. They've been goin' every chance they git."

"Good for them. I'll catch up with him

later. You hear anything about the pumps?"

"I just got a telegram this noon. They're on the way. Ought to be in Reno about Friday or Saturday."

"Then we'd better be there when they arrive. Just in case the outlaws decide to hit the warehouse and destroy them before we even get them on the wagons. Malcolm, do you have enough men to drive eight wagons, plus eight more to act as guards?"

"I think so. Especially if you're gonna build the same sort of iron thing fer the drivers like you did for Squint's stagecoach." He frowned. "The guards may be a bit harder to find. Even if we git men to go, they'll likely jump off and run at the first sign of trouble."

"We'll take what we can get. They're not the important pieces in our strategy anyway. I mostly want them to keep the drivers from running off."

"I plan to drive one of the wagons myself," Malcolm announced. "That might help stiffen the backbone of the men I do get."

The next day Marty and Squint sat at a table in the mule barn looking at some sketches Marty had made using the boilerplate as protection for the drivers of the freight wagons. Ross hurried into the barn, a concerned frown on his face.

"Marty, something fishy is goin' on."

"What's up, Ross?"

"Me and Ruud has been watchin' them four jaspers like you wanted. Up to now they have jus' lazed around town, not doin' much 'cept drinkin' and loafin'. Then this afternoon, the two new ones rode outa town on the Carson Creek Road. I followed along, stayin' well back like you said. Well, they stopped about a mile outa town and went up in the woods and hunkered down. I couldn't git too close. I watched 'em fer a spell, then rode past them stayin' on the road, sorta casual-like. They didn't do nothin', just stayed up in the brush. I watched 'em awhile longer. Then I circled way around and come to tell you."

"Where's Ruud now?"

"I don't know. He supposed to be watchin' them Sid and Jack fellas."

"Find him and keep an eye on the two still here in town. Maybe they'll tip us off to what's going on."

Ross hurried away. "Damn," Marty grumped. "Something's about to pop, sure as shootin'." He paced back and forth. "With the news about the pumps coming, it's probably no coincidence that they're up to no good."

About five, Ross and Ruud showed up at

the barn, finding a nervous Marty expecting to hear bad news.

"Them rats, Sid and Jack, done slipped away on me. I saw 'em ride outa town on the Carson Creek Road, but when I followed along, they wasn't on it. I went out until I hit the salt flats, four miles out. You can see fer miles in all directions from there. They cut off somewhere 'tween there and town. I'm shore sorry, Mr. Keller."

"Not to worry, fellas. You did your best. I told you not to get too close. That made it doubly hard for you. Something's up, that's for sure. You two stick around awhile. Let's see what develops."

Around sundown, Malcolm walked into the barn. "Marty, have you seen Colleen and Carson?"

A chill traversed Marty's spine. "Nope, sure haven't. Why?"

"They went ridin' this afternoon. They've never stayed out this long. Colleen was due to go to the Ladies' Wednesday Night Knitting Social at seven. She doesn't like to miss it, since she's sort of the president this year."

"Colleen and Carson are missing?" Squint came up and interrupted, having heard only part of the story.

"I didn't say that, exactly," Malcolm protested.

"You know where they liked to ride, Malcolm?"

"I think they rode out the Creek Road. There's a couple of hills out there where they can stop and look at some nice scenery."

"Ross, you and Ruud scout out that way. Take a look around where you lost those men. See if anything looks amiss. As soon as it's too dark to see anything, hurry back here. We'll be making plans in case you don't run into them. And take some medical supplies with you, in case they had some sort of accident and need tendin'."

He turned and put his hand on Malcolm's shoulder. "Malcolm, you go on over to the doctor's office and have him make you up an emergency kit for the boys to carry."

Marty waited until Malcolm had hurried out the barn door. "Look hard, fellas. I've got a feeling our four bad men have kidnapped the youngsters. If they have, they've signed their death warrants."

CHAPTER 22
KIDNAPPED

Marty and Malcolm were standing on the front stoop of the office the next morning, when a riderless horse trotted down the street and turned toward the barn.

"Oh, Lord," Malcolm whispered, "that's Colleen's hoss." He ran to the horse and grabbed its reins, calming the nervous animal. Running his hands over its flank, he made the observation "It's been sweating pretty hard. It's either come a long way or run some afore it got to town."

Marty was right behind the stage line owner. He grabbed a kerchief tied to the saddle horn. "Look, Malcolm. There's a note tied to the scarf."

Malcolm grabbed the scarf. "That's Colleen's. I saw her wearing it yesterday. What does the note say?"

"It's addressed to you."

"Read it, read it."

Marty squinted at the hurried handwriting. "Your gal's fine. So is her friend, a young fella named Carson. You jus' stay away from Reno and don't try to make no freight shipments to Virginia City till we tell you. If you do what we say, yur gal won't be harmed. Mess with us and she will pay the price. We ain't kidding."

Marty looked up at Malcolm. "That's all it says. I'm sorry, Malcolm. I never expected the skunks to do anything like this."

Malcolm's face flushed and his eyes darted wildly from Colleen's horse to Marty in panic and despair. "What are we gonna do, Marty? Them poor kids. They must be scared half outa their minds." He called for Squint. "Come take care of this hoss. He's been used hard."

Squint listened as Marty explained the arrival of the horse and the note. "I shore would like to git my hands on them varmints. I'd squeeze the life outa 'em on the spot."

"Squint, soon as you put her horse away, go find Ross and Ruud. They're in that cantina just down the block. The one with the rooster sign out front."

"El Gallo? Sure, I know it. I'll be right back with 'em."

It did not take long before the two scouts were seated at the rectangular table in the business office. Marty had a map of the local area laid out in front of the two men. "Show me where you last saw the outlaws, Ross."

Ross frowned at the map. "I ain't much fer reading a map, Marty, but I'd reckon it was right around here." He pointed at a spot near the Carson Creek Road. "Wouldn't you say so, Ruud?"

"I think so. To be real honest, I didn't see 'em go up in the trees, I jus' know they got off the road somewhere around there."

"Come first light, you two show me," Marty instructed.

"Sure will. Shall we bring any of the boys?"

"Not yet. Tell Johnny to have as many as he can get ready to be standing by, here at the barn. I don't want to stumble upon the outlaws with a full-blown search party just yet. I'll join you two and we'll make a quiet look-see first. If we find anything, we can send for the rest."

"Ya want I should come along, Marty? I know that part of the country pretty good. I prospected all over it a year ago, afore I went busted and started workin' fer Malcolm as a driver."

"Stick close to the barn, Squint. Maybe the other horse will show up. If so, try and follow its prints and bring the boys with you. I'll be back before dark and if nothing's come up by then, we'll make a new plan."

Marty and the two scouts rode out to where they had last seen the outlaws. The ground had been freshly disturbed, but as they followed the tracks of six horses away from the site, the trail disappeared.

"Somebody went to a lot of trouble to hide their tracks, it seems to me," Ross commented.

"If they did kidnap Colleen and Carson, they damned well better have," Marty commented. "Their goose is cooked if we can catch them holding the kids against their will. That's enough to warrant a rope dance in most folks' opinion."

"If they know it's likely to git them hung, they're liable to not wanna give in to us if we come upon 'em, wouldn't you say?"

"I have no doubt about that," Marty answered. "Well, the tracks are gone. Let's spread out and make a sweep. If you run across anything, come for me, but keep it quiet. I don't want to give anything away."

Colleen and Carson sullenly were led by their captor into the darkness of the tunnel. The mine looked as if it had been shut down for a good spell. Dust had settled on the support beams and spiderwebs were in abundance. But the most predominant presence was the blue, sticky clay that covered the floor and walls of the mine. The clay was everywhere.

"What on earth is this stuff?" Colleen asked as they reached the end of the drift and sat down on the sticky substance.

"Mr. Hearst said it's a kind of clay that comes up from the earth. All the mines in Virginia City are plagued with it. They have to continually keep mucking it out, or it will fill up a shaft." Carson glared at the masked man who had escorted them to their current location. "How long are you going to keep us in here?"

"You jus' keep yur mouth shut, sonny. You'll live longer that way. We'll let ya go when we decide, not a minute sooner."

"Well, can you take these ropes off? It's damned uncomfortable, trying to sit with my hands tied behind my back."

"I tell ya what, sonny. I'm gonna untie yur hands, but if you or the little lady show yur face at the front of this mine, I'm gonna fill yur gut with lead and fill the gal with somethin' else."

Carson jumped up, his face livid with rage. "You slimy bastard. You touch one hair on her head and I'll see you hang or kill you myself, I swear it."

The outlaw said nothing, just walked over and slapped Carson a vicious smack to his head, knocking him over a small box sitting on the floor, next to Colleen. He knelt beside the stunned man and deftly sliced the rawhide strip that bound Carson's hands, and then did the same for Colleen. As he stepped out of the yellow circle of light cast by a thick candle stuck on a large rock next to a wooden support beam, he snarled at the two prisoners, "Don't fergit. Don't show yourself to the mouth of this mine iffen ya know what's good fer ya."

Colleen knelt beside Carson, who was trying to get to his feet. "Oh, Carson, don't antagonize them over me. They'll just make it worse for us." She looked around. "How are we going to get out of here?"

"Look around, see if you can find anything I can use as a weapon." Both searched their small space and Carson found a worn, rusty shovel, while Colleen found a piece of drill steel, about three feet long. Either one would be a fearsome weapon in a close, hand-to-hand encounter. "For the moment, we'd better hide these. We don't want to make our move too soon. Let's see what happens for a while." This they did, hoping the outlaws would not find the crude weapons as the kidnappers came and went, checking on the two of them.

"What time do you think it is?" Colleen asked. "I'm pretty hungry, so I'd guess it's well past dinnertime. Papa must be awfully worried for us."

"One thing I do know, Colleen, is that Marty and the others are looking high and low for us. They'll find us, I'm certain of it. The men who captured us are the same ones Marty had men tailing already. He'll find us. We can count on it. We have to be ready to act, as soon as he does."

They continued to discuss ways of escaping or helping the hoped-for rescuers when one of the guards brought them some bread, ham slices, and water.

"What is the lady to do about using the convenience when it becomes necessary?" Carson demanded.

"Figger it out. She ain't comin' outa the mine, so you two'll jus' have to figger out somethin'."

"You swine," Carson murmured. Colleen put her hand on his forearm in warning. "All right. What about a blanket for the lady? We're going to have to sleep soon."

"See that box thar? It's got some stuff in it you can use. Make yurselves comfy, 'cause you're gonna be here fer a spell."

293

Carson mumbled all sorts of dire threats under his breath as the outlaw left. "We'll see about that." He spoke louder as the sound of the outlaw's footsteps faded in the darkness. He pried the top off the small wooden box and found two blankets, a jug of water, another candle, and several matches.

"Colleen, we'd better try and get some rest. You take the candle and go up the shaft a ways and relieve yourself. Then I will. After that, we'll try and get some sleep. Marty'll be coming tomorrow, I know it."

As soon as they were ready to settle down, Colleen whispered to Carson, "I'm so scared. I just don't want those vermin to know it."

"I swear to you, Colleen, I'll die trying to keep you safe. Don't you fret over this. It'll soon be over. Marty is gonna find us, I know it."

"Oh, Carson." Colleen kissed Carson, so hard and passionately that it took his breath away.

The young dude from Cincinnati vowed to sell himself dearly for the woman in his arms. "Good night, rest easy."

"Good night, Carson."

As Colleen settled down on her simple bedroll, Carson took up the shovel and started piling the thick, cloying clay in a pile just beyond the circle of light cast by the candle.

"What are you doing, Carson?" Colleen inquired. "Come on and get some rest."

"I'm making a little surprise for our captors. If one of 'em comes back here and hits this clay, he might fall or something. We might be able to use the opportunity to make our escape. I won't be long. Try and rest."

"Carson, I won't rest a second until you're right here beside me. What can I do to help?"

Marty and his scouts returned just after the sun set, tired and discouraged. "We couldn't pick up a trail, Malcolm. We rode up and down the Creek Road, to no avail. We'll get some rest and start out again tomorrow."

Squint and Johnny Harper walked into the office, just as Marty finished his statement. "Hi, Johnny. How many men have we got?"

"Every man, Marty. They're all outfitted for three days on the trail. Just say the word."

"I don't know where to go, Johnny. They could be anywhere."

"No, they ain't," Squint answered quickly.

"What?"

"I was cleanin' the missy's hoss jus' now. I shoulda done it last night, but I was too excited by all the happenin's. I'm sorry I didn't. I coulda saved us a lot of worry."

"What are you talking about, Squint?" Marty asked again, exasperation evident in his voice.

"I told ya I had a small minin' operation goin' back up in the hills east of here afore I started with Mr. O'Brian, didn't I?"

"Yes, you mentioned it."

"Well, I ran into a seam of blue clay, damnedest stuff you ever saw. Thick and gooey as glue and twice as hard to git rid of. I musta mucked five tons of the stuff outa my diggin's and still it came oozing back in as fast as I dug it out. I filled up a small hollow behind my shack with clay afore I give it up."

"And?"

"The damned stuff was so thick that rainwater wouldn't soak through it. Rain would pool up and stand thar for months at a time, as natural a water hole as a body could find. My ole hoss used go down and drink thar when the stream dried up, which was most of the time. He'd stand on the edge of the clay to drink and sink clear down to his fetlocks and deeper. I was always afeered he'd git stuck, but he never did. Anyways, when I was puttin' the missy's hoss away, I noticed that her forelegs was covered in that same kind of blue clay. I ain't never seen clay like that anywhere else but in my mine. I swear, Marty, I think them varmints may have the two kids in my mine."

"By God," Malcolm exclaimed, "maybe we've got the break we need."

Marty did not hesitate. "Johnny, have the men ready to ride as soon as the sun clears the horizon. Squint, you know how to get us to your claim without alerting anybody there that we're coming?"

"Sure do. Know more'n one. I could take us there in the dark if need be."

"Daylight's soon enough. I do want to move in real quiet on 'em. We're gonna save the kids, not give the skunks a chance to hurt them. If we move in quiet and unseen, perhaps we can catch them exposed and vulnerable."

"I'm riding with you," Malcolm proclaimed.

"Fair enough, Malcolm. You have the right. Just understand, I expect you to obey my commands just like Johnny and his boys do. You don't have any problem with that, do you?"

"Nope. I just want to git my little gal back,

safe and sound."

"That's the only thing on my mind. You can take that to the bank."

CHAPTER 23
RESCUED

Marty had his men slip out of town a few at a time the next morning, just in case anyone friendly to the outlaws happened to be watching. He, Squint, Malcolm, along with the two scouts, Ross and Ruud, left last, meeting at the designated rally point, where the men had trained the previous two weekends.

From there, Squint and the two scouts took the point and the rest followed as they climbed into the mountains east of Reno, mostly following a narrow game path or sometimes, no path at all. Finally, about midmorning, Squint came riding back to where Marty led the others in the column of fighting men.

"We're close, Marty. I stopped just over the hill from my mine. Ross and Ruud are sneakin' down the side of the mountain, to see if they can see anything."

"Can all of us move in close to your claim

without being seen?" Marty handed Squint a small stick and pointed at the dust at his feet. "Make me a sketch of your place."

Squint drew a crude outline of the mine, his cabin, and the stream. "I reckon that if we leave the horses back on this side of the hill, we can sneak down to within forty yards or so, maybe thirty. There's trees a-growin' across the creek on this side all the way up the hill." He marked the trees in the dirt sketch.

"Where's the clay pond?" Malcolm asked.

Squint made a mark with the point of his stick. "Right here."

Marty looked at the hastily drawn map. "Then, if we come straight at them, and they run, they'll have to either retreat into the mine or go north, into the trees across the creek."

Marty looked up at Johnny Harper, standing next to him, listening to the discussion. "Johnny, take four men and work your way around to a position where you can blast anyone who tries to escape your way. Squint, you lead him. Johnny, you have a watch?"

Harper pulled out a silver pocket watch. "Yep."

Marty looked at his watch. "It's ten thirty now. I'll give you until eleven to be in position before I start. You keep quiet until you hear my first shot. Then add on."

"Understand. Come on, Squint. Show me the way." Johnny, Squint, and two others moved off, leading their horses.

Marty turned to Pat Quinn. "Pat, who's the best rifle shot among the men?"

"Luther Hatfield. He can shoot the eye outa a squirrel at a hunnerd yards."

"Get him here."

Quinn softly called out, "Luther Hatfield, come up here."

A lanky, mop-haired man with a thin face that sported an impressive hooked nose protruding over a dark mustache moved up beside Marty and Quinn. "Yeah, Pat?"

"I told Marty here you was one of the best rifle shots I ever saw. Don't make me a liar."

"No, sir." The lanky man gave Marty a quick smile." I was a sniper fer Blake's first Tennessee Brigade durin' the war. I usually hit what I aim for."

Marty handed Luther his big Sharps with the brass scope mounted on it. "Ever use one of these?"

Luther grabbed the heavy rifle. "Nope, but it sure has a nice feel to it." He raised the rifle to his shoulder and looked through the scope. "My, oh my. What I coulda done with one of these during the siege of Vicksburg."

301

"I want to find a place where you and this rifle can cover the mine opening. I don't want anyone running into the mine, once the donnybrook starts. I'm hoping you can bring that person down before he can get to the girl. Understand?"

"Yep. You can count on me."

Marty turned back toward the top of the hill to watch as the two scouts scrambled over the top and ran toward him. "We seen the mine." Ross panted as they stopped beside Marty. "Three men was there and another just rode up, leading a pack mule. Probably bringin' supplies fer the bunch of 'em."

"Any sign of Carson or Colleen?"

"Nary a one. I think thar's someone in the mine, though, as one of the outlaws is sittin' in a chair right by the openin'."

Marty nodded. "All right. Can you lead us down until we're close without being seen by the skunks?"

"If we take it easy, sure."

"You find a place to leave the horses?"

"Just over the hill. There's a openin' that's plenty big fer all of them."

"That's it, then. Lead the way."

The men dismounted and followed Ross and Marty over the top of the hill and to a small clearing just on the eastern side of the crest. Marty tried, but could not see the mine because of the pine trees and undergrowth covering the hillside.

Marty instructed the men to tie off their horses and take their weapons. "We go the rest of the way on foot, and quietly. Keep your fingers off the triggers until we reach our objective." He looked at Luther Hatfield. "Keep your eyes peeled for a place where you have a clear view of the mine and cabin." Then he turned to Ross and Ruud. "You fellows have done your part. You stay here and watch the horses."

"Mr. Keller." Ross shook his head. "I think I oughta go on down with you and make sure you get to the spot where I was. I had a clear shot across the creek from there. Ruud here can handle the hosses."

"All right," Marty agreed. "If you want to, it's fine with me. Ruud, if any get away, I'll fire three shots, then three more. You bring down as many horses as you can handle, so we won't have to climb back to the top to chase after them. Make certain my gray is one of them."

"Yessir, Mr. Keller."

Marty waved his hand and arm in the universal "Follow me" sign and started on down the hill. Carefully, methodically, the armed men made their way down the hillside, weaving between trees and through the heavy brush. Finally, the far hillside was visible through the trees and the men knew they were getting close to the bottom. The creek, shack, and mine shaft opening should be coming into view any moment.

Someone touched Marty's arm. It was Luther. He pointed toward an outcropping of bare rock that stuck out over a sudden steep slope, off to Marty's right. "I think I can get a good spot up there, if you'll wait until I climb up."

"Go ahead. Just don't let anyone down below see you."

Luther hurried off, while Marty held up his hand, his fist closed, silently telling the men to stop in place. The men settled down, alert for the unexpected, and watched as Luther carefully climbed up the rock face of the outthrust. Finally, he reached the top of the exposed rock and slowly eased forward until he had a view of the ground below. He hoarsely whispered down to Marty, "It's about a hundred yards to the bottom. I can see the mine and the cabin. Go ahead, I'm ready."

Marty put his hand on Pat Quinn's beefy forearm. "Pat, it's time we spread the men out. You take the right side, I'll take the left. Wait for me to start things rollin' before you open up. I'm gonna give them a chance to surrender, if I can."

"I understand, Mr. Keller. Will we be charging the cabin?"

"I hope we don't have to. But if you see my men coming out, you charge as fast as you can."

"I'll do 'er."

The way the ground sloped toward a steep cut in the hillside, it forced the approaching men to slide to the right as they worked their way down the hill. Marty came to the edge of the tree line and wiggled the last few feet on his stomach. He was about twenty yards from the small creek, maybe fifty yards from the cabin, and twenty more from the mine opening. He had a clear view of the front of the cabin, but the back door was not visible. He hoped Johnny Harper and his men could cover it from their position. He checked his watch. It was five minutes until eleven.

Marty eased his rifle up to his shoulder, peering around the trunk of a tall pine tree. Suddenly, the door of the cabin opened and a man stuck his head out. "Sid, check on them kids. I don't want 'em gittin' into mischief."

Luther had his sights on the man by the mine opening, just as Marty instructed. He saw the man turn and step into the shaft. Luther's view was of the back of the unsuspecting outlaw's head. Remembering Marty's orders, the Tennessee mountain man quickly squeezed off a shot. Just as he fired, Sid slipped on a small rock and lurched to the side, reaching out to catch himself on the wooden support beam just inside the shaft entrance. The bullet meant for his brain clipped off his left earlobe, stunning the outlaw and hurting like the very blazes. He instinctively ducked inside the shaft, to the cover of a twelve-inch-thick post supporting the opening. Luther quickly reloaded and fired into the darkness of the mine, the bullet smashing into the support beam with a resounding *thunk!* but not hitting the outlaw.

The outlaw staggered, but Marty was not certain whether the man was down or not. From where he lay, he could not see any sign of the outlaw. The ball had started, whether he was ready or not.

"Hello, the cabin!" he shouted. "This is Deputy Sheriff Martin Keller. You are surrounded. Throw out your guns and come out with your hands up."

For a few agonizing seconds there was silence after the echos of the rifle shot faded away. Then ever so slowly, the door to

Squint's old cabin opened a crack and a rifle barrel reflected the bright sunlight of midmorning. Before Marty could make another appeal, the morning stillness was shattered by six shots sprayed around the trees where Marty and his men were concealed. The thunder of their return fire was awesomely resounding.

The chips flew around the door and windows at the front of the cabin as lead bullets pounded into the dried wood and river bottom rocks from which Squint had constructed the cabin. Unfortunately, old Squint had built the place soundly and the deadly bullets failed to impact any of the three outlaws hidden inside. Gunfire erupted from the windows and from a small notch cut into the heavy, wooden door.

After a few minutes of continuous but futile firing, Marty called out to his men, "Cease fire! Cease firing! You men in the house, give it up, you haven't got a chance. I promise that if you surrender, I'll take you into Carson City and see that you get a fair trial." Again his appeal was answered in hot lead.

Sighing in frustration, Marty sent half a dozen shots into the shattered windows of the cabin, as did his men from their various positions along the tree line. A single figure burst out the back of the cabin and ran toward the woods to the rear, awkwardly firing over his shoulder as he ran. He had not taken a dozen steps before he fell to the bullets fired by the men positioned at the rear with Johnny Harper.

Sid, his bleeding ear cupped in his left hand, stayed in the cover of the mine and recovered his shaken senses. He surmised that if he had the girl in front of him as a shield, he might make it to his horse and effect his getaway. Tentatively backing deeper into the shaft, he turned and ran toward the back of the shaft, panic and fear clouding any rational thinking.

Carson and Colleen listened in eager anticipation as the gunfire outside echoed around the dark mine shaft. "Didn't I tell you, Colleen? Marty's found us. He's come."

"What should we do?" she asked. "One of the outlaws might come back here to kill us before they give up."

"Roll up my blanket and put it under yours, like I'm inside. Then sit next to it. I'll hide here and if someone rushes in, maybe I can bust him with this drill rod." Carson wedged himself into a shallow depression in the rock wall until he was almost invisible. He hefted the heavy drill rod in his right hand. All they could do now was to wait and be prepared for whatever happened.

Sid hurried back toward the spot where they had put the two youngsters the day before. He was in such a hurry that he did not see the pile of gooey clay on the floor or realize that the girl was sitting beside a dummy. As his foot sank in the clay, he slipped and stumbled forward, falling to one knee, nearly losing his pistol in the process.

He barely glimpsed sudden movement out of the corner of his eye and did not realize what was happening until Carson's swing, intensified by his excitement and anxiety, slammed the heavy bar into the back of the unfortunate outlaw's head, killing him instantly.

The dead outlaw fell silently, sprawling facedown in the dirt, never to move again. Colleen sat with her knuckles crammed into her mouth, trying hard not to scream as the dead man's fixed stare looked into her eyes.

"Come, on, Colleen," Carson ordered as he grabbed the outlaw's pistol and belt with extra cartridges. "Let's give Marty a hand." He led the shaken girl toward the front entrance of the shaft. He carefully put Colleen behind a wooden support beam and then took a position where he could see the cabin. The two outlaws left inside were not expecting a threat from the shaft opening, so they were careless to their vulnerability from that side.

Carson waited, marveling that anybody could survive the fusillade of gunfire poured out by Marty and his men. The two outlaws inside had talked it over. They knew they would hang for kidnapping the girl, so they determined to fight on, hoping that some miracle might befall them and allow them to escape.

One of the outlaws edged close to the side of the window to take aim at someone up on the hillside. It was the target Carson was waiting for. He shot, his bullet hitting the outlaw in the arm. The wounded man spun around, crying out in pain. This made him an easy target to one of the men farther down the firing line from Marty. His bullet drilled the outlaw square in the back and the doomed outlaw lurched over, dying faster than the blood could spill from his wounds.

That was enough for the third outlaw. He slung his pistol into a corner and stepped to the door, starting to open it and shout out his surrender. A heavy buffalo slug from Luther's Sharps ripped through the wood and buried itself in his chest, knocking him back against the far wall of the cabin, to fall against the stone fireplace. Slowly, ever so slowly, he slid down the smooth rocks, leaving a crimson smear of red the entire length of his body until he sat on the floor, his chin resting on his chest. For a few seconds his head rose and fell with his labored breathing; then suddenly it was still.

Marty held up his hand and shouted over the dim of the gunfire, "Cease fire! Cease fire!" The firing gradually ceased, followed by an eerie silence. Marty squinted toward the gun smoke floating in the still air, then shouted toward Pat Quinn, "Pat, you see any movement in there?"

"Nope. Ain't seen nothin' fer several minutes."

"Hello, the cabin. You boys ready to give it up?"

Silence was the only answer. Marty rose to one knee, keeping the thick trunk of the tree between himself and the cabin. "In the cabin, give yourselves up. Your last chance.

"Luther," he shouted. "Can you hear me?"

"I hear ya."

"Keep a sharp eye. We're gonna charge the cabin. You see any movement, blast 'em."

"I gotcha."

Marty gave the command. "On your feet everyone. Ready, let's go."

He led the charge as the ten men in his party splashed across the creek and toward the still, silent cabin. Pat Quinn slammed his heavy body against the door and it flew in as easily as a feather blown by a gale. Marty was right behind him, his pistol at the ready.

It was unnecessary. The occupants of the cabin were too busy answering to the Almighty for their transgressions to pay Marty and his men any mind.

CHAPTER 24
THE PUMPS ARRIVE

Right after breakfast the next morning Marty assembled Malcolm, Carson, Squint, Johnny, Pat, and Luther to meet with him at the O'Brian office. The men made it very clear they were all grateful to see Carson and to know that Colleen was recovering nicely from the ordeal. Marty waited until the general hubbub died down and then stood up from his position at the head of the long conference table.

"I thought we ought to sit down together and talk over yesterday's operation, the rights and wrongs. What we need to do to make it better the next time, because believe me, it's coming and soon."

A discussion had ensued for over an hour as they tossed ideas back and forth when a young man walked in. "A telegram for you, Mr. O'Brian." He placed a brown envelope in Malcolm's hand. Giving the men gathered around the table an inquisitive look, the messenger walked out while Malcolm tore open the envelope and read the contents. As he finished, he passed the message to Marty, who quickly scanned it.

"The pumps will arrive on Friday, gentlemen. Phase two of our plan is now ready to commence." Marty turned to Malcolm. "Malcolm, would you get the map I drew, please?"

"Right away, Marty."

The men waited silently while Malcolm went to retrieve the map. Each man considered the deadly possibilities in the coming confrontation. During the gunfight at Squint's cabin, none of them had even been scratched. Now fifteen men were going up against two dozen or more. Their chances of everyone in their party escaping serious injury again were pretty slim.

Malcolm returned with the map and he and Carson laid it flat on the table for everyone to see. Marty began to brief his men just as if it were the precursor to a military operation, which in effect it really was. He pointed out where he thought the outlaws would wait for the freight wagons, their route in and out of the killing zone, where he wanted Johnny to position his men, and on and on, with precision and detail.

"You can't let any of your men get behind and above the outlaws, Johnny. When the Gatling gun starts, it'll spray bullets to hell and gone, all over. You'll have to come in on their flanks, and even then you'll have to watch them carefully to make sure they don't wander into the impact area of those bullets. Once that gun shoots those bullets, they'll destroy whatever they hit, friend or foe."

"I understand, Marty." Johnny and Pat exchanged quick glances. They were going to have their work cut out for themselves.

Pat spoke up. "What if they don't come to this exact spot, Marty? The ground is pretty rough on that mountain. There're a lot of places they could choose."

"I worry about it a lot, Pat. I'm hoping they'll be lazy and choose an old familiar place, but that's where you and the scouts come in, Carson. You'll have to find a location where you can watch the road from the Peavine line shack, and then trail the outlaws into the hills until they take up an ambush site, then hustle back to the rest and move our men into their firing position."

"We can do that, don't worry." Carson's voice was full of youthful confidence.

"They mustn't see you, Carson. There will

only be the three of you. If they turn on you, you'll not stand a chance."

Carson nodded, his face somber. Marty resolved to talk to Ross and Ruud separately, away from Carson, before he left for Reno. He turned back to Johnny. "You'll have to leave your horses well back, so they don't give you away. Make a slow careful approach on foot to your final positions."

Johnny nodded, studying the map, fixing the position in his mind. "We might be able to open up on them before you even get there with the wagons, if you want."

"I don't want. There will be too many of them. That's what the Gatling gun is for, to whittle down their numerical superiority."

Squint spoke up. "What about the drivers, Marty? We gonna expect 'em to jine the fightin'?"

"I don't think we can count on them for very much. I plan to build them boilerplate protection shields like I did for your stage, but if they'll simply fire their weapons in the general direction of the enemy I'll be satisfied."

Malcolm asked his question, "How many guards do you want on the wagons?"

"I'd like two per wagon, but I wonder if we can find that many in Reno. Once they see the pumps arrive, everyone in town will know that the showdown is coming, and may not care to be involved."

"I'm pretty sure I can get eight men who are trustworthy and willing to join us."

"If you can get eight, I'll be satisfied. Squint and I will be driving the gun wagon, and, Malcolm, I think you ought to drive the last wagon, to make certain none of the drivers get cold feet and turns back. That suit you?"

"Whatever you say, Marty."

"Any more questions?"

None of the men answered. Marty nodded, satisfied he had made a good start to the completion of his plan. "Carson, I'll send you a telegram from Reno telling you what time we're leaving town. You must leave the day before and take up a position in the mountains. From the time we leave until we get to the suspected ambush site is five hours. You have to be there plenty early so you are ahead of the outlaws. Be certain you respond so I know you got the message. And" — Marty held up his hand for emphasis — "slip the men out a few at a time. I don't want anyone noticing that fifteen heavily armed men are headed for the mountains."

"I understand, Marty."

"Malcolm, you, Squint, and I will leave

tomorrow for Reno, to get things set up at that end. Johnny, have the men all ready, plenty of ammo, food, and water. We may be out for several days."

"I will, don't worry."

"All right, then, that's that. You may as well get on with your personal affairs. I'll see you men on the hill. Godspeed to you all."

The men left and Marty turned to speak to Malcolm. He glimpsed Colleen standing just inside the doorway to Malcolm's office. He smiled gently. "Anything you want to add, Colleen?"

She shook her head, her eyes shiny with moisture. "Just try and keep Carson alive. Please, Mr. Keller."

"I'll do my damnedest, I promise." She turned away and was lost to his sight. Marty looked at Malcolm. "Mr. O'Brian, you're about to become a father-in-law. You know that?"

Malcolm gave him a mischievous grin. "I've knowed it since the boy arrived. I'd guess you approve of him, don't ya?"

"I absolutely do. He'll be a fine addition to your family."

Malcolm nodded his head. "We ridin' horses tomorrow, or do ya want to take a stage to Reno?"

"Let's take the stage and make a mail run out of it."

"Good enough. I'll have Squint ready to go at eight tomorrow mornin'."

"That'll be fine. Now I'm ready for a cool beer. Interest you in one?"

"Why not? In fact, I'll buy."

"Well, lead on, then."

Vern sat behind his massive desk he had recently installed in the office of his ranch house. It was even bigger than Stoddard's. He looked tired, anxious, out of sorts. Charlie girded himself for a reaming. However, Vern's voice was calm and collected. "Charlie, call in the boys from Virginia City. I want a maximum effort when we go up against the freight wagons. O'Brian is bound to get all the armed men he can find to act as shotgun guards."

"I'll git right on it, boss. You want any of the men guardin' the O'Brian gal?"

"Nope, let her be. When Slim picked up the supplies, he said everything was good, so we'll let them stay there."

"Maybe O'Brian won't even ship the pumps, he's so scared of losing his gal?"

"I don't know. Maybe. I told Cotton that he's to put one of his men in town to keep an eye on O'Brian. He'll report if O'Brian acts like he's gonna go ahead with the shipment. If he don't go, Hearst will have to put them pumps on anything with wheels, so Clem Atkinson should get the contract. I made certain Clem knows to agree to ship the pumps, if Hearst asks him."

"If Hearst does that, it'll shore make our jobs easier."

"That's why I took the gal. Either way, I want everyone here and ready to ride at a moment's notice. And send word to the lookouts in Reno. I wanna know the minute anything happens."

"I'll do that too, boss. I reckon I'd best git started, I got a lot to git done."

The stage ride to Reno was as uneventful as a Sunday morning surry ride to church. The stage rolled in exactly on time and Malcolm quickly delivered the mail to the Reno postmaster, whose office shared space with a saddle shop just off Main Street.

Marty checked on Sergeant LeCroix and Corporal Blue. Both of the soldiers were in the stage barn, putting the finishing touches on their gun box, for want of a better word. They had taken a heavy freight wagon and built a wooden box of four-by-eight-inch mine support lumber. The box had a twelve-by-thirty-six-inch opening to accommodate the Gatling gun's six rotary barrels, and a slot just above that for the gunner to see his target. It had overhead cover and a small opening opposite the gun port, allowing the two soldiers to enter and exit the enclosure.

The two soldiers proudly showed their creation to Marty and demonstrated how they could aim the gun and sweep a wide area with its deadly fire. "It looks mighty good, fellows. Don't forget you'll be shooting uphill. Make certain you can elevate the barrels enough." He climbed down from the wagon and walked all around the makeshift mobile fort. "Mighty good job, men. Mighty good." He looked hard at Sergeant LeCroix. "Has anyone made inquiries as to what you and Blue are doing here?"

"No, sir. We stuck pretty close to the barn and ain't had much contact with any civilian folks."

"Very good. Well, I've got another project for us. I'll tell you about it when I get back."

Marty headed for the freight office. He needed to find some boilerplate for the wagon driver's shields. The office manage, Clyde, acted as though he was pleased to see Marty. "I just spoke with Mr. O'Brian. He says you're gonna take the pumps up to Virginia City shortly."

"That we are, Clyde. Keep it under your

hat for the time being, however. I don't want the word to get out just yet."

The office manager nodded. "I understand."

"I need to find some boilerplate. Any ideas?"

"Like for the stage?"

"Very similar. For the wagon drivers."

Following Clyde's directions, Marty walked over to a warehouse where metal was stored prior to being shipped to the mines in Virginia City. He contracted for delivery of ten pieces of four-by-four-feet, three-eighths-inch-thick plate to be delivered to the stage barn.

Satisfied that he had what he needed, he returned to the barn and showed the two soldiers the shield he had put up for Squint on the stage. LeCroix nodded his head, his eyes gauging the improvised bullet barrier. "I reckon we can put somethin' similar on them wagons. We'll need some good rope or thick rawhide." He appraised the heavy Springfield-style freight wagon and how the driver's seat was fastened to it by way of twin leaf springs. "Maybe some lumber, to make a mount."

"I'll get it for you right away. The iron will be delivered this afternoon. If I'm not around, get started without me. We have to put it on all the wagons, including this one."

Marty was attaching the last shield with LeCroix and Blue when Malcolm walked into the barn. He allowed Marty to show him the way the boilerplate shields were fastened to the uphill side of the driver's box so that they provided protection against any bullets fired at the driver.

"Bad news, Marty. I just went over to Clem Atkinson's place and tried to rent five freight wagons. He said he was sorry, but it was no deal. He had strict orders from Ransom Stoddard not to rent me anything, no matter what I offered. To make matters even worse, all his wagons are on the road except two, so there's not enough anyway."

"How many do you need, Malcolm? I mean to get the minimum number of pumps to Virginia City?"

"I suppose four wagons. That would be enough wagons to haul two pumps. It would mean we'd have to make two trips. Even then, I'm still short a wagon."

"Why don't you and I take a little walk over to this Atkinson fellow's place? I want to talk with him. Sergeant, you two can finish up here without me?"

"Yes, sir, Mr. Keller. That we can."

Marty walked quickly the six blocks to the Atkinson Freight Office with Malcolm. He shook the freighter's hand when Malcolm introduced him. The man was square and sturdy, with strong arms and hands, a typical freighter. Marty gave up on the handshake first. "Quite a handshake there, Mr. Atkinson. You've done some heavy lifting in your day, I suppose."

"I did me share. What can I do fer ya, Mr. Keller? I done told Malcolm my hands was tied about renting my wagons out to him. I'd like to help, but I jus' can't."

"I can appreciate that Mr. Atkinson. You and Malcolm are caught in the bigger struggle between two hardheaded mining men, and I can see your problem. Malcolm, would you excuse us for a minute? I want to talk to Mr. Atkinson alone."

As Malcolm walked out the door, Marty put on his game face, the look he gave to wanted men when he ordered them to surrender or die. "I think I'd like to rent a wagon from you, Mr. Atkinson. I think if you were to say no, I might have to resort to harsher measures. Malcolm has had his wagons shot up and pushed over cliffs until he's on the verge of bankruptcy. I'm not gonna allow that to happen on this next load. We're gonna deliver George Hearst's pumps to Virginia City, and I'm gonna kill anybody who tries to stop me."

Atkinson squared his broad shoulders and glared right back at Marty. "Young man, I may be a little bit scared of your threats, but I'm still man enough to kick your butt into next week iffen I have a mind to. You try anything with me and I'll stuff that gun up yur nose and give you change. However, I like Malcolm too. He's always been a fair and honest competitor. I can't rent to him, but nobody said anything about you. I'm gonna rent you that wagon and mules, fer a dollar a day. The next time, you might ask politely first, before you git yur nose out of joint."

"Thank you, Mr. Atkinson. And excuse me for trying to put the bluff on you."

"Hell, I knowed it all along. And call me Clem. I think we're gonna be friends afore this is all over."

"I agree." Marty grinned and held out his hand. "We'll take that wagon now, if you don't mind. I'm making a little modification to the driver's box. Come on by the barn sometime in the next couple of days and I'll show you."

"I just might do that, thanks."

"And, Clem, keep our little deal under your hat. I don't want it getting out that we're about to make our move."

Marty and Clem walked out of the office

and found Malcolm hovering close, afraid of what might be happening inside. "Come on, Malcolm. Marty here has rented one of my wagons. Why don't you pick it out and select the mules you want for him? I doubt if he's quite the freighter you are."

Malcolm's jaw dropped. "Well, I'll be. I figgered you two was gonna come bustin' through that door and fightin' and squallin' like a pair of alley cats after the same mouse."

"Me and my friend Marty, fightin'? Come on, Malcolm, you hurt my feelin's."

"You and your friend Marty? Now you two really do have me a-dancin' to strange music."

Malcolm drove the Atkinson wagon back to the barn and turned it over to LeCroix and Blue to modify like the others.

"Get your drivers and guards, Malcolm. If the pumps arrive tomorrow, we'll make the shipment to Virginia City on Monday. Get the best eight men you can find."

Marty walked to the train station with Malcolm the next morning to watch the westbound pull in. The pumps were there, encased in heavy wooden crates measuring five by five by five feet, chained to two flat-bed railroad cars. The two men watched as the chains securing the boxes were released and, grunting with effort, eight men slowly maneuvered the crates to the siding of the depot.

Malcolm went to get the wagons to transport up the pumps from the depot while Marty walked to the telegraph office and wired Carson that the wagons would leave on Monday morning for Virginia City. He played a hunch and told Carson to send Luther Hatfield to Reno and to bring Marty's big rifle.

He explained his reasoning to Squint. "I got to thinking that we may want to put some carefully aimed fire on a target, even though the Gatling gun is spraying bullets everywhere."

"Ya don't have to convince me," Squint answered. "The more guns I got around me, the better I like it."

As they talked, a lone rider was hotfooting it straight to Vern Barton with the news that the pumps were already being loaded on the wagons for delivery to Virginia City. Marty did not know it, nor did he care. The plan was in motion and it was time to stir the kettle. Stuff was about to hit the fan. He rubbed the palm of his hand on his mustache in satisfaction. He was ready. He almost felt sorry for the outlaws. What a surprise they had in store. For many, the last surprise of their rotten life, if he had anything to say about it.

CHAPTER 25
RIDING INTO DANGER

"Well, there they are, all loaded, all armor protected, all ready to go." Malcolm crossed himself and stuck out his hand. "Here's wishin' ourselves good luck, Marty. And may the devil himself strike down our enemies." He climbed onto the driver's seat of the last wagon in line, as Marty had instructed. Behind the wagon, six extra mules were securely tied, in case any of the wagon mules were killed by the outlaw's fire.

Marty slowly walked the line of heavy, freight wagons. Each driver sat next to a shallow V-shaped protection of hardened boilerplate. The drivers were protected from any bullets fired at them not only from the side, but also from the left and right fronts. Even after showing the drivers their shield, Marty had no confidence the drivers would stand and fight any attack. The shotgun guards were four brothers, out of work and desperate for some quick cash to tide them over until they could get a job in the mines.

Marty was quick to hire them because he felt one would not run off and leave the others to the mercy of the outlaws. "Remember what I said," he told them for the last time. "If shooting starts, get behind the pump boxes. They'll protect you from any bullets fired your way. You've got plenty of shells. Keep those 'greeners' smoking." The deadly fire from the sawed off ten-gauge shotguns would deter any outlaw assault on the wagons.

Marty wanted the outlaws to stay above them, in the trees where the fearsome Gatling gun and the fire from his reaction force, under Johnny Harper, could do the most damage. He stopped at the wagon carrying the soldiers, LeCroix and Blue. "You men ready for what's coming?"

"Yessir, Mr. Keller," LeCroix answered. "Wait until you see what ole Betsy here can do." He patted the bronze receiver group of the Gatling gun with proud affection, as if it were a pet.

"I'm counting on it, Sergeant. Once you open up, just keep sweeping the area where the outlaws are hiding until I tell you to quit."

Marty reached up and patted Luther on

his skinny knee, the only part of the man he could reach from the ground with Luther sitting in the driver's seat, carefully cradling the heavy Sharps rifle and its long sniper scope in his arms. "You'll have to get on the ground once the wagon stops, Luther. I want you to take on targets of opportunity as they appear. You'll have a lot of gun smoke to look through to see what you're shooting at."

"I understand, Marty. I'll stick close to you, jus' like we talked."

A crowd of people standing along the streets of Reno watched the little procession as the men prepared to pull out. Marty wondered if the outlaw spy was among them or if he had already galloped off to report their departure to the outlaws.

He climbed onto the wagon, settling himself between Luther and Squint. "Well, my friend, let's get the party started, shall we?" At Squint's tight-faced nod, Marty stood and shouted, "Roll 'em. Let's go."

The first driver, Malcolm's most reliable of the four he had hired, snapped his whip and shouted a command to his mules. The sturdy animals put a strain into the harness and off the wagon went, quickly followed by the others, the gun wagon in the middle of the column, just as Marty wanted it. The five wagons rolled out of Reno and turned south on the Virginia City Road, headed for a bloody showdown. The die was cast, for better or for worse.

Vern and Charlie were standing by the door of the cabin when the two men acting as lookouts in Reno galloped across the rolling grassland to the Peavine line shack as if the devil were on their tails.

"They're coming, Mr. Barton. They had the wagons rolled out and all loaded. They was movin' through the town when we reached the tree line and I took a quick look back."

"How many, Waco?" Call asked.

"Five wagons. Each with a big box lashed on it. And only a driver and a guard fer each wagon," he finished, anticipating Call's next question.

"Only two men per wagon?" Vern questioned. "Either they're havin' trouble gittin' drivers and guards, or O'Brian is up to somethin'. And only five wagons. That means he's only got two of the pumps. We'll be able to git the others in Reno or from Atkinson once we wipe out O'Brian."

"Most likely they can't git anyone to risk his life fer a water pump," Charlie answered.

Barton took out his pocket watch. "What's

our time?"

Call patiently answered the question. He was used to being in complete charge of these things, but this time Barton had insisted on coming along. "They'll reach the ambush site in about four hours. Waco and Sam took an hour and a half to git here. We'll take almost an hour to reach the site, so we'll be there an hour or better afore the freight wagons arrive."

"Very well. Assemble the men. Let's git on the trail. Tell the men to leave their bedrolls and stuff here. We'll come back here after the job's finished before returnin' home."

Call hurriedly assembled his twenty-five outlaws. The only one left at the V bar B was Cookie. Even the big boss rode along to add his gun to the tally. Barton was determined the pumps would not get through.

Charlie and Barton led the way, riding in front of twenty-five cold-blooded, calloused outlaws toward the mountains to the west, where the road to Virginia City wound its way up the slopes to the mining boomtown.

Carson shifted in his saddle. He was perfectly situated to watch over the trail leading out of the ranch's line shack. Ross had found the high ground with a perfect view earlier that morning and they had arrived just after sunrise. Only twenty minutes earlier, two men had galloped down the road from the direction of Reno and cut off the trail. Since then, nothing had happened.

Carson and Ross waited patiently, just like the other men who gathered in a clearing about a quarter mile from where Marty anticipated the outlaws would make their attack on the freight wagons. Carson passed the time worrying about what he would do if the outlaws went some other direction. He had talked about that very real possibility with Johnny and the scouts while they rode away from Carson City the prior day. They finally decided to stay in one bunch, near their horses until the outlaws settled into their ambush location, then sneak up on them on foot.

Just before dark the previous day, Carson, Johnny, and Pat Quinn had walked to the suspected ambush site and looked things over. They found a location above and to the south of the outlaws' probable location, where they could cover most of the terrain the outlaws would use to hide in and still be outside the firing area of the Gatling gun. Carson silently prayed that the outlaws were as overconfident and lazy as Marty had said they were likely to be.

Ross elbowed Carson and pointed toward the road below them. "Lookie thar. A bunch of riders headed our way."

The two counted as the riders came closer. "Damn, there's twenty-five of 'em, at least," Carson said.

Ross said nothing, simply nodded his head and continued to watch, his face impassive. The snaking column of men rode on the Ranch Road for a couple of hundred feet, then turned off into the wooded slopes of the hill where Carson and Ross hid. The men were visible now and then as they worked their way upward, following the game trail that Marty and Carson had followed down from the top of the mountain only a couple of weeks earlier.

"By gum," Ross whispered softly, "it shore looks like they're a-headed right fer the very site Marty said they'd use." Ross chuckled. "That fella is somethin' special, let me tell you."

"No need to convince me," Carson answered. "Come on, let's follow 'em a little ways just to make sure."

Carson and Ross slowly trailed after the outlaws, content to just catch a fleeting glimpse of a rider every few minutes. They did not need to stay close, just maintain enough contact to ensure that they knew exactly where the outlaws stopped to set up their position for the coming ambush.

Shortly after Ross and Carson crossed the summit of the mountain, a long ridge with a tabletop flatness, Ross held up his hand in warning. "Carson," he whispered again, "they've gotta be there by now. Be careful — we don't want to stumble right into 'em."

They swung off their horses and tied them to the branch of a small cedar, then eased their way on foot toward the outlaws. They heard them before they saw them. The outlaws were talking and laughing as if they were out on a social gathering rather than a killing mission. As Carson and Ross peered from behind the trunk of a towering pine, they heard a harsh voice. "You gals shut up yur cacklin' and get ready. Them wagons'll be along in an hour or less. If I was you, I'd make myself a little cover to fight behind. Them guards is liable to be firing double-ought buckshot yur way afore this is over."

"They'd have to shoot it outa a cannon to get through this here tree I'm hidin' behind," some wit called back, and a nervous twitter rippled through the trees back to Carson and Ross.

The two men slowly retreated toward their horses and, leading them, walked the quarter mile to where the men of Marty's re-action force awaited. Johnny and Quinn were the first to greet them. "You see 'em?"

"Yes," Carson answered. "They're exactly where Marty said they would be. Ruud, light out now and reach Marty before he gets to the ambush site. Tell him we're ready, above and to the south of the outlaws. Tell him there are about twenty-five of them. Get going now."

Ruud rode over the hill. He had to work his way down to the Ranch Road, ride like the blazes around the mountain where the fighting would occur, and then find Marty and the wagon train. Carson watched him disappear in the woods, and then pulled out his pocket watch. "Marty wants us in our position thirty minutes after the outlaws take up theirs. It took me and Ross about ten minutes to get from there to here, so we need to go in about fifteen minutes."

One of the men spoke up loud enough for Carson to overhear him. "Twenty-five of 'em, huh? That's sort of long odds fer us, ain't it?"

"Not after that Gatling gun does its work," Carson quickly pointed out. "By the time it gets done, we'll have the advantage, believe me. If each of you finds just one man and puts a well-aimed shot into him, we'll not have any left to chase off this mountain. Take your time, get some good cover, and wait for Johnny's command, then pour it on 'em. We'll be just fine."

It was not a particularly hot day, but Marty Keller was sweating like a hog wrestler in August. In his mind he could name a hundred reasons why his plan would fail like a rusted-out water bucket and not many reasons it would succeed. He went over and over in his mind what he would do if the outlaws did this or that, until his head was aching like a Sunday morning hangover.

He was so absorbed in his mental gymnastics, he did not see Ruud galloping up the road from the rear toward him, flailing his horse with his sombrero. Luther had to call the approaching rider to his attention. Marty signaled for the wagons to stop.

"Hello, Ruud. You got news?"

"Yessir, Mr. Keller. Young Block sent me. We saw the outlaws. They're right where you said they'd be. Carson says there's about twenty-five of them. He said to tell you that he's got the men above and to the south of the outlaws and he'll be ready."

Marty signaled for the guards and Malcolm to come to him. As soon as they arrived, he repeated what Ruud had told him.

338

Marty looked at the faces of the men, his headache forgotten. "You Sorensen brothers, you need to put the pump box between you and the hill there." Marty pointed with his forefinger up the hill to his front. "The outlaws will fire at the drivers first, but they'll have the protection of the boilerplate. You won't, so stay behind the boxes. I've told you about the Gatling Gun. It will sweep the area where the outlaws are, without letup. But if you see a good target, cut him down. Do not let the outlaws get to your wagon. You understand?"

The four sandy-haired brothers all nodded in unison, as if tied to the same string. Marty smiled encouragingly at the brothers. "I'm counting on you to stop any rush toward the wagons. We cannot lose the Gatling gun or any of the pumps to the outlaws."

"Ve unnerstand," the oldest brother replied. "You can count on us, by gum."

"All right, I will," Marty answered, and stuck out his hand. The big Dane nearly crushed it with his handshake.

Marty turned to Ruud. "You want to take off now, Ruud. You've done your job, and mighty well too."

Ruud shook his head. "Nope, I don't think I will. I'd sort of like to see this thing through with the rest of you."

"You certain?"

"Damn straight, I am."

"Very well. Ride at the last wagon. Do all you can to protect the extra mules. We may need them once this thing is over."

Ruud and Malcolm headed back to the rear wagon. Marty watched, a faint smile on his lips. He admired courage, whenever he found it. He looked at the lanky sharpshooter. "Well, Luther, shall we get this little shindig started?"

Luther shifted the Sharps rifle in his arms, his face deadly serious. "Once, long ago, I kilt a bunch of good men fer a bad reason. I reckon it's time to kill some bad un's fer a good one. Let's get her on."

CHAPTER 26
WHO'S AMBUSHING WHO?

"Luther, it's time we got some cover ourselves. The ambush site is just at the top of this slope." Marty checked up and down the column of freight wagons. He could see the four Danes crouched behind the huge box of pump parts in their individual wagons, their shotguns at the ready. He glanced inside the portable fort the two soldiers had made for their Gatling gun on his wagon. They were looking out the viewing slot, intently scanning the ground above the road, trying to visually pierce through the dense screen of trees and undergrowth.

"You two ready?" Marty asked. "It should be any minute now."

"Yessir, Mr. Keller. Ole Bess here is cocked and loaded." Sergeant LeCroix fondly patted the bronze butt of the heavy machine gun, a wide grin on his coal-black face.

"Good. Remember, don't wait for my

command. Once you hear the first shot, open up, sweep the area from side to side, and pour it on until I tell you to quit. If one of you is hit, call for me, and I'll get in there to replace you."

"We'll be jus' fine, Mr. Keller. You needs to worry 'bout them outlaws, if you wants to worry a'tall."

Marty looked at Luther. "You choose any target you can find, Luther. Keep an ear cocked for my command to fire at a specific target."

"I'll be listenin', Marty. Good luck to ya."

"Same to you, Luther."

Neither said another word as the mule teams struggled to pull the heavy wagons up the final yards of the steep slope to the level ground near the summit of the mountain.

The wagons proceeded up the steep slope, each driver trying to stay close to the wagon ahead. Marty could almost reach out and pat the noses of the lead pair of mules on the wagon following his, they were so tightly bunched up. Malcolm, in the last wagon, was almost as close to the wagon ahead of him. The two lead wagons slowed down after they crested the steep slope so the other wagons could catch up. He nodded in satisfaction. If this indeed was where the ambush would occur, his drivers had done all they could to put themselves in the best defensive position possible.

As the last wagon crested the hill, a single shot rang out. The lead driver ducked behind his boilerplate shield. The shot signaled for the entire line of outlaws to open up. Gray-white, greasy gun smoke boiled from the woods and bullets clanged off the curved iron of the shields, slammed into the boxes containing the precious pumps, or zipped past the heads of the crouching guards.

Marty was gratified to hear shotguns firing back at the assailants from the wagons. The four Sorensen brothers were answering the gunfire with fire of their own. Marty ducked his head and shouted at LeCroix, "Any time, Sergeant."

"Yessir," the veteran soldier replied, flashing Marty a quick smile of white teeth against ebony skin. "We're determinin' the extent of the firing line up thar. As soon as we gets the target identified, we'll let 'er rip."

"Make it count." He flinched as a bullet ricocheted off the top of the box just above his head. He looked over at Luther, who was peering around the pump box, searching for a good target. "See anything?"

"Yep. I got one spotted. Here goes." He quickly aimed and fired, the heavy *Boom!* of the Sharps buffalo gun overwhelming the fire of the guards' shotguns. Luther flashed a quick grimace at Marty. "Got him!"

As if to punctuate the remark, the Gatling gun open up in all its fury. Sounding like hail hitting a tin roof, the gun belched fiery death up the slope toward the shocked outlaws. Chewing up dirt, scattering leaves and wooden slivers from tree trunks like a deadly tornado, LeCroix swept the gun from right to left and back again, showering the outlaws' position with a rainstorm of death-dealing lead.

Both sides momentarily stopped their firing to gape in awe at the destruction wrought from the gun. Realizing they were in desperate peril, the outlaws directed their fire toward the little mobile fort housing the gun. Bullets from twenty rifles slammed into the green lumber fort, to no avail. The two soldiers had built their fortress too well. The bullets flew so fast and furious, the gun smoke was so thick that Marty and Luther leaped down and crouched at the front of the wagon, hoping to get a shot at an exposed outlaw. Squint rose just long enough to fire both barrels of his shotgun, then dropped back behind the safe cover of his iron shield while he reloaded.

"Damn, but that device do make a racket," he shouted at Marty, a grin splitting his gun-smoke-darkened face.

Luther fired Marty's big rifle again, another quick nod of satisfaction, another outlaw down. The Tennessee mountain man's eyes never blinked; he was too busy killing to take the time.

Scanning the hill, Marty saw one of the outlaws lose his nerve and start to run toward his horse. Marty dropped the man before he had taken three steps. "Sorry, fella. You ain't been excused yet. You started this little dance and you're going to have to stay put until the music quits playing."

"What's that ya say, Marty?"

"Nothing, Luther. Just keep shooting." Marty squinted to see through the cloud of gun smoke created by the Gatling gun's firing over three hundred rounds of black-powder cartridges a minute. "I wonder where Carson and Johnny are," Marty shouted up to Squint. "Do you see any sign of 'em?"

Marty glanced to the right and left. All his men at the wagons were steadily banging away at the outlaw positions. Already, Marty could tell there was a dramatic drop in the volume of fire from the hidden killers above him. He heard Luther fire again, but did not see the result. He aimed and fired at a bush where an orange-red twinkle of flame indicated someone was firing down at the wagon train. A bullet skipped off the wood front of the wagon box, too close for comfort, so he ducked back behind the welcome cover of the heavy Springfield freight wagon.

Over and over, the Gatling gun swept the hillside, the din and smoke almost as unbearable as the deadly slugs it spit out of its rotating circle of hot barrels.

Carson and Johnny had halted their men about a hundred yards from where the outlaws had gone into hiding. "We'll wait here until they start firing," he whispered to Johnny. "Once they start, move everyone up fast and get into position. Then let the bastards have it."

Pat Quinn and the rest of the men crouched behind the thick trunks of old pines and awaited the orders to move up. Johnny Harper moved to the end of the line of men opposite to Pat, while Carson stayed in the middle. Fighting their nervous anxiety, the men awaited the order to move.

Carson nervously flinched at the sudden onset of the battle. He motioned with his hand and the line of determined men moved forward, darting from cover to cover as they closed in on the outlaws' position.

The stunning impact of the machine gun's incessant roar of death and destruction caused the men to pause for a moment, but they quickly recovered and moved on, knowing the outlaws' attention would be on the gun and not on their approach.

Carson saw a man lying prone behind a tree truck, then two more. He hoped every man in his command had sight of some of the outlaws. The excited young man dropped to the ground and crawled a few feet until he had a tree trunk in front of him. He looked to his right and left. The rest of the men were settling in behind whatever cover they could find, picking their targets and awaiting the order to commence firing.

Only one man among the outlaws had ever seen or heard a Gatling gun before, in the Union army several years earlier. He was one of the first killed by the initial volley of fire directed at the outlaws: he could not advise Charlie on what to do. Most of the men were panicked and terrified by the deadly hail of bullets that swept over them as the gun traversed the outlaws' firing line. Some tried to fire back as the gun's path took the bullet stream away from their position, but all that seemed to do was bring the swarm of lead hornets back their way again.

Carson watched as the gun swept the far end of the outlaws' position. As the gun moved its hammering shower of .45-caliber bullets toward him, Carson called out, "Open fire."

Most of the outlaws taken under fire by the flanking line of Carson's men did not know they were under attack before the first bullet or bullets hit them. As the Gatling gun's trace took it back toward the far end of the line, Carson's men shifted their fires to follow it. The results were devastating. Half the outlaws were dead or severely wounded before Vern realized they had been flanked and were in danger of being wiped out. The roar of the guns, the smoke, the deadly missiles of death that were hitting all around him sapped him of his last reserves of courage. "Charlie," he shouted. "We gotta git outa here." Illogically he thought to himself, *Who's ambushing who?* Without waiting for an answer from Charlie, Vern hotfooted it up the hill toward his horse. When he reached it, he climbed up and waited a few seconds to see if anyone else was coming. Charlie Call and five men were all that reached the horses alive. Twenty men lay hors de combat where they had confidently awaited the arrival of the freight wagons only ten minutes earlier.

"Jesus, what was that, Vern?" a shaken Call asked. "It sounded like a hunnerd men were in them wagons."

"It had to be a Gatlin' gun. I heard about them but I never saw one afore."

"I hope to hell I never see one agin," Call replied. "Whaddya wanna do now?"

"Come on, let's git outa here fer a start." Barton galloped away from the bloody scene, his heart racing faster than his horse was running. The five remaining outlaws followed, none concerned about those left behind. As the panicked men reached the Ranch Road, Barton slid his horse to a stop. "Charlie, you come with me. We'll ride to Virginnie City and tell Stoddard what happened. We'll git some money from him to rebuild the gang and then git back to the ranch. You fellows head fer the line shack and gather up all our stuff that's left there. Then take the back trail to the ranch. If anyone comes nosin' around, claim you ain't been off the place in a week. Me and Call'll rejoin ya just as soon as we git done."

The outlaws split up, and both groups rode hard, trying to put as many miles as possible between themselves and the men who had dealt them such a savage blow.

Marty sensed a sudden cessation in the fire from above. He waited for a few long seconds without seeing a single telltale sign that anyone was shooting from the outlaws' position. "Cease fire," he shouted, calling again and again until the firing stopped. The only sound he heard was the braying of a wounded mule, somewhere ahead. And the almost musical ping of hot metal cooling. Cautiously, he stepped out from behind the wagon. "Carson, Johnny, can you hear me?" he shouted up the hill.

"We hear ya, Marty," Johnny shouted back.

"See any sign of them?" he called back.

"Not alive, I don't," Johnny answered.

Marty headed up the hill, followed by Luther. "Squint, check the mules and see if any need replacing."

Marty met Johnny, Pat, and Carson at a dead outlaw's body, his head split open by the heavy bullet from the Gatling gun. "God." Johnny spoke for everyone. "This is awful, it makes me sick to my stomach." The men somberly looked at the crumpled bodies of the dead outlaws, each feeling the same nauseated reaction to the carnage.

Carson held his arm tightly to his side.

"Carson, you hit?"

"A scratch, honest. I'm fine."

Pat Quinn spoke up. "I think he was nicked by a piece of bullet that broke off when it hit a rock or something. It had to be the Gatling gun. I don't think any of the outlaws ever fired at us. I got a bandage on it."

"One did," Johnny answered. "Billy Walters took one in the throat. He's dead, over there, by that big pine with the split trunk."

"I'm sorry," Marty answered. "Did we get all the outlaws?"

"I don't think so," Pat Quinn broke in. "I saw half a dozen or so runnin' up the hill from my spot. I shot at 'em but I don't think I got any of 'em."

"Ruud," Marty shouted. "Bring your horse and get up here."

"Right away, Marty," the scout shouted back.

Marty turned to Johnny. "Where's Ross?"

"He's watchin' the horses, about a quarter mile back there." Johnny thumbed toward the rear.

"Pat, would you take some men and bring your horses up? Meet me at the wagons."

"Sure thing," the big Irishman answered, and took off at a quick step across the rocky, pine needle–covered slope.

Ruud showed up, leading his horse. "We

had three mules hit, Marty. Squint's changin' 'em out now."

"Ruud, a half dozen took off over the hill. I want you to follow them to the Ranch Road, and see where they're headed. Then wait for me. I'll be there as soon as we can get everyone mounted."

"Gotcha, Marty." Ruud climbed on the back of his dark bay and headed up the hill, his eyes sweeping the ground for sign.

Marty led the others down the slippery slope to the road, where Malcolm and Squint waited with the other men.

"We git 'em all, Marty?" Squint asked as soon as he saw Marty break out of the brush.

"All but about six," Marty answered.

"Whooee," Squint shouted. "That'll show them varmints."

"We have anyone hurt?" Malcolm asked.

"We lost one man, and Carson got a nick in his arm."

"Thank the blessed saints. That's better than I'd hoped, fer certain." Malcolm hurried to check out Carson.

"What's next?" Squint asked.

"I'm going after the ones who got away. I aim to finish this thing here and now, just like I promised." He watched Pat and the others lead their horses out of the woods toward the wagons.

"Carson, I'll ride your horse. You and Malcolm get this load to Virginia City right away. You shouldn't have any problem between here and there. Keep the drivers and guards on duty with weapons until Hearst takes delivery of the pumps."

"Aw, Marty. I want to go with you. I'll be all right."

Marty shook his head. "I'm sorry, son, orders are orders. You know the rules. Besides, I need someone to make certain Malcolm fulfills his contract. You'll be the most valuable making certain the pumps arrive safely."

Marty clamped his hand on Carson's good arm. "I'm counting on you, Carson. Luther, you come along with me. We may need some long-range shooting before this is over. Sergeant LeCroix, Corporal Blue, you two did marvelous work. Have a look before you go on into Virginia City."

Squint spoke up. "Marty, I wanna go on with you to finish this. We ain't gonna be needed the rest of the trip to Virginnie City."

"You can't get that big wagon over the hill, Squint. There's no road and it'll never make it through the trees."

"We'll go around. There's a cutoff 'bout a mile or so back down the road. We'll meet ya where the outlaw trail cuts the River Road. Take us 'bout half an hour, maybe twenty minutes."

"All right, Squint. Get one of the Sorensen brothers to ride shotgun and get goin'. We'll either meet you there, or I'll leave Ross to guide you to where we are."

Marty led his victorious fighters up the hill and down the other side, following the game trail until they reached the Ranch Road. Ruud was waiting for them there. "What's the story?" Marty asked.

"Two men went north, toward either Virginia City or Reno. Four rode to the line shack trail and turned in. They probably don't think we know about the line shack."

"Ross, follow the two who went toward Reno. Stop at the turnoff to Virginia City. Pick up Squint there and bring him and the Gatling gun to me. I'll go with everyone to the line shack first. See if you can determine if the two runners are going on to Reno or to Virginia City."

"I'll do her. See ya shortly."

Marty motioned to the rest. "Let's go. We've got some outlaws who need redeemin'."

CHAPTER 27
THE RIGHTEOUS
SHALL PREVAIL

The four fleeing outlaws slid their panting horses to a stop at the line shack. They had paused at the top of a small rise about two hundred yards in front of the cabin and watched their back trail, and saw nobody in pursuit. They rode the rest of the way to the cabin at a dead run, each anxious to be the first to rummage through the private articles of their dead comrades.

Being thieves and amoral, it was easy for them to completely disregard the fact that their friends and co-outlaws had just died a violent death only moments earlier. They felt safe now; nobody knew about their use of the line shack. They could take what they wanted from their dead friends, then leisurely ride the back way to the V-B, where they would wait for Vern and Charlie to return.

Ruud easily followed the tracks as they crossed the Peavine range toward the line shack. Marty slowed the pace as they approached the small rise to their front. If his information was right, the shack was just on the other side, backed up to an animal lean to, and a small corral, with woods about a hundred feet to the rear. He stopped as the shack became visible through the bunch grass. Four horses stood tied to the top rail of the corral, but there was no sign of the hunted men. A slight breeze barely stirred the bunch grass and the sun was directly overhead.

Marty motioned for Pat and Johnny to come forward. "Looks like the same situation as at the mine. Johnny, take five men and cover the back. Don't let anyone out. Pat, you follow me with the rest. I'm gonna stand off a bit and try and convince them to surrender. If they haven't done so by the time the Gatling gun gets here, I'll turn it loose on 'em. That oughta help them make up their minds in a hurry."

Johnny took five men and rode wide around the shack, disappearing into the trees. After ten minutes, Marty began to deploy his men in a wide semicircle around the sides and front of the log cabin. They all went to ground about two hundred yards from the cabin, within rifle range, but reasonably safe from anything but the most carefully aimed fire. When everyone was in position, Marty fired a shot through the roof of the shack. "Hello, the shack," he shouted. "You men inside, come out with your hands up, and you won't be hurt."

"Damn, where'd them fellas come from?" one of the outlaws inside the line shack complained. He headed for the back door and a quick exit to the woods.

An explosion of shots from the woods drove him back into the line shack, unnerved by his close call. "They're all around us. What'll we do?"

One of the more daring outlaws grabbed his rifle and knocked the glass out of the only window in the front of the cabin. He ripped off three quick shots as fast as he could fire and lever in another round. Then he fell dead to the cabin's dirt floor, a buffalo slug through his chest from Luther's scope-aided rifle.

The remaining outlaws were in a quandary. Intense arguments erupted as to whether they should try and fight their way out or surrender, or try something else.

Marty waited patiently, hoping the outlaws would use good sense for a change. Squint's wagon carrying the Gatling gun came rumbling down the trail, following Ross on his paint horse. The heavy wagon lumbered along as fast as Squint could make his tired mules trot. There was no way the stubborn animals were going to run, pulling their heavy load.

"Where do ya want us, Marty?"

Marty pointed toward a small knoll, about midway between his extended line of men. "Pull in there and wait for my command to fire." The little swell provided some protection to the mules and the wagon, while still allowing LeCroix plenty of visibility to fire his gun.

As soon as the wagon stopped, Marty shouted, "Let 'em have it, Sergeant."

The Gatling gun opened up, and so did Marty's men, firing with deadly abandon at the shack and its unfortunate occupants. Bullets flew through the shake roof, the busted window, or slammed into the round logs of the outer wall. The men inside dropped to the floor, covering their head with their arms, as if that might save them from a deadly wound.

Joaquin crouched below the window at the rear of the cabin. He risked a quick look out the window to ensure that none of the men in the woods to the rear were trying to sneak up on him and his companions. As he did, a bullet, probably from the Gatling gun bounced off a rock in the fireplace and nearly cut him in two. He died without a sound. That was enough for the others. One man tied his neckerchief to his rifle barrel and stuck it out the front door, waving it up and down to attract attention.

"That's it boys," Marty shouted. "Cease fire, they're quitting."

The two remaining outlaws filed out of the cabin, sullen looks of defeat on their faces. Marty quickly had them tied and separated from each other. Then he went from man to man asking the same question. "Where were Barton and Charlie Call?"

They soon had their answer. "So they're in Virginnie City." Squint nodded. "It figgers. That's where the moneyman is, Ranson Stoddard."

"Squint, you and Johnny take these jaspers down to Carson City and get 'em jailed up. I'll take Ross, Luther, and Pat Quinn and head for Virginia City. We may as well make a clean sweep of it."

"Don't ya want more men than that?"

"No, we'll make do. Any more and we might get in each other's way."

The four men hunters rode away from the line shack after the two remaining outlaws were secured to their saddles, preparatory to taking them back to Carson City. As they reached the cutoff to Virginia City, Marty laid out a rough plan to find and capture the two outlaw leaders. "I doubt if they're going to give in to my demands without a fight. If they start anything, don't hesitate to take 'em down on the spot."

The men rode most of the way in silence, still digesting the mind-numbing battles of the past two hours. They reached Virginia City in about an hour, where Marty split them up. "Pat, you and Ross start at the north end of town and Luther and I will start at the south. Keep your eyes peeled for the pair of them. You clear on what they look like?"

"Yep, if we see 'em we'll come git you right off," Pat answered.

Vern and Charlie had impatiently waited in Stoddard's office for him to return from an inspection trip to one of his smaller mines. The silver vein his miners had been chasing had inexplicably disappeared, and Stoddard's mood was foul and angry. He listened with barely concealed rage as Barton described the chaos at the ambush site and the loss of so many of his men.

"You've failed miserably, and now you want me to help bail you out? I must say, Barton, you've got your nerve. I oughta just throw you outa my office and wash my hands of you forever."

"Now, Mr. Stoddard, it ain't quite that bad. With a little money, I can rebuild my gang and we can continue raiding O'Brian's stages and such. I'll lie low fer a couple of weeks, let the heat die down a mite, and then it'll be business as usual."

"All right, Barton. I'm gonna go along with you, just this once. I may regret it, but I assure you, if you fail me again, you'll regret it the rest of your very short life." Stoddard turned to the large safe behind his desk and spun the twin dial tumblers until a soft click was heard. Then he swung open the heavy door and reached inside. He grabbed a stack of paper bills and threw them on the desk next to Barton's hand. "Here's two thousand. Now get out of my office."

Barton scooped up the money but did not leave. "Hold on, Mr. Stoddard. I'll need more'n that. It'll take at least five thousand to pay off my men and hire new ones and keep them paid till we can take enough from O'Brian to cover expenses."

"Well, you're outa luck. I don't have that much. Guess you'll have to take that and go on the dodge until it's safe to return."

"He's lyin', boss. I seen a big pile of money in his safe."

Barton's tone grew ugly. "You're not tryin' to weasel out of anything are you, Mr. Stoddard? Give me the five thousand."

Cursing under his breath, Stoddard turned to the safe, knelt down on one knee, and reached for the additional money. His eyes fell on the handgun he always kept in the safe. He paused. He could shoot the two of them and claim they had been trying to rob him. Then he wouldn't have to worry about their loyalty. He took the pistol and started to stand up.

Call drew and shot in one fluid motion, the bullet hitting the mining man in the lower back and coursing upward until it pierced his liver. Unable to move or even cry out because of the shock and pain, Stoddard slumped back to his knees. His head knocked against the upper shelf of the safe. He died the way he had lived, his eyes focused on stacks of paper money.

"What the hell?" Vern shouted at Call. "Why'd you do that?"

"He grabbed a gun. It was nickel plated. I saw it shinin' in the light. He was gonna shoot us."

"You don't know that. Christ Almighty. Now what are we gonna do?"

"Grab the money and light a shuck outa here. There's other towns and other places to do business."

Call reached in past Stoddard's head and pulled out the stacks of bills. He passed some to Barton and shoved some into his shirt. "There's better'n ten thousand here. That'll take us a long ways. Come on, let's git while the gittin's good."

The two killers dashed down the stairs and out of the building, headed for their horses. They nearly ran over Marty and Luther, walking slowly toward Stoddard's office.

Marty did not hesitate. "Barton, Charlie Call, you're both under arrest for robbery and murder. Throw down your guns and get your hands up."

Screaming in rage and frustration, Charlie Call clawed for his pistol. Smooth and steady, Keller shot him twice in the center of his chest before Call's pistol cleared leather enough to point. The horse they were running for reared and thrashed around the hitching rail, masking Barton's body from both Marty's and Luther's aim. Barton leaped on the back of the shying animal and spurred him hard. The horse took off running directly toward Ross and Pat Quinn, who were racing toward Marty and Luther as fast as they could.

Marty refrained from shooting at the fleeing Barton: there were too many innocent people suddenly gawking at the spectacle. "Pat, get Barton!" he shouted at the top of his lungs.

Vern Barton pulled his pistol and looked around. He was not about to stop for anyone. He aimed at the big body of Pat Quinn running into the street and snapped off a quick shot. Pat stopped and crouched, drawing his pistol as Barton thundered past. He never got off a shot. Ross calmly had aimed his rifle and put a bullet into the fleeing outlaw's side, knocking him off his horse, into a crumpled heap in the dust of Virginia City's main street. As the two outlaw leaders had sown, so did they reap.

CHAPTER 28
GOOD-BYE

"By gum, three trips to and from Virginia City in a week and not one hint of trouble. Marty, me lad, happy days are here again."

"I'm glad to hear it, Malcolm. By the way, Luther Hatfield wants a job as a shotgun guard. I told him to come by tomorrow and you'd talk to him."

"Good. That's four men from your force that's workin' for me now. I couldn't ask for any better. I got good news too."

"What's that?"

"I'm buyin' out Clem Atkinson's freight business. He don't have much goin' since Stoddard died. Say's he's ready to retire to his daughter's place in Fresno anyhow."

"Wonderful."

"I also saw George Hearst while I was in Virginia City. He paid me for haulin' the pumps up. Said he's already started puttin' out the fire in the Comstock with the water drained from the Little Bill Mine. He sent these for you." Malcolm passed over some ornately printed pieces of paper.

"What are these?"

"It's ten shares in the Little Bill Mine and ten more in the Comstock. Hearst says that right now they're worth fifty bucks a share and will go to two-fifty or more once the mines hit the mother lode." Malcolm smiled at Marty. "That means they'll be worth five thousand in a few weeks."

Marty eyed the valuable pieces of paper. "Mercy sakes, how does a body turn these into money like that?"

"You have ta sell 'em on the San Francisco stock market."

"I don't know how."

"Tell you what. He gave me some too. If you want, I'll get them to a broker in San Fran and tell him to sell when the market gets to two-fifty. I'll send the profits to yur bank in Dallas. That all right with you?"

"Great. All this high-finance stuff makes my head hurt."

Carson and Colleen walked out of the office together. They had been inseparable since the day of the gunfight on the mountain. Marty was grateful to see Carson using his wounded arm again.

"We were lucky," he had confided to Malcolm the night after the fight. "We could have lost a lot more men. Maybe, for once, the good guys got a break."

Two days later, Marty had sent Sergeant LeCroix and Corporal Blue back to the Presidio of San Francisco, each with a hundred dollars in gold coin in his pocket and a brand-new Winchester rifle, payment for their help in eliminating the outlaw gang.

Squint walked in after putting the stage in the barn. With his new source of funds from Hearst, Malcolm now had a stable man to help Squint handle the mules and rolling stock.

"Hey, Squint, how was the trip?"

"Nice and quiet, jus' like I like it. Pat's a great companion fer me when he rides guard. He don't talk much, so there's plenty of time fer me to git my say in."

Marty smiled. "By the way, Squint, when I was in Reno saying good-bye to our soldiers, I ran into Phil Diedesheimer, the mining engineer. He said that Hearst sent out that blue clay he was plagued with and had it analyzed. Said the reason it's so blue is because it's got silver in it. Enough silver to make it worthwhile to collect and smelt. Maybe your mine has the same stuff."

"By gum, wouldn't that be somethin'? I'll ride out tomorry and git a sample fer the assay office here. By gum, wouldn't that be somethin'?" Squint shook his head. "If it do have any silver in it, you're in fer ten percent of the first year's take, Marty, my boy."

"No, that's not necessary. I was just passing on information. You don't . . ."

Squint held up his hand. "I don't want no back talk from you, Marty Keller. I've made up my mind."

"That's mighty kind of you, Squint. Thank you very much."

"Hell, you earned that and much more, far as I'm concerned."

Marty watched him disappear around the corner, probably headed for Jack's Bar and a long cool beer or perhaps several. He turned back to Malcolm, standing beside Carson and Colleen. Marty smiled at his new friends, a warm feeling in his cold heart.

"As for me, dear friends, I think I'll hit the trail tomorrow. My job here seems to be done."

He waited out the storm of protest, and then continued. "You know why I have to move on. I'll try and stop by and visit you the next time I'm in the area."

"What about your profits from the stage line? Remember, it'll be worth a lot, and very soon."

"Malcolm, all I want from you is the

reward money for Luke Graham. Take the rest and give it to Carson and Colleen here, as a wedding gift from me." He smiled as both youngsters blushed a fiery red. "Carson, you'll do to ride the high country with. I'm proud to call you a friend. Listen, the mines in Virginia City are going to be using prodigious amounts of lumber with the new support technique Phil Diedesheimer has come up with. Take the money from Malcolm and buy yourself a sawmill. Get as many acres of timber rights as you can buy up. Don't forget the railroad will want ties for the tracks as well. You'll be a rich man the next time I stop by if you do this, believe me."

He stopped, his throat unexpectedly hoarse as he tried to say more. For him, friends were hard to find, and he regretted leaving them. "Come on, I'm buying supper for all of us. Anyone hungry besides me?"

Early the next morning, Marty rode Pacer to the end of the street and turned to head toward Reno. In his pocket was the fifteen hundred dollars, his goodbye gift from Malcolm. He looked back. Malcolm, Squint, Carson, and Colleen were still waving their hands in farewell. He blinked hard as Pacer turned the corner and they were lost to his sight.

ABOUT THE AUTHOR

Thom Nicholson was born in Springfield, Missouri, and grew up in northwest Arkansas and southwest Missouri. After college he worked in a uranium mine in New Mexico before entering the U.S. Army. He served as a Special Forces officer in Vietnam, South America, and Africa. In Vietnam he was an A-team executive officer, then a Raider Company commander. In 1996, with more than thirty years of commissioned service, he retired at the rank of colonel. A graduate of the National Defense University and the U.S. Army Command and General Staff School, he is a registered engineer and holds an MBA. After retirement, he started writing novels. He and his wife, Sandra, have five children.